C000175002

Timeline

T G Hancock

2nd Edition 2017

PAPERBACK
Timeline
© Copyright 2011
Thelma Hancock

The right of Thelma Hancock to be identified as
author of this work has been asserted by her in
accordance with the Copyright, Designs and Patents
Act 1988.

All Rights Reserved.
No reproduction, copy or transmission of this
publication may be made without written
permission.
No paragraph of this publication may be
reproduced, copied or transmitted save with the
written permission of the publisher, or in
accordance with the provisions of the Copyright Act
1956 (as amended).

Any person who commits any unauthorised act in
relation to this publication may be liable to criminal
prosecution and civil claims for damages.

While historical details are believed to be accurate, all
the characters in this book have no existence outside
the imagination of the author, and have no relation
whatsoever to anyone bearing the same name or
names. They are not even remotely inspired by any
individual known or unknown to the author, and all
the incidences are pure invention.

**A CIP catalogue record for this title is available
from the British Library.**

ISBN 978 1 9997425 9 1

EBook ISBN 978 1 9997425 8 4

Printed and Bound in Great Britain.

Dedicated to

Johnnie, Evan and Arthur of the FR

(1990 – '95).

Acknowledgement (2nd Edition)

Having had a number of comments about the previous cover not representing the railway used in the novel I challenged one of the detractors to produce a suitable sketch for me!

It has been described to me as a 'double Fairley hybrid'; being made up in part of the 'Josephine' - displayed at the Ottago Settles Museum in New Zealand - with changes, such as livery and gauge, to make it similar to a Festiniog double Fairley. I hope this appeases some of the critics.

Timeline.

Prologue.

'GEE UP HOSS!'

It might be the night before Christmas but no star or moon lighted the way and the burden wasn't life; but death.

It was raining again. But when wasn't it raining in Wales, he pondered.

The horse had been reluctant to leave the warm fug of the stable, and even more reluctant to turn its face into the wind coming off the Irish Sea.

'Come on.' He tugged at the lead rein and the horse snorted a protest, tossing long, stiff black hair out of its eyes, but it settled again, shoulder muscles bunched, to the task of pulling the heavy wooden cart. The wooden stays rang as it bumped across the metal tracks.

The man pulled his cloth cap more firmly down over his eyes, the collar of the thin jacket up around his grubby neck, and tucked his muffler more securely down into the gap between the two, so that only his wide mouth and unshaven chin could be seen. His leather soled boots with the segs in the toes, made a quiet counterpoint to the horse's shoes on the cobbles, like a couple of Morris dancers with inhibitions.

He continued to mutter imprecations admixed with encouragement to the beast as they all but felt their way along the recently made cart track parallel to the shoreline. The looming presence of the man-made barrier blocking the estuary provided darkness for this dark deed. He shivered with a mixture of cold from the rain and fear that he would meet someone.

He pulled on the leading rein again as they arrived at the large breach and manoeuvred the animal into the lee of the stones. It was little enough shelter for the horse, but he knew he would have even less once he started on his task.

The horse dropped its head and began to lip at the few tufts of grass which had found uneasy purchase in the crevices at the base of the wall. As the man walked round to the back of the cart and dropped the gate, he continued to talk, first to the horse and then to his grisly burden as he struggled with it, easing it to one side of the straw-covered trap's flooring.

'That's it, hoss. I won't leave you long. You just stand quiet here and don't go calling to your friends.' He pulled the tarpaulin off the base of the cart and shuffled a long, empty toolbox to the back gate, then with a grunt hefted it up.

'Jasus and I haven't even got the body in yet!'

He dragged the box down and shuddered as the wood screeched a protest like fingernails over a blackboard.

'I've gotta have a bit of light here, boy. Can't give you a burial in the dark.'

He flicked the shutter halfway across the metal of the acetylene lamp, revealing a tiny flame which he tweaked up slightly.

'Right then. You wait here, hoss, I won't be long.' The lamp sent a ray of luminescence dancing and bobbing over the rough stones as he approached the side of the Cob.

He looked around cautiously; the oily sea was still snaking its way through the tussocks of sand-blown grass to his left, and far off he could see what was probably a fishing boat returning to the harbour. He could just make out the green light winking outside the sandbanks. He turned the lamp even lower and shielded it with his body as he searched along the side of the edifice for the gap.

Porthmadog town was a dark blur further along the track. Not even the new-fangled gas lighting the council had installed on the main street shed enough light to penetrate across the barrier onto the shore line. He began to pull the box up over the rubble on the seaward side of the wall.

The McAlpine firm had been working on this breach since the hurricane in October. Wooden shuttering had been erected to keep the tide from eroding away the huge stones already placed to fill the gap. Last week the men had started to infill the bottom with any conglomerate they could find. The gap was protected by only a stone's thickness from the incoming tide.

He crawled over the stones and builder's rubbish, lugging his heavy burden behind him, his lamp, as it swung from his wrist, cast eerie shadows against the sides of the man-made cave. The box tipped sideways and fell into a gap in the stones with a clatter of falling pebbles. The man shuddered and cold sweat ran down his back. 'Oh God, don't let anyone come.'

The whisper echoed from the insides of the hole, a sibilant hiss drowned out by the rising tide. As if in answer to his prayer the wind began to pick up and tossed the sea against the outside so that spray was forced through the gaps in the planks and the soughing of the waves filled his ears.

Setting the lamp next to the box he pushed and shoved the rectangle more firmly into the gap parallel to the outside barrier. His hands were icy with fear and cold as he struggled with the unwieldy shape. 'Right then!' He crawled back out of the hole and went to pick up the body. A hand flopped over his face as he slung it over his shoulder.

4

Shuddering at the residual warmth, he dropped the burden back onto the cart tail and dragged the tarpaulin down, rolling the body into it.

'Oh, God! Oh, God, I'm sorry, boy. I didn't mean it, lad. You should have spoken ...'

Once again he hefted the body and again crawled over the stones through the gap, cursing, and with the breath shuddering out at each gasp at the feel of the dead weight over his shoulders.

He felt his way towards the box which sat wedged on a pile of sand tilted to one side as it had fallen just inside the great barrier. He dropped the corpse and shivered as the warmth trapped between himself and the body evaporated.

'Still shielding me, boy! You always tried to protect me. I should never have believed the tales.' He whispered the words, though who he thought might be listening was anybody's guess.

Opening the lid with the squeal of a thousand muted banshees, he pushed the still wrapped body inside then shut the lid again, pulling a gun from his pocket and stuffing it down next to the box as an afterthought.

'You told me it would bring me grief, boy. Looks like you were right.'

Pulling off the dirty cap he stood bare headed as he spoke a benediction over the makeshift coffin. 'You always said you loved the sea, lad. So I know you won't mind staying here.' He flipped the cap back on his head and began to tug rocks over the lid, piling them on and around the tool box and with the aid of the lamp, finding bits of driftwood to camouflage the box's shape.

He eyed the subsequent cairn from several angles, crawling around the sandy stones and debris. Eventually he was satisfied. He crossed himself. 'God grant you peace, boy. Now you'll excuse me if I don't linger, it's bloody cold and I'm bloody scared.' Crawling rapidly away he slithered out of the hole and, clucking to the horse, headed back towards the workhouse at Minffordd.

1

Present day.

'NOT MUCH LONGER.' THE voice was male and pure Oxbridge, a musical counterpoint to the sea lapping gently against the boulders of the great stone and earth barrier that separated the sea from the land outside the small Welsh town. The moon was full and the embankment crowned with two narrow lines of rail track, a rusty tiara twinkling on an ancient dowager.

A few birds rustled in scrub bush which grew along the bank near the rail track. Something else was rustling, and Willow shuddered slightly at the sound, imagining small pointy snouts whiffling, and skinny pink tails flicking; she hated rats. She fixed her eye on the scene before her in a determined effort to distract her mind from both the effects of her imagination and the rather beautiful voice.

'Sian must be half frozen. Late October in North Wales is not the ideal month for lying around outside.' Willow checked the water and trickled a minute amount through to the boiler as she spoke to the owner of the voice and her driver this night.

The girl she could see through the right hand glass spectacle of the train, appeared to be bound to the train track with thick cords. Her arms stretched along the lines and her knees bent over the second parallel flat-bed rail.

She was dressed in a diaphanous dress which Willow thought would have had Austen's maidens swooning with envy. Willow shivered, even though the heat from the firebox on the front of her legs was causing her overalls to steam gently. She reached out a hand to check that the pasties she had placed on the top of the firebox were warming through nicely; they too issued little puffs of steam, like baby dragons resting before breaking out of their eggs.

Morgan stirred at her movement, adjusting a lever with a firm hand. Willow watched him checking gauges, his hat with the insignia of the Ffestiniog Railway pushed to the back of his head, revealing a high forehead, at the moment creased in thought. His light, mousy hair was brushed back and tied in a small tail of curls at the nape of his neck with a handy piece of bootlace. A five o'clock shadow, more deepening of already dark skin than real bristles, was giving him a slightly piratical air in the dim light of the engine's cab.

He sported a red and white spotted kerchief round his neck looking like a very superior tramp, the kerchief lending colour to the drab navy blue overalls. They appeared clean; even the rag he used to wipe the gauges had hardly any grease on it.

Willow groaned inwardly as she looked down her own grubby person. How did the man do it? She transferred her attention to the scene outside their enclosed pocket of warmth, and watched the unfolding drama before her. It was rather like being on the lot of a miniature MGM; except this was real scenery and icy fingers of wind were seeking out areas of her anatomy only normally touched by herself and, in the distant past, her mother.

Moving around with cameras and microphone booms like large dirty mops on long poles, were several teenage boys. Mr Hughes, the male teacher with them, called out a new set of instructions. 'Deniol, ready?' There was a fresh flurry of activity.

A boy dressed in Edwardian garb rushed forward, the sideburns he was so proud of obscured by his high collars. Willow thought without the costume he'd look like a fifties' rocker, and sighed to herself. There were times when she felt very old, despite being only 27.

In a well rehearsed move he cut the ropes with an evil looking knife which glinted in the fitful moonlight. He pulled the young girl close with one arm while using a silver painted plastic sword to fight the villain with the other.

Circling the romantic pair, the villain, Lyndon by name, curled theatrically, a rather wonderful set of moustaches between finger and thumb. 'Poirot eat your heart out', thought Willow. Earlier in the evening that same hirsute adornment had given considerable trouble, showing a marked tendency to droop and drop off, but the benefit of modern make-up adhesive had cured that tendency. Though, if Willow was any judge, it was going to be rather painful to remove, she could almost feel her eyes watering in sympathy.

Lyndon swirled his black cape in a truly villainous manner and waved his sword, giving an evil laugh 'Blofeld' would have appreciated. A young girl stepped towards the camera and held up a sign saying, '*Ha, Ha, you won't escape*!' which Lyndon mimed in an exaggerated manner.

The hero pointed at him and mouthed, '*Die you dog*,' which was then shown in gothic script; and then another placard was held in front of the camera reading, '*I will save you!*' The hero ran his sword between the arm and chest of the villain, who hammed his way through the death throes by degrees and, overdoing the acting, stumbled around the railway line before falling to the ground. The heroine embraced her saviour in true silent movie style to the applause of the watching parents and school staff and Mr Huges yelled, *'Torrwch'*.

Willow smiled to herself. So much for teenagers who took drugs and got into trouble. These youngsters had had a great time making the film. She watched as, amid much laughter, the crowd of teenagers walked down the side of the line and came to offer their thanks to the pair on the footplate of the steam engine.

Morgan leant down. *'Deniol, wyt ti ddim yn medru actio o gwbl. Ofnadwy!'* He shook his head in mock horror.

Deniol, the hero of the piece, laughed up at him. *'Diolch yn fawr.'*

'Croeso.'

They came round the other side of the train, Deniol acting as spokesperson.

'Thank you so much, Miss Edwards. We appreciate all your help tonight. It's been great!'

'It was a pleasure, Deniol, and you too, Sian. I think that make-up is incredible.' She looked at the deep black circles around the girl's eyes. 'Just like 'Pearl White'.' The young girl blushed under the pancake make-up and grinned up at her. Not that Willow thought Sian would know who 'Pearl White' was! 'I hope you'll invite me to the opening night; it's bound to win the first prize.'

'Well, Miss, if it stops someone like my kid sister going off with a stranger that will be the real thing.' Deniol grinned at her. 'But we do want to win too.'

'I'm sure you will, you've all put such a lot into it. Now don't stand around, get a coat on, Sian. It's cold enough to see your breath. Go and celebrate, the lot of you!'

The group moved away, laughing. Willow could hear them repeating bits of the script and pushing each other. The hero and heroine, she noted, walked hand in hand behind the others. Sian seemed to have acquired Deniol's padded jacket as they walked the short distance to the Railway Station, her diaphanous gown was trailing like a bridal train as she stepped daintily between the rails.

Willow had never enjoyed, herself, the courtship rituals of the very young. She sighed and smiled to herself as she turned her mind to the tasks ahead. They'd be mortally offended if she suggested they were too young for such a thing; fifteen was such a vulnerable age, halfway between child and adult.

Mr Hughes stretched up a hand to Morgan. 'I too appreciate your help, as well as the railway's. The kids have had a great time. It's something they'll never forget, and without your backing the school couldn't have afforded to do something so ambitious.'

Morgan looked both annoyed and embarrassed. 'It really was a pleasure, so let's say no more about it, shall we?'

He glanced across at Willow, and saw she was listening with interest. 'Water.' He pointed at the small gauge. Willow followed the direction of the slim and elegant finger. The small glass gauges set above the firebox showed water at the half way level, well within the safety zone. She looked back at him questioningly, but he was now speaking in rapid Welsh to the teacher.

The teacher swung away carrying a case of equipment, and Morgan turned back to Willow. 'Right. Home.' He pulled the cord and the whistle echoed off the hills in a mournful manner, as if the little train didn't want to leave the party and fun behind. The regulator was pulled down, setting the train in motion.

The short trip to the sheds was at the far side of the long strip of stones that joined the town of Porthmadog to the other side of the estuary by means of the high embankment. The cylinder cocks sighed gently and the delicate little Hunslet picked up her skirts and began to glide along the rails.

Willow looked along the lines towards the Boston Lodge Works about a mile distant. A few lights shone down on the old sheds, glinting off the tin roofs, their power dulled considerably by the moonlight. *Craig Ddrwg* in the background was a black demarcation line between land and sky.

She eased open the lever and allowed the engine to burn oil, leaning out to check the colour of the smoke. The familiar smell of burnt diesel and hot Brasso assailed her nostrils, along with the faintest whiff of aftershave and healthy male. Studiously turning away from the scent she looked out towards the sea, sniffing the frosty air blowing in; it was going to be another cold night.

The teenagers had been trying to film for a week, but heavy rain and storms had not just battered the coastline, but coated the shoreline in debris, before cooking the lot in the foam of a bad tempered sea. This had been the first fine evening and the moon had obliged too; hanging low on the horizon and turning the black and white scene into a charcoal and chalk etching of the real thing.

It couldn't have been better, but the wind was picking up again now and blowing small icy gasps of air down her neck. She could hear the suck and rattle of the sea even above the engine noise, as that same wind hurled the incoming tide onto the consolidated walls of the Cob, in a tantrum at being ignored.

She spread her legs and planted her feet firmly on the footplate, holding on to the side panelling as the train picked up more speed, her eyes monitoring the colour of the smoke. She brought her gaze inside the cab while her eyes flicked over the pressure gauges. The wind whipped the short blonde fringe across her forehead and she absently shoved it back with a greasy hand, unaware she was leaving a light trail of soot across a smooth white forehead.

This was the first occasion that Willow had stoked for Morgan, despite the fact that they had both been volunteering for the railway for three years. She pondered the phenomenon of a clean driver while the train clacked and gently rocked her way along the high lines and, like an old lady venturing out in unaccustomed high heels, the train gathered speed with confidence.

Willow seemed to attract greasy oil the minute she swung up onto the footplate. She glanced across to the very masculine hand resting on the regulator. It appeared clean. She looked down at her own fingers and winced at the black cuticles. She looked as if she'd been down the mine for a week, without a shovel!

She leapt agilely off and down as they slowed to five miles an hour at the corner adjacent to the sheds, and swung the bob weight across to change the points. The train shunted across the pit in front of shed number six.

She could see Morgan in the high sodium lights, leaning over to pull on the brakes as she walked up the line towards the engine. Her steel toe-capped boots felt as heavy and awkward on the uneven surface, as if she were walking at the bottom of the Irish Sea instead of beside it, as she made her way towards the back of the engine.

As she approached there was a deafening whoosh as Morgan blew down over the pit and let the pressure go. Then he was jumping down without a backward glance and walking away to check-in the brass staff which gave them right-of-way up the line.

She walked up to extinguish the red light on the back of the engine, then swung back aboard. Having looked at all the gauges and turned the shutoff lever, she waited, leaning against the cab side wearily, for Morgan to return.

He came across the yard, picking his way between lines and oil spills, his boots crunching on the rough surface. She admired his six foot of sinewy strength from the safety of the cab, secure in the knowledge that he couldn't see her face. He really was a very handsome specimen of manhood, definitely man candy.

He swung aboard, easing back the regulator. 'Brake.' He nodded in her direction.

The train moved slowly into the shed and he stopped it expertly at the end of the line and looked across. 'Thanks.' he climbed down, disappearing into the gloom.

Willow loved the end of a day in the shed. The engine quiet, emitting little puffs of exhaust steam and clinking slightly as it released heat, the smell of diesel and hot metal. The almost stable-like peace of a spirited animal entering its stable for the night was very comforting and restful.

She knew it was fanciful, but she patted the blue livery as she turned off the front lamp and made the engine safe,

16

stumbling slightly over a rail and clutching her supper more securely as she walked towards the door into the repair shop. She had enjoyed herself helping the school kids, but she was tired now. She'd already done two runs up the line. The half-term specials were always busy. Her day had started at six that morning, prepping her own engine; this little jaunt had been unexpected.

DAI AND GAVIN HAD approached her in the station just before she'd gone off shift that evening. She'd seen Gavin's unsteady walk and wondered about it.

'You had too many pints already, Gavin?'

Gavin had revealed a right calf already turning red and purple with a nasty looking graze down the centre of its hairy surface. Willow had been put forcibly in mind of one of those exotic flower petals, the kind that attract, and live on, flies. She gave a small shudder.

'Whatya trying to do? Drive her wild with passion, man?' Dai hadn't been very sympathetic. He turned to Willow. 'You just can't get the staff!'

Whereupon Willow had chimed in with the old joke. 'The driver won't hand it over!'

She'd looked back at Gavin. 'Seriously, how did you do that?'

'Got in the way of a train and its rake. Those Norwegian couplings are hard.'

'Well since you're still walking on the leg I shouldn't think anything is broken.'

'The thing is,' Dai continued, 'Gavin here was supposed to be stoking for Morgan tonight, for the school children's run. How would you feel about doing it?'

SHE GRINNED TO HERSELF now as she pictured the scene when the foreman, Dai, had told Morgan who his fireman was. Especially as they all called her 'Will'. As she wandered through the deserted shed, detouring round machinery and pits in the half light, and through the small door into the workshops, she found herself thinking about her driver.

Morgan could be taciturn to the point of Trappism. She'd heard he didn't like women as well, but discounted it. Now she thought rumour might have been right; if his conversation this evening was anything to go by he could be classified as a misogynist on a par with Aristotle or Kant.

When he'd stepped up to the engine at six that night he'd looked annoyed, asking where his fireman was, even while he could see she was obviously employed in the preparation to set off. Of course he must know there were women working for the railway, but he always contrived to get a male stoker. Until now. His incredulous, 'Will!' as he'd looked at her had not been exactly complimentary, rather as if he'd found half a worm in his salad and feared for the fate of the other half.

He'd said very little throughout the evening, speaking to her only when necessary in that polite voice without its trace of Welsh accent. They'd gone across the embankment, called the Cob, in the evening dusk, and done some shunting in the station yard before going up to the first signal along the line to allow the teenagers to start that part of their filming.

Now she went through the main building and out into the cold air, shivering as she crossed obliquely to enter the passageway to the changing room. She could hear the shower running in the men's section. Bit of a dandy was Morgan, she thought. She debated for a minute using the showers herself, but decided she would walk back to her lodgings and get a bath there.

She sat down to remove her boots and then pulled the grimy overalls down and off with a grunt, hanging them in the locker and putting the boots back on. The cap followed the overalls and a thick honey blonde braid fell down her back to the narrow waistband of her jeans. She tugged, over a well proportioned figure, a navy pullover which had seen better days, then shrugged on a thin denim jacket, wishing she'd remembered to bring her heavy donkey jacket with her, as she flipped her hair out of its confines.

Her hands received a perfunctory wash with Swarfega and soap and then, wrapping a not too clean cream scarf, about her neck, she fished in her pocket for her torch. She slung her canvas meal bag over her shoulder and, gathering her supper which she vaguely hoped would keep her hands warm, prepared to walk along the dark road to her lodgings.

As she emerged Morgan appeared from the adjacent men's changing room. His hair was slicked back and curling wildly in the nape of his neck, little glints of water shining as if he'd scattered his head with tinsel, and he smelt expensive. He was wearing a heavy Harris Tweed jacket and dark brown Chinos. On his right pinkie a chunky signet ring winked in the unshaded bulb outside the changing room door. The engine driver had disappeared to be replaced by a man of the world. Willow glanced down her dishevelled person, feeling like the chimney boy who'd accidently fallen down into the parlour and disturbed the Lord of the Manor at his supper. She might have washed her hands, but the soot took some shifting and she smelt of diesel and degreaser.

Morgan looked down at her from his extra inches, as he came to a halt. She couldn't be much taller than his sister, and Jane was only five two. He hadn't been too pleased at the change of his fireman, but she appeared to know what she was doing and that was all he asked. She hadn't chattered at him, or gushed or flirted either. Now he came to look at her in the light, he saw she looked more than just grimy, she looked tired too, her big green eyes shadowed underneath, and smudges of grease and soot on her face.

On impulse he said, 'Do you want a lift back to the hostel?'

She looked up startled. 'I'm, er, I'm not at the hostel, but no, no thanks.' She stepped back out of his way.

'I'm going towards Minffordd. Are you sure?'

'Quite sure.' She stiffened and turned away, heading out of the door, walking swiftly through the pool of reflected light outside the window and disappearing into the shadows. He stood there for a second or two, somewhat surprised. He knew when he was being given the brush off. He wasn't a vain man but he knew women liked him, or his money anyway he thought with a grimace. He shrugged. Women! He'd never understand them.

He switched off the lights and went outside; walking along the tracks towards the small bach near the works Halt, outside which he'd parked his car. He pressed the key control as he strolled up and watched the lights flick on the sides of the new green Jaguar as the doors unlocked.

Settling in the bucket seat, he set the safety belt and inhaled the smell of new leather, it was a whiff of nostalgia. He grinned to himself; Jane would say he was like a kid with a new toy, but what was the point of earning money if he couldn't enjoy it? He flicked on the lights as he backed up carefully, and drove swiftly down the slope onto the main road.

Willow appeared in his headlights almost immediately. She was trudging along, her shoulders hunched against the icy wind. He pulled up several yards ahead in the left-hand lay-by and got out to lean against the bonnet while he waited for her to come up to him.

'You're cold, you're tired, and it's dark. Let me drop you off home. I promise not to steal your supper.' He nodded at the pasties she still cuddled between her palms.

Willow looked from the immaculately dressed man to the beautiful car and shook her head. She hesitated, obviously looking for a good excuse. 'No thanks. I'm filthy.'

'I'll begin to think there's something special about those pies soon,' he teased with a whimsical smile.

Willow looked astonished but said, 'You can have one if you want.' She held out one foil wrapped bundle.

'Oh no! Not unless you let me pay for it with a lift.'

She looked uncomfortable. 'I'd rather not.' She realised he was frowning at her. 'Thanks.'

Morgan didn't know why he was persisting, he shrugged. 'OK, but don't say I didn't offer.' He got back in the car, slamming the door and starting the engine. With a slight wave of the hand he drove off.

Willow looked after the red tail lights receding into the distance like a couple of evil eyes, and gave a faint shudder more from her thoughts than the cold, and started to walk again. She didn't trust men much, especially men with money. Morgan had seemed polite enough, but Barry, her ex, had seemed polite, till he started telling her what to do, how to dress, where to go. He'd had money too; maybe it was something to do with that, she thought, as she made her way along the roadway, maybe they thought they had the right to order people around, money and power seemed to go hand in hand.

She turned off and went along Quarry Lane by the side of the estuary; it smelt of sea water and decaying vegetation. A potent mix that had her mouth pulling down in disgust. The trees arched overhead, forming a tunnel and making it considerably darker than the main road she'd just left. She didn't like this bit of the walk at night, but it wasn't very far. She straightened up, walking down the centre of the road in deference to her self-defence teacher's advice and using her torch to signal her presence to any oncoming cars.

She was all the more astonished to see her shadow lengthening rapidly in front of her as car lights, travelling at speed, approached with little regard for any sentient beings that happened to be using the same space. She moved quickly to the side of the road stepping onto the grass verge, and groaned as her boots sank into icy water which lapped their tops.

A ripe smell rose up and she wrinkled her straight nose. Her feet made little sucking sounds as she stepped back further to avoid being splashed as the car passed within inches of her body. She heard loud, heavy metal music, coming from the interior and the draught of the car's passing pulled at her clothes, like an evil hand seeking to drag her under the wheels as it whooshed away into the distance.

Looking down to see if it was sheep droppings or a cow pat she had stepped in, she played the torch across her feet, pulling a face in anticipation, then froze at the sight of the decomposing corpse whose stomach cavity she just happened to have her left foot in.

She gave a small scream and felt the bile rise, turning her head away in time to throw the contents of her stomach into a bramble patch along with her carefully nurtured supper. Stepping hastily to the side she searched her pocket for her mobile, praying that reception wouldn't be obscured by the opencast workings from the Quarry looming further up the road.

'Great!' Her hands shook so that it was a major task to press 999. A canoeist or walker, washed up at the end the day, just what she wanted to find! The official voice who answered spoke, an island of calm against which her voice hurled itself.

'Fire, police or ambulance, Miss?'

'Hi. Yes, I want the police, please.' Her voice shook and she fished a crumpled tissue from her pocket and wiped her shaking mouth with a trembling hand. 'Yes, my name is Willow Edwards. I've found a body. I'm on the back road, next to the estuary between Portmadog and Minfordd, about halfway along Quarry Lane. No. I don't know who it is. It's,' she swallowed the saliva pooling in her mouth that tasted of hot metal, 'well, sort of, very dead!'

She listened to the friendly voice on the other end telling her not to touch anything and to stay exactly where she was, they would send a car out straight away but it had to come from Penrhyn, so to be patient.

She looked cautiously back along the road and then down at the ditch; there wasn't a thing she wanted to touch. She didn't need to be told. She shuddered. The moon chose that moment to come out from behind the clouds and illuminate the grisly scene; she swallowed afresh and averted her eyes.

That would teach her to refuse offers of lifts. Someone else could have found this body and she could have been soaking in her landlady's enamel claw-footed bath, full of hot water and aromatic bubbles, right about now.

Willow tortured herself thinking about hot suds and bright lights as she stood by the side of the road stirring from foot to foot to try and keep warm, shivering in the wind which brought the ripe smell of decomposition and a few spots of rain with every fresh gust. She felt sick and admitted to herself she was scared. Every little creak of a tree or rustle in the undergrowth had her heart bouncing up and hitting her front teeth with fear.

She looked away and found her gaze focused on the path up to the cemetery. *'Death in front; destruction in the rear.'* She couldn't remember who said it, but wished they hadn't, or better that she hadn't dredged it from her memory.

When the blue flashing lights of the police car with *'Heddlu'* on the side finally drew up she could have kissed the Welshman who emerged. Ah! Yes, of course, Lord Byron's Childe Harold. Willow, her mind suffering from shock, finally made the connection she'd been unconsciously trying to remember, as the Byronic figure of Sergeant Gareth ap Rhys appeared before her. How he would have reacted to that was a debatable point. His dark grey eyes, black hair and height made him seem like a rock that some women had shown a desire to cling to. He didn't care to be a rock.

He smiled faintly. 'Hello there, *Cariad*. What have you got for us then?' He gently took one of her frozen hands which showed a tendency to clutch at his uniform front. 'Show us where this body is.' The gentle musical cadences of his voice offered as much comfort and reassurance as his solid bulk did, by shielding her from the cold wind of reality.

Willow pointed into the ditch with her torch hand, turning her head away as soon as she was sure the light was picking up the body. 'That's it.'

'Right.' Gareth swung his own powerful beam into line and looked impassively at the remains. 'I think we need to get the inspectors from Caernarfon out here.' He looked at the young constable walking round the back of the car who had been busy at the boot. He turned back towards Willow. 'If you'll just get into the car for a minute.'

He held open the front passenger door of the car and Willow gratefully sank into the warmth. He closed the door on her. She watched as the two policemen conferred and the younger man began to string tape to a tree. The sergeant moved in an assured manner, pointing to various areas and getting some hazard lights and cones from the boot and setting them on the side of the road, before coming and sitting in the car next to her. He offered a quiet smile before picking up the RT and connecting to central control.

'Yes, this is ap Rhys here. Yes, we have got a body; and it's in a bad state of decay.'

He listened to the voice asking, through what sounded like someone frying chips, what he required at the scene.

'Is the body accessible or do you need to call out Mountain rescue?'

'No. It's on the side of the roadway; we'll need canvas, forensics, and floodlights. Can you inform the CID branch?' To further questions he denied need of ambulances for any others. 'No. I can't tell yet. It could be a walker got lost on the marshes or a swimmer got caught by the tide.'

He swung round in his seat. 'I'll need to take you to the station, Miss. I need a statement.' Willow nodded, her teeth clenched tightly together. She thought if she tried to talk at the moment her teeth would chatter like castanets. She was shivering with shock and cold now, and just wanted to be anywhere but on this lonely stretch of dark roadway.

'Fasten your seatbelt.' She tried, unsuccessfully, fumbling with the catch until he came to her rescue, snapping the belt together. 'My name's Sergeant Gareth ap Rhys, *Cariad*. What's yours?'

She opened her mouth and came out with a stuttered 'W-W-Willow.'

'Well, and that's a pretty name. English then, are you?'

She nodded again. Speech seemed to have deserted her for the moment. Gareth turned the key and started the engine. 'I lived in England a good few years; up North. Are you on holiday here?'

'N-no.'

He smiled across at her, and then looked back to the road, checking that his constable was carrying out his orders. Satisfied, he transferred his attention back to Willow. 'Well, don't worry, *Cariad*. You just tell us what you were doing and how you came to find the poor soul. You didn't murder him, did you?'

She shuddered, 'N-no!'

'That's alright then.' He smiled across again, and twisted a knob; the warm air began to circulate. 'Soon be there and we'll get you a nice *panad*.' The sergeant set the car in motion and Willow unconsciously sighed with relief as they moved away from the scene and she was enclosed in the darkness of the squad car and could allow her face to relax from the blandness she'd imposed on it, allowing horror to creep out and have a half holiday's play on her features.

The police station was modern, warm, and redolent of chips, reminding Willow that she hadn't eaten. Not that she had any appetite; the well sugared *panad* of tea in front of her, brown and strong enough to float horseshoes, was making her feel queasy enough. She was conscious of the ugly smell coming from her right boot and vowing she would buy new ones the very next day.

She sat facing the friendly Sergeant ap Rhys, on a hard wooden seat that offered as much comfort as a stone wall. A much scratched table in front of her was as unyielding for the arms she had resting on it, her hands tightly clasped in front of her.

She was in a small room with plain institutional green paint on the walls and a much stained brown cord carpet under her despised boots. A radiator clicked on one wall, sending out a smell of hot paintwork. A corkboard with various notices in two languages hung on the wall behind the sergeant's back.

'So.' He was all business now as he pressed down his ballpoint and smoothed down a fresh sheet of paper. He'd shed his thick blue jacket and cap and sat in his shirt sleeves, giving her his undivided attention. 'Tell me who you are and how you came to find the body. In your own words and in your own time.' He offered a gentle smile and evaluated his witness. She was nervous and uptight but that was understandable. He'd attended a few murders in his time, and finding a corpse unexpectedly was not exactly calculated to settle the mind.

Willow started slowly, her voice faltering a bit when she told how she'd stepped off the road to avoid the car and stood on the body. She explained about being sick and then ringing 999. Gareth wrote down all she said, checking her story and asking questions along the way. He'd have to take her boots and maybe her jeans he thought, they might have evidence on them. 'You didn't get the licence plate I suppose?'

'No, only two letters a 'DV', but it was a modern car with a red and white lightning stripe along the doors, and it had extra fog lights on the back, they were using them too.'

'OK, don't worry.' He made a note; they needed to find that car if only to back up her story, what's more he thought he recognised the description. But he didn't think she'd stood out there waiting for the corpse to rot before ringing the Police!

'How many years have you worked for the railway?'

''This year makes three.'

'How long have you been living at Minffordd, all summer or just for the short holiday season?'

'All summer.'

'Where did you stay previous years?'

'In the new hostel.'

'So why the change?'

'It got rather noisy there at night sometimes.' Willow was aware that this wasn't the whole truth, but didn't think telling a policeman that she didn't want her ex to come looking for her was relevant.

'What's your occupation when you aren't volunteering on the railway?'

'Oh! A radiographer.'

'So where do you do the radiography then?'

Willow sighed. 'I haven't actually got a job at the moment. I did Maternity cover for a year and then I took some time out to think about where I wanted to go next, my mum was ill so I stayed home. I was engaged for a bit, but it fell through.' She offered the information and hoped that that subject could be dropped.

Gareth paused in his writing, looking at her steadily; his grey eyes gave nothing away. He wondered what was behind the sudden evasion. Up until then she'd been answering the questions without hesitation. He made a mental note to circle back to that failed engagement if possible, not tonight, but he'd have to get back to it.

'So, tonight. Do you often go that way home?'

Willow sighed thankfully under her breath; the question of her engagement obviously wasn't relevant, thank God. 'Sometimes. Not usually when it's dark, but I wanted to get home quickly. I was cold and tired.'

'And the car made you jump back and you stood on the body?'

'Yes.' She nodded.

'And, aside from the vomiting, you didn't touch anything?'

She nodded again.

Gareth asked a few more questions and then sat back, eyeing Willow. Aside from that one hesitation, she seemed to him to be an honest and reliable witness. Gareth had learnt his interview technique from a detective he considered one of the best. He didn't think this young woman had committed murder, but he did think she had something to hide. People always did, and Detective Inspector Bell, his old mentor, had said that you have to find out what they're hiding, just to make sure it isn't relevant.

'Well that all seems quite clear. I'll just get this typed up for you to sign. We shall need your boots, *Cariad,* and maybe I can have a look at your jeans to see if they've got any evidence on them.' He saw her swallow visibly but carried on with his comments, facts were facts and he needed those boots. 'One of the cars will take you back to your lodgings. We might need to talk to you again in a day or two. *Paid a phoeni,* it'll only be to check on a few details.' He smiled at her. 'Can I get you another hot drink?' He looked at the untouched mug of tea.

Willow shook her head and leaned back in the chair as he went out. He left the door open and she heard him talking to someone in Welsh. But aside from the basic hello, goodbye, and thanks, she hadn't mastered much of the language despite her father being a Welshman; he'd always spoken English to her mother and herself.

She felt she had been sitting on the hard chair for hours. She was adjusting her bottom to the unyielding wood for what seemed to be the hundredth time and trying to distract her mind by puzzling out the words on a poster on the far wall; it seemed to be something about a *'Noson lawen'*, whatever that was, when he returned with several closely typed sheets of A4 paper.

'If you could read it through and sign at the bottom of each page and at the end, if you agree with what's written? Then the constable here will take you home. I've brought you a spare pair of boots from lost property, if you could change ...?'

Willow gave a small smile and bent to unlace her boots, setting them on a sheet of paper he'd laid on the ground in front of her and putting on the battered pair he offered, before turning to read through the pages. Gareth sat opposite, watching her carefully. She scrawled her name and stood up, lifting her jacket from the back of the chair. Sergeant ap Rhys came round and helped her on with it. 'Alright, *Cariad*. Go home and get some sleep. It will be alright.'

SHE'D ANSWERED THE ENQUIRIES about the filming when she'd arrived back to her lodgings with as much enthusiasm as she could, but the subsequent events had somewhat dulled her recollections. She definitely hadn't wanted to talk about those events to the garrulous woman who had greeted her return so kindly. Mrs Jones was as curious as a cat, her thin nose sniffing out gossip for any choice titbits. Trying to explain why she'd been brought back in a police car had been difficult. Why she'd handed over her boots impossible.

The woman had sat her down in front of a huge, blue, china pot of tea and fished out a packet of cigarettes from her paisley coverall. 'Now you tell me all about it, my dear,' she said, striking a match and applying it to the dangling nicotine. Her curlers had positively bristled about her head as she waited for Willow to explain.

'I found a dead body. The police think it might be a lost walker. I had to make a statement.'

'*Bechod*. You poor thing.'

Willow could see her lining up her story for the delectation of the coffee morning in the chapel.

'And will there be an inquest, do you know?'

'I suppose so.' Willow hadn't really thought about it. Indeed she didn't want to think about it. She felt she would quite like to flee the country, but since she had little money and nowhere to flee to, she would have to stay put and meet the curiosity of her fellow railway enthusiasts with as much *sang-froid* as she could raise.

There was no way she could keep her finding of the body secret if there was to be an inquest. Like all small groups it was an almost incestuous community, sharing every little detail, but also supportive of its members.

She had eventually escaped the inquisition to a bath and her bedroom and now here she sat, wondering what she would do if her name got into the papers and Barry turned up. He'd already made one scene at her old lodgings, showing a temper she had only dimly suspected to exist before.

She sat on her bed, upstairs in one of the row of quarrymen's cottages. The room smelt slightly of mothballs and lavender furniture polish. It wasn't 'alright' because she couldn't get the picture of the body out of her head, or the squelchy feel and sound she'd experienced when she'd stood on it. The smell, despite the hot and sweet-smelling bath she'd taken, still seemed to be in her nostrils, refusing to be ousted by lavender.

She pulled her fleecy and very serviceable dressing gown more tightly round her and tucked her pyjama-clad legs underneath a counterpane and several thick blankets. It was cold in the room with its minimal furnishings of wooden bed and chest of drawers. She could see the beginnings of frosty ferns growing up the window, even though there was a radiator on the wall underneath; but she was willing to admit, if only in her mind, that that wasn't the source of her cold and goose-bump covered skin.

The curtains might be thick blue velvet but they only reached to the bottom of the window frame, allowing a nasty little draught to blow over her upper body, that wasn't the reason for the goose-bumps either. The draught teased among her wet hair which dangled down her back as she alternately combed it and played the small hairdryer across it. She wriggled on the bed, releasing a few strands she had been sitting on. She ought to get it cut; it was a bit of a nuisance, but it seemed such a waste of time going to a hairdresser.

Sergeant ap Rhys appeared to be a pleasant and understanding man but the police had been less than sympathetic when she went to them last time, with complaints of abuse. She had no bruises or broken bones; Barry had only slapped her once. That had been enough to bring her to her senses and break off their engagement. Trying to explain just how he had treated her, his jealousy and the possessiveness that had sapped her confidence in herself, had proved difficult to express and that was part of the reason for the deep seated cold in the pit of her stomach.

She could hear her landlady's clock ticking solidly away downstairs, making the night seem full of small sections of fear and horror. Willow put down the hairdryer and picked up a rapidly cooling mug of cocoa, wrapping her hands round it. Someone was dead and she'd found their body, that was the source of the coldness; a mix of pity, horror, and the thought of someone dying alone.

A pile of letters, written in a spidery hand, lay on top of the sheets. She thought that she would give a lot for the bustle of the hostel tonight. She certainly couldn't concentrate on reading them, though she had tried in a desperate desire to distract her mind, like concentrating on a finger splinter to take your mind off a broken arm. Finishing the cocoa, she put the mug down on the floor and gathered the letters together, placing them in a plastic file and sighing; she'd never find out what they said at this rate.

She pulled the covers up over her shoulders and stuck her face under the covers, trying to breathe warm air into the pocket of space her body was currently occupying. Eventually she gave up and lay looking at the yellow neon light just peeking round the side of the window where the curtains gaped, her eyes wide open, wishing she dared to go to sleep. It had taken most of her store of courage to run this far; she wasn't sure she had the reserves to run again, financially or otherwise.

WILLOW WASN'T THE ONLY one having trouble settling in for the evening. Morgan Williams' resting place, however, was much more comfortable and much less open to the inquisitive. In the rather exclusive village of Portmerion; an Italianate conglomerate of rescued buildings set incongruously at the side of the sea on the West Coast of Wales, were to be found hotels and private villas. Morgan was seated in a small but very well appointed cottage. He had rented it for a month, preferring its quiet anonymity to the hostel or lodgings.

He could go to the hotel in the centre of the village for meals and a very obliging student was available to keep the place clean and tidy. He sat now in a deep leather chair, his feet stretched out towards a cosy log fire which crackled cheerfully. He'd put some music on the CD player, but hardly heard it.

He was deep in thought, his hand warming the small shot of brandy in the deep glass and pondering the behaviour of Miss Willow Edwards. He had driven away from her that evening because he believed that when a woman said no, that's what she meant. He didn't think women required anyone to make their decisions for them. He hadn't been happy, though; to leave a fellow creature in the cold and incipient rain, and especially a woman. It made him feel very uncomfortable.

She had looked rather fiercely at him from those huge green eyes, her stance that of a cat protecting its litter of kits. He was still trying to figure out why a simple offer of a lift should have brought that expression to her face, when the phone rang.

Taking up the receiver he spoke. '*Nos da*, Morgan Williams here.' He listened to the honeyed tones on the other end.

'Yes, Mary, I'm back from playing trains for the day. Is there anything spoiling in the office that needs me?'

His secretary of seven years knew what he wanted to be told. And what he needed to be told. 'The merger is coming along nicely. I've set up the final meetings for ten days time when you get back, Morgan. Your sister will be back from New York at the same time and Hamish will hold the fort in the meantime.'

'So why the phone call, Mary?'

'The American company, Morgan. You'd think they'd be more go ahead. They didn't like Jane being your representative, and there was an e-mail wanting to know when you would be available to talk to them.'

'I won't be back for ten days.' His voice had reinforced steel girders running down the middle. Mary didn't quail. She'd heard that tone before; she knew he wasn't angry with her. 'So long as Jane hasn't mucked things up, and I don't for a minute believe she will have, they can wait on my convenience. I'm incommunicado, Mary, unless it's family trouble. You'll reassure Jane for me, won't you? I'll speak to her myself as soon as possible.'

'Fine, Boss. That's what I thought you'd say, but I also thought I'd better keep you in the loop.'

'OK. Anything else I need to know?'

'No. Hamish's his usual competent self. Everything's under control otherwise.'

'Great. Ring me if you need me. Bye, Mary.'

Morgan replaced the receiver with a sigh. He had built the engineering firm up from a small but struggling family concern at his father's death, to a multinational organisation. He believed in delegation; he just wished there weren't so many chauvinists in the workplace.

He laughed at himself. 'And what are you then, Morgan? You won't have a female working with you on the railway?' He picked up his brandy and swirled the rest of the liquor round the balloon glass before swallowing it. 'Yeah, and you know why.

They like the money too much, boyo!' He mocked himself as he set the glass down with a clink on the side table and stood up.

He had an early start tomorrow driving a Farlie double engine. There was a coach load booked at both ends of the line. It looked like being a busy day on the trains.

As he went to lock the doors he looked out at the now teeming rain and wondered how the fugitive Willow was; he hoped she was tucked up snugly for the night. He locked the door and turned towards his bedroom, reflecting that she hadn't been a bad fireman at all. He wouldn't mind having her on the footplate again provided she just did her job. Then he wondered just why she should be haunting his thoughts.

2

SERGEANT GARETH AP RHYS was having a very busy night. Having disposed of his witness he returned to the corpse. Gwyn had done a good job of cordoning off the scene. The tapes were strung like a ticker-tape parade and police swarmed over the area like ants over a pile of sugar. This area of Wales wasn't exactly geared up for a death in mysterious circumstances, so some of the police were strangers to Gareth, but not all of them, unfortunately.

'OK, Gwyn, I'm back. Has the medical examiner arrived yet?'

'Just arrived, Sarge.' Gwyn pointed with his chin at the elegant man approaching, case in hand and a gloomy look on his face.

'Oh Lord! Him. Ah well, Gwyn, beggars can't be choosers.' Gareth went forward to greet the Medical Examiner and fill him in on the circumstances, before they moved the body to an equally chilly location for the post mortem.

'Don't know why you called me in.' The morose man wiped the rain from his face and gazed down at the mortal remains. Gareth stood stoically, his waterproof leaving a puddle of rain at his feet, and soaking trousers where the jacket bottom rubbed against the tops of his legs.

He could have said, 'because I need an ME to confirm death no matter how manky the corpse,' but he saved his breath. The ME continued to gaze down at the exposed chest cavity and then he looked up at the black haired copper waiting for him with monumental patience. And given Gareth's size, monumental wasn't difficult to achieve he thought. 'Well he's dead. I don't know how long, but given that degree of decomposition, over a week. You can scrape him up and take him away. Send him to Liverpool for the coroner.' He turned away and began walking back to his car.

Gareth wiped rain off his face and looked at Gwyn. 'Didn't even get his hands dirty.' He gave another glance at the corpse. 'You heard the man. Has the wagon come yet?'

'Not yet, Sarge.' Gwyn took off his cap and shook the wet from the brim before speaking, he was, if possible, wetter than the corpse, and he'd been standing around waiting for someone to arrive in the dark and rain. He was not always sure of his moves, being a very young policeman, but Gareth was a good trainer. 'I radioed for extra men as you see, forensics are due any minute. I've cordoned and sent those who have arrived to canvas

43

the nearest houses.' He looked like a pup expecting praise for not wetting on the carpet.

Gareth half smiled. 'Fine. I shouldn't think we'll be in charge for long. The DI division will take over pretty quick. You get an impression of those tyre prints like I asked you too?'

'Yes, Sarge. Took some photos with the digital too.'

'Good, because I think I might just know who it was who caused Miss Willow Edwards to step into the ditch. If we can't catch murderers, Gwyn, we can catch dangerous drivers.'

Gareth turned away at a hail from one of the other policemen. 'Yo.' He went over.

Gwyn stood watching him talking, he liked the sergeant, the man might be tough but he always thanked you, and what's more he didn't expect you to just do something, he gave an explanation where he could. He took his eyes from contemplation of Gareth as a small cavalcade of police vehicles arrived and began to disgorge men, in the manner of the *Keystone Cops.* The business of solving a suspicious death could really get going now.

GARETH SLUNG HIS JACKET into the back of the squad car and settled the belt around his chest. 'Right Gwyn, take us to Blaenau. I'll tell you where after that.'

Gwyn, nothing loathe to leave the miserable scene behind them, put the car in motion, and set off. He was conscious that his superior was in a foul temper. He just hoped he wasn't the one to have provoked it. He drove steadily, thinking about his activities for the last couple of hours. He couldn't think of anything, finally he said, 'Sir, Did I forget to do something? Only I'd rather you told me, then I can not do it.' He gave a quiet gulp as Gareth swung around in the darkened car and he became aware of the grey gaze fastened on him.

Gareth took the comment in his stride. 'Do you think you did something wrong?'

'Er. No, well, maybe, only I can't think what. Only you're er ...'

'You're going to have to stop second guessing yourself, Gwyn. Have a little confidence, lad. I wouldn't have left you to guard the scene if I didn't think you were capable.'

Gareth sighed. You didn't, in his opinion, rake down a senior officer in front of a junior one. It was a courtesy he'd learnt, and believed in. However, he'd had his opinion and actions challenged in front of half the men in the Gwynedd area that night, and he didn't appreciate the sympathetic looks he'd been given, anymore than the odd smirks.

Gareth had transferred out of Wales once before, because of the attitude of Detective Inspector Jenkins. He didn't know why the man took such a delight in antagonising him, but Gareth always had a strong desire to go and have a shower after prolonged, or even short, contact with the Jenkins presence. The man made him feel unclean with his oily attitude to those higher up, and the dirty looks he gave those lower in the ranks.

He returned to watching the steady swishing of the wipers as they struggled against the Welsh weather. He addressed the windshield, careful to keep his voice devoid of emotion. Nevertheless he offered praise and reassurance, 'It wasn't anything you did, Gwyn. You prepared the scene well; the senior sergeant was telling me he thought you'd done a good job.' He nodded at the bridge just emerging in the orange lighting. 'Turn and head along the main street, we're going to pay a visit to the Evans boys.'

A car with red lightning flashes along the sides was parked half on the pavement. Gareth climbed out, pulling his jacket on and snapping the poppers over his flak jacket. He glanced across to see if young Gwyn had his flak fastened. The Evans boys could be nice; then again they could be nasty, it depended on the quality of cannabis they were currently smoking.

Gareth nodded approval. Gwyn, despite the bulky rainwear was making sure his baton was to hand. They stood on the pavement and knocked briskly on the door. Lights were shining from both upper rooms and the front room. The upper rooms suddenly went dark. However the door opened and a teenager poked his head out cautiously. He looked from Gareth to Gwyn and then his eyes settled back on Gareth.

Gareth was a big man. Not just tall, but broad. He filled the view in the same way that the slate tips that hung over the town did. You couldn't miss him and you couldn't get past him.

'Hullo, Sarge, did you want something?'

Gareth sniffed the air in a marked manner, the unmistakably sweet smell of cannabis was thick in the room in front of him. 'Well now, I might just be wanting a word ...'

BACK AT THE CRIME scene men were being deployed. DI Jenkins was proceeding to annoy as many men as possible in the shortest period of time. The forensics team largely ignored him, which he didn't like either. 'How much longer are you going to take to process this scene? It's just some silly sod who doesn't listen to weather forecasts. Keeping decent folk from their beds and causing us to stand around in the rain while you mess about.'

The SOCO glanced at his men and nodded for them to continue while he walked over to the detective. He wasn't a member of the force; he was employed by the Home Office. He didn't give a 'monkeys' what this detective wanted; the scene would be examined carefully and correctly.

'It might just be a 'silly sod' to you, but he's a human being and my men will treat his remains with respect, and find out how he came to be where he is, before we release the scene.' He paused just long enough to make the, 'Sir,' sound like an afterthought. He spoke quietly. 'I suggest you go away and arrange for your men to start a house to house. The body has been lying in that ditch for about sixteen hours by the sign under him; I want to know why no-one noticed him earlier. Perhaps if you did your job we could get ours done more quickly.' He turned and walked away.

Jenkins opened and shut his mean little mouth a time or two, which, combined with his small eyes, made him look like a hooked hake. Then he turned and began to harass the officers standing watching the quiet confrontation.

THE STORM SEEMED TO have blown itself out next morning when Willow woke. She had a free day and had planned to do mundane things like the washing and shopping. Now, however, she stood at the window, shivering in the chill, and gazed at the picture postcard sky with its scattering of white nimbus. This promised to be too beautiful a day to waste. She wasn't a great believer in the spiritual rewards of early rising but today might just prove her wrong. She hurried through her morning ablutions, partly to escape the cold and partly because she was anxious to get going before anyone came to ask questions.

She would go for a walk, she decided. She skipped down the central runner of the narrow stairs. 'Mrs Jones.' She put her head round the kitchen door and addressed the paisley-clad rump presented for her inspection as her landlady bent over the fridge.

'*Bore Da*, what would you like for your breakfast?' The voice echoed from the interior as the woman continued to rummage in the cold box. She emerged with a crock of eggs in her work reddened hands. 'Could you fancy a couple of eggs on toast?'

Willow nodded. She hadn't eaten since midday the day before, between work and dead bodies. 'And do you think I can have a packed lunch? It's too gorgeous to spend time indoors.'

'Of course, *Cariad*. Where will you go?' Mrs Jones bustled about preparing breakfast for her lodger, while Willow sat at the prettily set table and drank a cup of the strong brew favoured by her landlady.

'I don't know; it was nice on the seashore the other day. I found quite a few caves along the bottom of the cliffs I thought might be worth exploring.'

'You be careful! That tide has caught a few explorers in its time. You could try the walk on top of them, it's an easy climb and a bit sheltered.' Mrs Jones put a steaming plate of toast in

49

front of her, with fluffy scrambled eggs piled high atop. 'Or you could walk across; you can go into Portmerion. Pretty it is there, no matter what time of year.' Mrs Jones nodded her head in agreement with herself. She stood with her hands on her ample hips, making her shadow look like an eighteenth century panniered dress, as she watched her young lodger pick up a knife and fork.

Willow nodded her thanks for both food and information. This was why she stayed, despite the woman's curiosity and garrulousness. Mrs Jones' cooking was the stuff of a gourmet's dreams and, despite the antiquated plumbing, her house was spotless.

A short time later, replete with breakfast, clad in the ubiquitous jeans and with a thick, green, waterproof jacket and a light backpack on her back, she set off. She had debated going to fetch her father's old Morris Minor, but it hardly seemed worth the trouble of driving it from the hostel yard.

It had carried all she possessed when she moved down to Wales, but, aside from one or two day trips, had lived a hermit existence in one of the old carriage sheds for most of the time since. She felt rather guilty about that; her father had lavished such loving care on it, polishing it every Saturday morning.

As she strode along the main road she mused on those happy times as a child. She wondered what he would have made of the events of last night. She had no inclination to take the bottom road today. She took the path up through the gardens of the old stationmaster's house and crossed the line at the Halt, heading up onto the top cliffs. She'd had to stop briefly to allow the double to steam past. Morgan was driving and she gave him a wave, but she didn't think he'd noticed her.

She was wrong; he'd spotted her as soon as they'd rounded the curve of the line. So had his companion. 'Isn't that Willow? She's a pretty girl, don't you think, Morgan?' The statement was accompanied by a sly smile over the top of the boilers at his driver. He knew, as did everyone else, that Willow had fired for Morgan the previous evening. And everyone knew that Morgan always asked for a male fireman.

Morgan grunted but didn't take his eyes off his gauges. His fireman was a nosy sort and Morgan wasn't about to give him fuel for gossip. He smiled quietly to himself; she was a pretty girl. When she wasn't covered in oil and soot!

Climbing the hillside through oak and ash, busy littering the path with their unwanted leaves, Willow wasn't conscious of her looks at all; she couldn't see the pink cheeks and sparkling eyes which had attracted the notice of the fireman. She climbed higher up the path, stopping occasionally to look at the view of the sea outside the estuary entrance. It slowly slunk its way towards the land through deep gullies, a leopard approaching its prey, ready to whip and tear the unwary who walked by its shores.

She was only distracted by the scene occasionally, being deep in thought. She'd come to this part of Wales at the beginning of the summer because it was familiar and was where her father had been born. She hadn't anticipated the language problem though. It hadn't seemed such a problem when she was only down for a few weeks at the height of the season. But a full summer had shown a difference. She was mulling over how she might learn a language which appeared to be as slippery as an eel to get hold of, and whose words changed their beginnings apparently as randomly as the Welsh weather.

Her reverie was rudely broken by the curious behaviour of Deniol and Sian who she could see further up the hill. They appeared to be carrying rucksacks and, while she had one herself, she couldn't imagine what they wanted with something big enough to accommodate a double duvet, between them. They appeared to be unaware of her presence, arguing somewhat fiercely as they stood at a wooden kissing stile, the arms waving, as if signalling the commencement of battle at Trafalgar, and, it seemed to Willow, that war might break out any minute. Sian stood on the far side of the gate as it separated the path from an open field, scowling at her friend.

As Willow came up to them she admired again the dark Celtic looks of Deniol contrasting with the almost Scandinavian blondness of Sian. They fell silent as they became aware of her presence.

'Hi, you two. Are you going camping for the weekend?'

Deniol looked embarrassed. 'Well, not exactly, Miss Edwards.' He turned to Sian, and muttered to her in Welsh. Willow caught her name and the violent shake of the head Sian gave.

He continued in Welsh addressing Sian, 'Well, I say yes. We need someone who can drive, and she can!'

Willow looked from one to the other in surprise, in her experience the Welsh were polite to a fault, always reverting to English when they were in the presence of those who didn't have the Celtic tongue.

'Can I help you two in some way?'

Sian shook her head violently again, but Deniol nodded at Willow but spoke again to Sian. 'We have to tell someone; he's too sick for us to deal with.'

He turned to Willow and spoke in English. 'It's like this, Miss. We found a walker late Thursday afternoon. He didn't seem to speak any Welsh or English and he hadn't got the right clothes on for the weather. He was cold and wet, and seemed scared. So after a bit of trying to understand each other we tried to get him to come back to town, but he wouldn't budge from the hillside, and it was getting dark.' Deniol stopped. 'We have to be back by six my *tad* says. It's not he doesn't trust us you understand.' He coloured. 'Anyway, we didn't like to leave him, the walker, so we showed him how to get into one of the empty holiday cottages.'

'We didn't mean any harm, honest!' Sian was going almost as red as her Aran jumper as she interrupted. 'They houses sit there empty, and the English don't care that we can't afford to get our own houses 'cos they've push the prices up beyond our wages.'

'Sian, this isn't the time for that!' Deniol was now beetroot red. He turned more fully to Willow, one of the despised English. 'Sorry, Miss, we don't count you.' He took Sian's hand and stopped her from speaking with a look. 'So, anyway, we showed him this house, and we went up yesterday to see if he'd gone, but he was still there, and he hadn't eaten anything, so we went and got some food. And then we went back today with some more.'

Sian, brushing her ash blonde locks from her face, took up the tale. 'Only he'd fallen, see, sometime last night I think, and what's more I think he's broken his leg, only he's hot and he won't wake up, see.' She looked embarrassed. 'I don't think he'd want us to call an ambulance and, anyway, he's in someone's house and we said he could go in and – oh, Miss, we don't want him to get into trouble,' she gulped, 'nor we don't either.'

Willow looked at the two earnest and worried faces in front of her and came rapidly to a decision.

'Here's what we'll do. OK? You take me to look at him and then we'll go from there.'

The two youngsters looked at each other, exchanging some sort of silent message, then Deniol nodded with relief. She gestured for them to lead the way. Deniol gallantly helped her over the stile and they set off across the rough tussock grass of the field towards a far gate leading into what Willow had assumed was a small copse.

'It's back here, Miss' His words were almost whipped away by the stiff breeze as they climbed higher up the hill, past sheep that stood stoically, their backs into the wind, and watched the humans scrambling past.

Willow could see a small bach-type cottage set amid the trees, with a miniature square of dry-stone walling forming a somewhat dubious barrier against the incursions of curious sheep and barbed brambles. 'I wouldn't have even known this was here.' She stepped carefully around the trailing plants which were encroaching onto a cinder path leading to the front door.

'It was a shepherd's cottage, Miss, and then some incomers bought it. They only visit a couple of times a year.'

'How do we get in?'

'Round the side, Miss, there's a door. It's not locked.'

Now that Willow was with them a good deal of their confidence was returning. 'My *tad* says you have to dress properly to go walking in Welsh hills even if it's only for a daytime walk.' Sian offered the information over her shoulder as she opened the door and stepped into the stone-flagged kitchen. 'And you should be aware of the weather at all times and seek shelter if necessary.' Sian almost chanted the advice so obviously drummed into her head.

'All sound advice. Now let's see what this young man of yours has done to himself.'

A couple of chairs and a small table comprised the furnishings, along with a very ancient and somewhat grubby black-lead stove which was set into one wall. Willow's nostrils were assailed by the scent of dry-rot and damp wafting up from the red tiled flooring.

'Through here, Miss.' Deniol led the way through another door. This room was better furnished with three mismatched but comfortable looking chairs and a small coffee table. A Welsh dresser obscured most of one wall with willow pattern china set out on its shelves. Everything had a thick layer of dust on it, like velvet on a deer antler.

As they entered Willow got her first look at the young man they had been talking about. He was lying on the carpet, covered by a couple of multicoloured blankets.

'He was over near the door with his leg all bent, Miss, so we sort of tugged him onto the carpet then covered him up. We couldn't decide what to do, so we thought we'd get my Dad maybe to help us only ...' Deniol stopped and took a gulp of air. 'We shouldn't really be in here.'

'OK, let me have a look; in another life I was a radiographer.' She smiled at the pair of faces looking hopefully at her.

Carefully pulling back the covers she examined the specimen of manhood before her.

'You can see, Miss, he hasn't got the right clothes on.'

And indeed Willow could see; his clothing was very thin for a Welsh winter. T-shirt and three-quarter-length trousers, both of indeterminate hue, light canvas shoes with no socks. She looked around. 'Had he got a coat or jacket or something?'

'He'd got this.' Sian pulled at a rather moth-eaten ribbed jumper in a faded green which was folded and being used as a pillow.

Willow was doing a rapid survey of her new patient. 'You're right. He's got a break to his upper thigh bone.' The man gave a quiet groan as her probing fingers felt the crepitus under the skin. She spoke to him but he didn't rouse. She took his pulse and then started a quick overall body exam to see if there was any other damage.

'Oh!' She drew in a sharp breath. 'I'm sorry, my dears, but if we don't get him to hospital fairly rapidly your friend might die. You see those little spots?' The youngsters peered at the small red spots on his chest.

'What is it, measles?' Sian stared, fascinated at the hairy chest with its crimson embellishments.

Willow wondered if it was the spots, or the chest looking not unlike a horse ready for the knacker's yard, that was holding Sian's gaze, but didn't ask. 'No. I'm pretty certain he's got a clot of fat that's escaped from his leg bone, stuck in his lung. And that could kill him. I need to phone for an ambulance and get him to a doctor. Do you two want to disappear before I do that?'

The two of them looked at her, then at each other. Deniol spoke, 'No, Miss Edwards, we wouldn't leave you alone with him, and anyway we got him into this mess. It wouldn't be fair to go off now.'

Willow nodded. 'I'll phone then.' She pulled her small mobile out and for the second time in twenty four hours was asked which service she required.

Deniol had to take the phone when it came to giving instructions. The place wasn't exactly easy to get to by vehicle; it would require a small trek across a boggy field by the ambulance brigade.

The three of them settled down to wait. Deniol put a comforting arm around Sian's shoulder as they all crouched on the floor. 'We brought some sandwiches for him, Miss Edwards.' Sian proffered foil-wrapped bread with ham and lettuce visible round its edges.

'That's alright. I was planning on a picnic so I've got food.' Willow smiled at them. They'd both begun to look anxious again, they needed distraction she thought. She had what she considered a brainwave.

'You could help me if you like.'

'Do we need to shift him or something?'

'No, this young man needs to be kept as still as possible. No. I've got some letters and they're in Welsh. Maybe you could translate some for me, while we wait.'

Willow rummaged around in her rucksack and pulled out the small clear zip packet. 'These were in my parents' house and when my mother died a couple of years ago I found them. I can't read them. I've been trying to, but your language isn't easy.' She grinned at them.

She pulled out a notebook. 'You can see what trouble I've had. Every time I look for a word it starts with a different letter!' She grimaced. 'I thought maybe I could learn the basics and that would help, but what with mutations and a different alphabet ...' She shrugged.

Deniol had been trying to decipher the closely written scrawl on the first letter she'd handed to him. 'It's old, Miss.'

'Deniol, call me Willow. I feel like your teacher with all this 'Missing'.'

He coloured. 'Yes, Miss - I mean, Willow.'

Sian cast Willow a dark look but Willow ignored it. 'You would both be doing me a huge favour. They're from my grandfather's brother, I think. And the last one is dated November 1927.'

'Coo, you must be old, Miss!' The grin was gamine.

Willow wasn't sure if Sian was being ingenuous or just cheeky, but she grinned back at her. 'Well, perhaps not that old!'

'I can't really make it out, Willow. It seems to be just a personal letter. He writes about a crane that won't go under a bridge and there's a bit about cricket. Oh! We lost against New Zealand.' Deniol sounded as disappointed as if the event had happened the day before.

'Is that the bit with *Zealand Newydd*? I wondered what that was all about. I thought maybe that's where my great-uncle went.'

'No, Miss, it's the cricket. But there is a bit about Australia - maybe he went there. It says ...' Deniol turned the paper round, with a frown gathering, 'no, that's something about Canberra and their parliament opening.' He turned back to the letter. 'There's something about the General Strike. I remember reading about that in the history books.' He seemed awed by the fact that history was real life to some people. Sian was reading another letter.

'Maybe he went to Beddgelert; I can read that word but what the rest of the sentence is ... oh, a hurricane! No, that can't be right, we don't get them here.' She frowned, turning the page upside down, and then over, in and an effort to read the crossed pages. 'I wonder why there's a bit of candle wax stuck to the back.'

'Maybe his candle dripped.'

Sian was puzzling over some phrase. Willow could see her mouth forming words but she didn't look up. 'It says here that there is a shortage of horses for the farm since the war and they have to haul stones on sleds. You wouldn't get many stones on a sled and the plastic would soon break.'

'It wouldn't have been plastic then.' Deniol looked at his girlfriend in disgust. Then he frowned. 'Which war would that have been then? Was it the one against Hitler?'

Willow started to speak and then heard the tramp of approaching feet.

The two youngsters had also heard the noise and looked at her for guidance. '*Paid a phoeni.* Have I that right? Don't worry!' She smiled reassuringly at them.

Deniol nodded. 'Yes, Miss.' He handed the letter back but still looked anxiously towards the door.

'Go and bring them in, Deniol.' She turned towards Sian as that young lady handed the other letter over, her white face reflecting her fear. 'Let's get your friend to hospital. If you hadn't been caring enough to come and check on him he would probably have died up here on his own. No-one is going to shout at you. I'll deal with them. OK?'

'Yes, Miss. Willow, I mean.' Sian tried to smile as the ambulance men entered.

Willow set the conversational ball rolling. 'Hi, fellas, did you enjoy the hike over the field.'

'Oh, yeah! Wading through fields of sheep droppings is my idea of a fun Saturday morning.' The young ambulance man had a strong Liverpudlian accent and a twinkle in his eye, but despite the comment and accompanying grin on his long thin face he was focused on his prospective patient.

'The call said it was urgent. What is it, hypothermia?'

'Well, probably he's suffering from that a bit, but I'm more concerned by the advanced signs of a fat embolism from that broken femur.'

'You a doctor, Miss?' They obviously weren't going to take her word for it. Willow donned her professional mask and pointed out the betraying marks as the men began to unwrap a space blanket. 'I think you'd better blue light him, lads. I'm a radiographer, so I do know what I'm talking about.'

'Right ho! Give us a hand here, George. We'd better splint it before we move him.'

'Don't try to stretch it!' Willow put out a restraining hand. 'Just stabilise. Trust me; you don't want to puncture his artery to add to his woes.'

'What's his name, Miss?'

'I have no idea. My young friends found him with this broken leg and asked me to help them.'

'Do you know him then, son?'

Deniol shook his head, he glanced across at Willow. 'We just found him and saw his leg was broken and went for help, and Willow came to help us.'

Sian chimed in. 'We don't know anything about him at all.'

'OK, don't worry. Someone is bound to claim him once we get him to hospital.'

George, obviously the older and more experienced, flicked a cowlick of grey hair out of steady brown eyes as he assessed the situation.

He knelt down at the side of the passive body and took a pulse, monitoring the breathing at the same time. 'Could do with a bit of oxygen here, Quinn.'

Quinn flicked the catches on the black box he'd brought in, while George shifted to the task in hand, holding the limb steady and directing his willing helpers to get the man onto a stretcher. Quinn, his opposite number, slid a board under the injured man's back before fitting a mask over the white face of their patient and holding his head steady.

'Right, you kids, you're doing great. Now I want you to lower him onto his back without twisting him. Together, on three. One, two, three.'

The combined group settled the inert young man onto the stretcher and George wrapped him snugly in the silver blanket, then piled pale blue aertex ones on top, strapping black belts around to secure the resultant bundle and placing a small oxygen tank at the side of his upper body. The gentle hiss marked a counterpoint to the harsh rasp that the stranger was now emitting from his labouring chest.

'Thanks.' George nodded at the trio. 'You take the front, Quinn.' The two men raised their burden and prepared to leave.

'Where are you taking him?' Deniol looked anxiously at the man who lay strapped to the stretcher between the two ambulance men, swinging like a hunter's trophy.

'*Ysbyty Gwynedd* at Bangor.' George offered a smile and they headed out the door.

Willow looked at her fellow conspirators. 'See, I told you it would be alright. I'll ring up later and find out what's happened and let you two know. I can take you to visit if you want?'

Deniol and Sian looked at her and then at each other. 'That would be great, Miss. Maybe someone will find out who he is by then.'

'Right then, let's put this house to rights and make it secure. Then we can all have easy consciences.'

The teenagers set about gathering up the blankets and packing them away into the large rucksack. Willow, meanwhile, went through into the only room she had yet to see. As sparsely furnished as the rest of the cottage, it contained a three drawer chest with a blue rug on the floor in front of it. The dresser top had a comb, a pen and an open writing pad beside a small leather wallet. It all smelt slightly of unwashed clothes and the all-pervading damp.

The wallpaper was a horticulturalist's nightmare with large bunches of what might be supposed to be roses, if they'd been viewed by someone on expensive and illegal drugs. Dark lines of mould ran up this designer's excrescence to add further to the dismal scene and give a clue as to the source of the invasive aroma.

A metal framed double bedstead was the only other furnishing; the mattress had been covered by an eiderdown that had seen better days, presenting to her discerning eye the appearance of a moth's banquet. A very old, slightly-stained, striped bolster along the top of the headboard completed the coverings of the bed.

The young man had slept on the top of the bed by the looks of the crumpled covering. A small rucksack in an indeterminate brown was sitting at the foot of the bed, its drawstring open to reveal a shabby and much faded red plastic anorak. Willow, feeling like an intruder, gathered up the few things from the dresser. And closing the pad which was covered with what she assumed was writing, and which reminded her vaguely of Pitman's shorthand, she stuffed them in the top of the bag and pulled its strings tight.

She walked back into the living room. Deniol and Sian stood holding hands, the anxious look back on their faces.

'I wish we'd looked in the bedroom before they took your young man away. I've found some more of his possessions!'

She showed the bag to the two young people. 'Never mind, we can take it with us when we go and visit him.'

'Perhaps it'll tell us who he is, Miss.' Sian looked at the bag with ill-concealed curiosity.

'Probably, my dear, but let's leave him a bit of privacy.' Willow hefted the bag along with her own rucksack and headed out the door. The pair followed her and Deniol pulled the door shut behind them, dropping the metal latch in place.

'What shall we do now, Miss?'

Willow stood looking about her; she was no longer in the mood for walking and, besides, she now had an extra bag. 'I think if it's alright by you two, we'll head back into town and have something to eat. My treat.' She accepted their nod of agreement, and the three of them set off down the hill.

'After that, I'll ring the hospital and find out what's happening. How does that sound? It usually takes about three hours to get seen and put on a ward.'

Stumbling slightly, they all walked by the still incurious sheep, Deniol leading the way. Sian walked beside Willow. 'Miss,' she waited for Willow to nod, 'what will we tell my *Tad*? About the man.' The words were almost snatched away by the wind which had turned quite cold and brisk.

'Well, if I were you I should tell the truth. After all, you were only trying to care for him. Your Dad should be proud of you. Do you want me to come with you, while you explain?'

Sian nodded again. 'It's just about letting him into the house, Miss. We don't mind the rest.'

'Well, I think it was very sensible of you both.'

Willow looked out across the estuary as they reached the woodland path she'd come up the hill by. 'It's going to rain again. Maybe it's just as well I'm not heading across the top today.'

'You can always tell what the weather is going to be if you look across to Black Rocks, Miss. It gets really black when the rain is coming in.'

Deniol held out a hand to Sian and they walked ahead of Willow down the path. Willow looked in the direction of Black Rocks, where the black clouds clustered in a dark threatening armada.

The pair in front of her still seemed a bit subdued. As the path widened she came abreast of them. 'Are we catching the down train at the Halt or walking across the Cob? I think you're right about the weather, Deniol. We'll be rather wet if we take too long walking into town.'

The pair looked at her 'Er ... it's a bit,' Deniol hesitated 'Well we haven't er ...'

'Oh!' Willow looked at the two young people who suddenly seemed ill at ease again. 'Freebie! We'll ride in the guard's van, just this once.'

'Cor! Thanks, Willow.'

They waited in companionable silence for the down train, Deniol and Sian sitting on the wooden bench under a small half shelter. The teenagers where obviously worried still, about the part they had played in the recent drama, since even the prospect of a free ride didn't lift their gloom entirely. Willow, her back to the line, was looking up the estuary towards Snowdon, but she looked down at them as they remained silent. 'Come on kids, your Dad isn't going to eat you for being good Samaritans!'

'No, Miss. But he can shout!' Sian obviously feared her father's wrath. Willow foresaw an interesting afternoon looming; she wasn't too good at confrontation, but she'd do her best.

The train, when it huffed to a stop, was a single, with a small rake of carriages filled to bursting with eager passengers. The guard stepped down and gave Willow a friendly, 'Hi.' Willow could hear an American twang say something about the cute little fields, as she waved to the driver and hopped aboard the wooden guard's van with her two travelling companions. These grinned shyly at the guard as he stepped back inside after blowing his whistle. The van had only recently been refurbished and still smelt strongly of varnish, its woodwork gleaming in the single electric lamp. Sian wrinkled her nose at Deniol, who grinned at her.

'Stowaways, Willow?'

'Hi, Alex, the Stars of the movie last night,' she waved a hand at Deniol and Sian, introducing them in turn. 'I met them up the hill and now we're all going for a meal to discuss how we're going to share the Hollywood rights.'

'Yeah, right! You going to share with Morgan too?'

'Oh, no! He was only the driver, he didn't do that much! It's the fireman that controls an engine.' Willow grinned at Alex, deflecting his curiosity.

'Oh, Miss!' Deniol laughed. 'Mr Hughes said, Morgan said, you were a good fireman too.'

Alex raised an eyebrow at her under his guard's cap. 'He did, did he? Ain't that interesting?' he drawled, betraying his New York origins and sounding like a thirties gangster.

'Mind your own business, Alex.' Willow could feel the colour mounting her cheeks as they grew warm.

She changed the subject slightly as she glanced out of the little window upon which spots of rain were now beginning to fall. 'It looks like you two got the best night of the week for your filming; this looks as though it's going to set in for the afternoon.'

Deniol, following her look, nodded glumly, 'We're back at school next week, so I don't care if it does rain, 'cept maybe for the rugby.'

The train rattled its way into the station at this point, the three jumped out behind the guard and followed him up the platform as he unlocked doors. 'Thanks, Alex.' Willow waved as they reached the shop and turned in.

'Do you two want to eat in 'Spooners'?'

Deniol exchanged a look with Sian, sniffed the air like a hungry wolf, and said, 'Chips?'

'Yeah. And tea.'

Deniol took Willow's two rucksacks from her while she went over to the counter.

They found seats while Willow ordered, then she brought mugs of tea across. 'The advantages of getting off first,' she said, and settled into her seat as the massed hordes from the train flooded the café and started to line up, waiting for service.

'Now, when we've eaten, do you want me to come with you? I really don't mind, but I think we'd better get it over with soon before you both suffer chronic indigestion.'

They laughed, as she'd intended, and seemed to relax a bit, noticeably brightening up as they ate, and by the time they had finished the mugs of tea both seemed resigned to explaining their morning to both sets of parents.

Having dealt first with Deniol's parents, Eirlys and David Myrddin, who proclaimed that both teenagers had been sensible, they went down a nearby back street, its road still cobbled and glistening in the now fairly heavy rain, to Sian's house.

Willow smiled brightly as she stood on the doorstep, the rain dripping off the ends of her fringe and causing her to blink the moisture away. Sian seemed the more nervous of the two, so Willow braced herself to meet hostility.

'Hi.' She held out a wet hand to the brawny specimen who opened the door in front of her. Sian's father, clad in shirt sleeves and dark corduroy trousers, looked just a bit harassed; the hand gripping hers was hard and callused. 'Your daughter asked me to come and help her explain a little problem.'

'Sian?' The voice was gentle and soft. He turned to Willow. 'Won't you step inside, Miss …'

'Edwards.'

'Miss Edwards.' He held open the door to a room directly off the street, comfortably furnished with a three piece suite in muted shades of blue. Removing jackets and wiping feet took a moment or two, then Sian looked across at her Dad as they all sat down. 'Miss Edwards hasn't the Welsh, *Tad.*'

'Well, if she's here long enough she might learn, darling, but for now we'll manage in English, though if I'm honest I'm not comfortable with it, not knowing many English to speak with.'

He smiled across at Willow. 'So what has this young lady been up to now?'

'Nothing bad at all.' Willow smiled back at him, then nodded at Sian as she sat next to Deniol on the settee.

'Well, *Tad,* it was like this...' Her hand crept across to be met halfway by Deniol's. 'You know how you said if we ever got caught in bad weather we should seek shelter and sit it out.'

'Yes, darling.'

'Well we found this ...' she hesitated, looking at Deniol for inspiration.

'Hiker,' he supplied.

'And,' she continued, rushing her fences, 'he didn't speak English and he hadn't got proper clothes on, and he didn't seem to understand that the weather was getting worse, so we showed him an empty cottage of one of the incomers.' She was rather red by now and Willow could see the hand holding Deniol's was gripping tightly.

'Well, that sounds sensible, *Cariad,* but why not bring him back here?'

'He wouldn't come, *Tad*. We asked, honest! So we sort of opened the door for him. It wasn't locked; and then today when we went to see if he'd gone, we found he'd broken his leg, and the ambulance men took him, and Willow said he was really sick.' She paused for breath. 'But we didn't ask the people if we could use the cottage and I suppose we should have, but we didn't take anything, and we left it all neat, truly we did.' She sighed with relief at having confessed all.

Mr Davies looked across at his daughter and then at Willow. 'Are you the *Heddlu* then? Are they charged with the breaking and entering?'

'I'm not the police, and technically I broke and entered too.' Willow grinned at him. 'I shouldn't think there would be any repercussions.' She saw his glance at his daughter. 'Any problems,' she amended, 'from our actions. But we thought you'd better be prepared for the worst. We did leave everything tidy and nothing was taken from the house.'

'But ...' she looked at the pair on the settee, 'I intend to go and see the *Heddlu*,' she stumbled over the word, 'after I've rung the hospital. Because,' she held up a hand to silence Sian, who would have spoken, 'it occurs to me that this young man when he comes round will be rather friendless, and rather frightened, if we don't supply what little information we have to the authorities.'

She turned to the teenagers. 'I've been thinking about it, you two, and how I'd feel if you all spoke Welsh to me all the time. I'd be really frightened, especially if the police came asking me questions I couldn't answer. I think we'd better go on being this man's friend, don't you?'

The pair nodded soberly. 'However,' Willow turned back to Sian's father, 'I'll keep these two out of it if that's what you'd prefer, Mr Davies.'

'No, I don't think they've done that much wrong, and we're not quite so fanatical these days in supporting Owen Glyndwr. Even if my daughter can be a bit vocal about it.' He smiled across at his daughter. 'Go and make a *panad*, darling, and *paid a phoeni,* you haven't indulged in all seven deadly sins.'

His daughter grinned across at him 'OK, *Tad*. Com'on, Deniol.'

'Call me, Gwillim.' Sian's father looked at Willow. 'She's a good girl really, just … well, a teenager.' He sighed 'Her mam died two years ago of the cancer. I thought you were going to tell me she was pregnant or something. She and Deniol have been an item nearly since junior school; he saw her through her mam's illness and they're very close.' Willow looked across at him as he pushed the hair back from his face with his fingers. 'It's not easy being a single parent and trying to hold a job down too.' His face and eyes showed his frustration, but also his sadness.

'I can imagine. They are good kids and they didn't intend harm. I promised I would take them to see this young man. Is that alright with you?'

'*Iawn, iawn.*' Gwillim Davies nodded his agreement.

'If you can give me the directory I'll phone the hospital and see how he's getting on.'

Gwillim passed a thumbed copy of the phone book, and Willow rifled through it until she came to hospitals. Excusing herself she pulled out her mobile and dialled.

The youngsters returned with delicate china mugs of steaming tea, and biscuits on a plate whose pattern was revealed in seconds, it seemed, as they munched happily now that their cares were relieved. They stopped eating, however, when they heard Willow say, 'Oh, if that's the case we won't come today. Thank you for the information.' She switched off the small machine and flipped it closed.

Turning to her companions she said, 'He's very ill. They have him in intensive care at the moment and it would be better if we don't go.' She sipped at her tea. 'They say the police have no record of anyone of his description missing. But apparently they need to contact other districts.'

She looked across at Deniol. 'Do you want me to ring you up when I go? I'll ring them tomorrow and see if there's any news.'

They chorused, 'Yes, please.' Then Sian looked across guiltily at her father. Willow drank the warm sweet brew in her mug and watched the love for his daughter glowing in Gwillim's eyes.

'Yes, darling. If Miss Edwards is happy to take you, you can go and visit this young man.'

Willow looked at the small gold watch at her wrist. 'I'm going to do some much neglected shopping, so if you'll excuse me, I'll disappear.' She put down the empty mug and stood up; gathering her rucksack, then looked at the other small duffel at the side of it. 'I'll take this to the police station on my way home. OK?' At their nods she gathered that up too, and offered a hand to Gwillim Davies. 'Thanks for the tea.' Then she headed out the door with the teenagers thanks ringing in her ears, and walked down the wet street back towards the station. She intended to catch a lift to Minffordd station on the next train.

Having bought such thrilling things as toothpaste, and considered the delights of the Edinburgh Woollen Mill as she passed, she decided it was long gone time to get home. She still had to visit the police station. She hoped the friendly sergeant was on duty again at the local station. She'd go and get her car and see.

SERGEANT GARETH AP RHYS WAS indeed at the desk - standing filling in a form, his burly figure looking even bulkier by virtue of the bullet-proof glass which separated the public from the offices.

'Hello, *Cariad*. Found another body for us have you?' He smiled across the counter at her. Looking from her slightly wet hair to her rain soaked jeans.

Willow gave a wry grin back. 'Well, actually ...'

'You haven't, have you?' He looked faintly astonished.

'Well, not a dead body, but certainly a body.'

The sergeant came hastily round the counter and unlocked the glass door, inviting her in and showing her into the same room as the night before. He went from friend to authority in a blink, reminding Willow of certain consultants she'd worked with.

'So tell me all about this body that's not dead. But first where is it so that we can check it out.'

'Oh! It's in *Ysbyty Gwynedd* now. So you don't have to turn out the troops.' Willow seated herself at the table opposite the friendly face, whose grey eyes regarded her gravely as Gareth assessed her statements.

She began her tale, from when she'd decided to go for a walk and how she'd met the teenagers. She concluded, 'If you want to clap me in irons I'll understand.' She held out her hands as if waiting for the cuffs to go on.

Sergeant ap Rhys laughed, 'I'll let them know at Caernarfon what a desperate character we have in these parts. No, on the whole I think you all acted for the best. There was no intent to steal or cause malicious damage - even the trespassing can be excused. I'll have to make a report, but I don't think anything serious will happen. I'll find out who owns the property and give them a ring and explain. They may want to prefer charges, but I shouldn't think so in the circumstances. They really ought to keep the place locked up, it's inviting squatters, to leave it unsecured like that.' He put down the pen he'd been making notes with. 'Let's have this duffel bag, *Cariad*.'

Willow swung it up onto the table. 'I put the things in the top as I told you. I didn't look in the wallet and I only shut the notebook. I didn't read anything.' She grinned at him. 'I couldn't have, it's in a foreign tongue; and I don't mean Welsh.'

Gareth pulled open the string at the top and began to remove the few possessions he found inside. As well as the wallet, notebook and a sketch map which Gareth frowned over for a minute, it yielded very little; an anorak, spare pair of trousers in an unremarkable grey, a very thin grey jumper with a frayed cuff, and three socks, each a different shade of white, one with a hole in the toe. At the bottom the sergeant pounced on a flat package wrapped in a plastic bag. 'Treasure trove!' His big hands prised the plastic away delicately.

'Oh!' Willow gazed at the prize thus revealed. 'How lovely. It's an icon.'

'Is it now, Miss, and what's one of those? It looks a bit religious to me! In fact I'm sure I've seen one before.' Gareth directed a disapproving look on the gold and blue pictures in his hand. He sniffed with the minor disdain of 'chapel' confronted with 'popish works'.

'You get them in Slavic countries, Sergeant. They're used to help people pray, like beads and...' she searched her memory, 'and incense and candles and things like that.'

'Well, that might help us find out who the poor soul is and where he comes from anyway. If it's the Catholics; they keep an eye on their parishioners. I'll have them check out the churches with his description.'

The sergeant had been looking in the wallet as he spoke, and now dropped it on the table, the meagre contents held in his hand. 'A railway ticket stub. A piece of paper with numbers on. They look like a telephone number,' he muttered to himself, 'not local anyway, probably a mobile.' He picked up the wallet and inserted big fingers into the various card slots, pulling out a crumpled stamp. 'And that's not British either, and not much help to me.' He finally dropped the wallet on the table, poking at the discarded wrapping. 'Ha! Nearly missed that.' A photo lay revealed. His forefinger pointed accusingly at an inch-square photo of a young woman.

'She's pretty.' Willow stretched out a hand. 'May I?' At his nod she picked it up and examined the picture closely. 'And pregnant, I should say.'

'Eh! Let me look at that. Hmm, you could be right.' He began gathering all the things, carefully putting them into a neat pile. 'I'll get this to the Caernarfon men, they can go and see your young man and try to find who he belongs too. Thank you for coming in, *Cariad*.'

He led the way out, pausing at the door as Willow asked, 'I don't suppose you know any more about my first find?'

''No, it's early days yet. The inquest will be sometime next week.' He looked at the teeming rain queuing to land outside and inquired if she had transport home. On his being assured of that they parted, Willow going back to a belated tea of crumpets before the fire, and then to struggle with the Welsh language.

Gareth went back inside to ring his opposite number in Bangor and arrange to reunite the well-travelled duffel bag with its owner. He also rang round several Catholic priests, but all denied having misplaced a young male parishioner. Gareth shook his head as he replaced the receiver on the fifth 'Father' and addressed a young constable bringing him a mug of tea.

'*Diolch*.'

He sat looking at the triptych for several minutes, wishing he could speak to someone about it. If he'd been up in Cumbria he'd have known just who to ask. DI McInnis would have had the answers in minutes. He wasn't surprised to find he missed the Cumbrian men, even though they spoke English all the time.

'It looks old, Sarge.'

Gareth nodded. 'I'm wondering if it's stolen, Rory.' He turned it over and examined the minute engraving on the back, but it didn't help him much. 'It looks like Russian writing, but I'm no expert at that.' He sighed and laid the three pictures carefully down, folding them onto each other.

'Oh! Is that how it goes.'

Gareth nodded. 'It's meant to fold up, like that. I should think it's worth a lot of money, Rory. But by what Miss Edwards tells me, and the state of the rest of the things in this duffel, the man who had it in his possession was almost destitute. Where's the nearest Russian orthodox church around here?'

Rory gave him a blank look. 'No idea, Sarge.'

Gareth grinned, 'Don't worry, I'll find out.' He nodded dismissal of his satellite and returned to his examination of the rucksack's contents. The picture of the pregnant woman held his attention next. 'Pretty. She'll be worrying. We'd better find out who you are quick, lad.' He addressed thin air. Then picked up his mug and fell into a reverie thinking about his own girlfriend. She was back in Cumbria and he was definitely missing her. More than a bit.

He set the mug down and looked at the sketch, trying to spot any landmarks. But it was only a few roughly drawn lines. What he'd taken at first to be a clue to the identity of the area, he eventually realised, after turning the map upside down, was a picture of a bed. It still didn't give him any idea of where it was.

Maybe the man was a burglar and this was the place the icon was stolen from. He'd have to set the wheels in motion, see where it had come from. He'd get a picture out to all the stations and have them check at the port authorities for anything like it that might have been lost or stolen.

He took the map through to the other room and took a photocopy. Then he carefully filled it in his report book before turning to the details of his report on the young men up a Blaenau Ffestiniog.

3

WILLOW LOVED SUNDAY MORNINGS, especially when she didn't have to get up. She could hear the wind hurling the rain in hard and angry pellets against the windows, like a lover trying to get his girl's attention.

She got out of bed and went to draw the curtains back then, shivering, dived back under the blankets, promising herself she would get up in just a minute. Her cold feet burned, even after this very brief contact with the lino, and she rubbed them together, and then giggled to herself as she thought of a recent nature film. 'I feel like a grasshopper!' she muttered out loud.

She gazed at the rain flowing down the pane, obscuring the grey clouds scudding by in the sky. 'I guess I won't walk to church today.' She shivered. 'Breakfast, then we'll see how 'the mysterious stranger' is doing. I do hope someone has come forward to claim him. I wonder if the picture was his wife.' She lay for a minute longer then crawled out of bed again, and, shivering, went to have a bath.

Coming back pink and warm she shuddered at the thought of removing her dressing gown and getting dressed. 'Com'on, don't be a wuss,' she adjured herself as she began to rapidly strip and re-dress. 'Bet I could rival a quick change artist this morning!' She covered the goose bumps with her best soft, light blue cashmere jumper and teamed it with a calf-length blue cord A-line skirt, then struggled to tie her long hair back into a braid. The slippery strands refused to co-operate and she gave up, tying the whole lot into a pony tail with a piece of blue ribbon. Her hair fell down her back in a silken wave.

She presented herself to Mrs Jones ready for the day, and breakfast.

'*Ofnadwy*, the weather.' Mrs Jones pointed her chin towards the window as she came to the table with her hands full of toast and butter. Even Willow could follow that bit of Welsh and had to agree with it, it was awful. 'Will you be in for your lunch then, *Cariad*? I've got a nice bit of Welsh lamb from the farm down the lane.'

Willow didn't mind meat, but the thought of eating some of the little lambs she'd seen skipping in the fields on her arrival in Wales, caused her to shudder slightly. 'No,' she looked at the kindly, crumpled face of her landlady, the unlit cigarette trailing from the side of her mouth, 'I might have to go into Bangor with some friends, so I'll eat out. But thank you anyway.'

Mrs Jones shrugged. 'That's fine, you know you're welcome. I'll be going to Chapel. Joseph will be here to pick me up in half an hour. So if you have everything you want,' she looked assessingly at the groaning board, 'I'll go and take off my pinny and put on my hat.'

As she went out the door Willow grinned to herself. There was enough on the table to feed several people, including the rather malnourished specimen she'd sent to hospital, reflected Willow. Thinking about it she poured a second cup of tea and got up to fish her mobile out of her jacket pocket.

Stirring her tea with one hand, she held the small machine to her ear with the other. '*Ysbyty Gwynedd*? Intensive care? I'd like to make enquiries about a young man who was sent in yesterday with a broken femur. No, I'm not a relative. I did find him and arrange the ambulance though.'

The voice at the other end quacked at her officiously.

'We can't give information to strangers.'

'Well, can I come in and see how he is?'

'It would be better if you didn't just at the moment.'

Willow heard various bleeps and buzzers going in the background. Then the voice continued, 'We are extremely busy at the moment. I think you'd better wait until a relative can speak to you.'

The phone clicked, and Willow looked at the empty screen in surprise. 'Talk about being given the bum's rush!' Mrs Jones, entering at this moment in a hat Nora Batty would have died for, looked at her curiously. 'Did you want something, *Cariad*?'

'No, it's OK. I just wanted to speak to someone, but I seem to have been cut off.'

'It'll be the storm; it'll have taken out a line, perhaps. The telephone people will soon fix it.' Thus Mrs Jones solved the problem and ignored the miracle of satellite communication. 'I'll be off,' she continued. 'Don't forget your key in case you come back while I'm out.' She left in a swirl of lavender water and righteousness.

Willow finished her breakfast in a leisurely fashion, debating whether to chance a visit to Bangor without the benefit of an invitation. It was miserable weather to be driving very far. On balance she felt it was probably better to leave it until a less busy, or perhaps more helpful, nurse was available to talk to her.

She'd call on Deniol and let the teenagers know the latest news, then decide what to do with her day. If she stayed in, then she might be obliged to eat lamb, and she couldn't face that. Perhaps she would go and see the progress on the line out Beddgelert way. The lads from the Welsh Highland Railway had been talking about some of the line clearance they were doing, and she hadn't seen the famous grave yet. It was one of those tourist things she hadn't got round to because she was living in the area. Yes, that's what she'd do. With the decision made she cleared her breakfast things away and went to get her waterproof jacket.

With the weather moderating, a brisk walk round the road brought her to the entrance to the Minffordd Yard. She crossed over the railway lines and walked past the hostel, exchanging pleasantries with several volunteers sitting outside. As she crossed the yard to get her car from the carriage shed, several ribald comments came her way; mostly the words were along the lines of how some people never did any work. She smiled back. 'It's ten in the morning. How come you're not at work then, Iwan?'

'Ah! Well, I'm busy supervising, you see.' He drew on his cigarette, the tip glowing red in the damp air.

Willow had had more than a few obscure sequiturs come her way on the wards, she was more than a match for Iwan. 'Supervising what? This lot of layabouts in how to do it properly?'

Iwan took a few seconds to process that thought, then burst out laughing, along with the others standing around in the lee of the roof, having a quiet smoke out of the rain.

'She got you there, Iwan!'

Still smiling to herself she continued on her way. It seemed the jungle telegraph hadn't transmitted her revolting find of Friday yet. She brushed the rain off her face and hunted in her shoulder bag for her car keys.

The old car started without a hitch. The familiar scents of home enveloped her as she drove away. She smelt the faint scent of crushed rose petals that her mother had stored the blankets in, clinging to the travel rug; the aroma of her father's pipe tobacco which seemed to have permeated the fabric of the car's upholstery, and the slight odour of wet dog from her mother's pug.

She sniffed, 'Pugwash, you were a scruffy animal and yapped too much, but I miss you sometimes!' She felt the familiar sadness as she acknowledged how much she missed them all. That was one of the reasons she was here in Wales, to try to track down the only remaining relative she knew about. Not that she expected to find him alive. But he might have married, there might be cousins or second cousins she could call family. She hoped so. He'd been born in 1898, her grandfather's older brother, last heard of working in this area. It would be good to have some family. Not even to herself would she admit to being lonely.

She waved to the group still lounging outside the hostel and drove carefully over the lines and out onto the road towards Porthmadog. The little car made good time as it approached the large causeway across the estuary. Willow noted the high profile police presence as she passed Boston Lodge Works.

HER CAR WAS IN turn noted by Gareth ap Rhys, just on his way back from works to the original scene. He'd been interviewing a few of the volunteers in the works, trying to find anyone who might know about the foreigner found by Deniol and co. the day before. He looked down from his elevated height on the railway lines at the passing automobile traffic, as he waited for a goods train to shunt by. He mentally registered the number plate and make as he spoke to one of the other senior men.

'I agree with you, Robin, he's a pain to work for, he cuts corners. Thank God there are others around who will make sure the job is done properly.'

'Yeah. We've got over sixty combing the area now; half of them don't have the Welsh either so it's to be hoped the interviewees all speak English. But let's be grateful anyway. No-way could our section deal with this on their own. What's he detailed your station to do?'

'Oh, I'm to keep the peace and keep my nose out of business I can't possibly have the brains to cope with.'

Robin swung around catching the grin Gareth flashed at him. 'He never said that did he?'

'Yep.'

Robin used a descriptive and colourful expression to describe his senior officer.

'Tut. The man can't help it if he's a *Saeson* and doesn't have our advantage of birth. Don't fret Robin.' They continued to stroll along the roadway until they arrived at a massive 'Scene of Crime' van parked up on a small car park, and partially obscuring an already closed road. As they approached, a torrent of men jumped down, one by one, making the whole vehicle rock like a steamer in a force ten. They stood back as the final man stepped down. He looked at them as Gareth spoke.

'What's up?'

'Prelim. It's officially a murder.'

'Ah! No wonder Jenkins was in a panic. He must have known that when he spoke to me. Are they bringing in the big guns?'

'Not yet. But the team is to be increased to a hundred men. The search area is to be widened and combed for anything and everything. Bloody Londoner, he hasn't got a clue about tides.' He shrugged, then waved a hand at the water lapping to the edge of the road. 'My men aren't going wading into that without a bit better equipment than I've got at the moment. What's more I want a diving team down for the middle. So he'll just have to wait, and so I told him.'

Gareth offered both men another grin, his grey eyes sparkling a bit. 'I think I'll just go and do some peacekeeping in my nice warm station.'

The other two sniffed and grinned back. 'Lucky B.' Robin snapped the poppers on his yellow, police-issue rain jacket, and strolled away towards a squad car with the other man.

Gareth made his way to his own squad car and threw his outerwear on the back seat. He settled back, turning up the heating and flicking on the windscreen wipers as a petulant spray of rain came his way.

If he was honest he would love to have a hand in the murder that was shaping up on his patch. But having to work under DI Jenkins was enough to put the keenest man off. He headed along the road back to the police station at Penrhyn.

THE WINDSCREEN WIPERS WERE working overtime in Willow's car too. Clearing and re-clearing the rain away, but eventually the rain eased off and the delights of the Welsh countryside were revealed to her uncritical eyes.

A brief halt at Deniol's had found the teenager still abed. Deniol's father had promised to pass on the current state of play, and then she'd been on her way again.

Sodden fields were sprinkled like cakes, with the black and white dots of sheep. Herds of Friesian cattle huddled together, steaming gently in the fitful sunshine. As she drove further along the narrow winding road alongside the river Glaslyn she wound the window down, the better to enjoy the spicy autumn leaves floating off the trees and attempting suicide under her wheels.

There was a gang of volunteers working at Bryn Y Felin, the site of a new railway bridge. Willow pulled over and, getting out, leaned on a convenient gate to watch. Seeing them doing battle with bramble bushes, rolling the stalks into huge reels with tractors reminded her of a picture she'd seen of tanks laying barbed wire in the trenches in the First World War. She said as much to Barbara, the forewoman who'd come over to speak to her.

'I don't know about that. It's certainly holding up our progress and fighting back pretty viciously.' She examined a deep and rather dirty scratch on her hand. 'Blooming thing went right through my gloves.'

'You'd better get that cleaned, or it'll go manky on you.'

'Oh! I'm up to date with my tetanus.' Barbara was middle aged, never seen out of overalls and, rumour said, had no legs, since no man alive had seen them. Even her husband said he couldn't remember when he last saw her in a dress. Now she brushed her wiry iron grey locks out of her face and looked at Willow from serious grey eyes. 'Talking of 'manky' I hear you found a body.'

Willow felt her stomach lurch. 'I had hoped that hadn't got round yet.'

'I don't think it has spread far. I had to report some vandalism up the line and saw Gwyn. He mentioned it.'

Willow hadn't connected the young policeman with Barbara's nephew before, but did now. She continued. 'I haven't mentioned it to anyone else, its none of my business. I only mentioned it now because I wondered if you were OK.'

Barbara was notorious for mothering half the young men and women who volunteered on the line; she would have done the same for Willow, if allowed.

'No, I'm fine. Bodies, as such, aren't that much of a novelty. Not that I'm exactly hardened to them.' She smiled wryly. 'I'm just not looking forward to the inquest.'

'Well, you know you can always come and talk to me and it won't go any further.' Barbara, who'd been keeping a weather eye on her band, offered a smile, then shouted across to one of the men. 'Take it across to the left.' She gestured with her arm. 'Hopeless, they can't hear me with the defenders on. I'd better go and sort them out.' She patted Willow on the shoulder. 'Take care of yourself, darlin'.'

The smile lingering in her eyes, Willow went back to her car and continued her journey to Beddgelert. The road was clear and the sun now seemed disposed to peep out from the clouds like a shy maiden round a fan, darting behind again as the wind scudded big cumulus clouds across, like huge warships massing for battle.

Beddgelert, when she arrived, proved to be a typical Welsh town. Strung out along the road its buildings were constructed of solid grey slate with small gable windows in some of the more prosperous houses. Willow pulled across the road and parked in behind the hotel, eyeing its faded elegance as a possible suitable venue for lunch.

She was just walking across the expanse of parking spaces towards the exit when a familiar car turned in, Morgan's green Jaguar. Skipping hastily to the side, she hoped he hadn't seen her as she carried on out the gate and down the road towards the bridge at the far end.

Despite the end of season and inclement weather there were still a number of keen walkers about. A least she thought they must be keen, since it wasn't exactly balmy. She shivered slightly and fastened the zip on her jacket. She must be mad, she thought. She could be toasting her toes by the fire with a good book, waiting for her dinner to be cooked for her. Ah, yes, the lamb! Now she knew why she was out in the wilds with the wind whipping around her kneecaps and her hair blowing all over the place. She put up a hand and held a few stray strands out of her eyes as she looked around her.

Having walked the length of the village and peered over the bridge at the rushing river, its turbulence swollen with the week's rain quota, and a certain degree of tourist debris, she crossed the main road. If the postcards were anything to go by Beddgelert loved dogs, especially the brave kind. The Post Office abounded in teacloths and cuddly toys for the discerning. She wandered along the high street, window shopping until she came to the track leading to Gellert's grave.

The wind, bringing with it a spattering of rain, whipped about her and covered the area in leaves. A slab of slate set into the ground seemed hardly worth the effort of visiting, even if the story was true.

She stood reading the inscription. Well, it was a love story of a sort, and she was always a sucker for a love story. A wolfhound set to guard the young prince, falsely accused and slain for killing him, and the grief of the father when the truth was revealed.

She was oblivious to the approaching footsteps whose noise had been masked by the worsening weather. The first indication that she wasn't alone was a faintly familiar and musky scent. Then Morgan spoke. 'The moral is good, even if it is cloaked in Victorian sentiment.'

Willow looked across the grave at his tanned face, the twinkle in his eyes belying the serious tone of his voice. 'I might have known you'd take all the romance out of it!' She indicated the grave, with a moss-green mittened hand. 'It's not true then?'

'Probably a Victorian idea. According to local legend it was a local publican hoping to climb onto the Victorian tourist bandwagon, who had the grave built.' Thus Morgan disposed in cynical fashion of both Victorians and legend.

'But if you want to believe it don't let me stop you. This is a delightfully chilly spot to meet you again, Willow.' They turned and walked together back along the path to the entrance, their feet making a gentle shushing sound as they walked through drifts of leaves. 'Are you here for any special purpose or just to view the grave?'

Willow looked at him as he held the gate open for her. His black cashmere topcoat was beautifully tailored and lay across broad shoulders, and the hand that held the gate so politely was sheathed in finest calfskin. He looked, she thought, exactly what he was, a successful business man. He was definitely more at home in the boardroom, today, than the driver of Friday would have been.

'I came to see the grave, but aside from that I came to look at the Welsh Highland Railway progress, the track-bed is still very badly overgrown, isn't it? I need to buy a new pair of boots too; I'm told there's a place that sells pre-loved ones that don't cost a fortune.' She shivered in the rising wind and rain, thinking of the reason for the new boots, which added a separate dimension to the shivers and caused her to pale slightly.

Morgan followed her through the gate and they swung up the main road again. Willow, in an unconscious effort to escape from her companion and seek some warmth, turned into the first shop they encountered. She was somewhat surprised to find herself confronted by a canoe and a rack of wet-suits.

'Did we come in here for anything in particular?' Morgan surveyed their surroundings and sniffed at the overwhelming smell of rubber coming from the wet-suits. He wasn't into fetishism, and this place would have kept several of that particular inclination, believing they'd landed in paradise.

'Er, I was wondering about a hat as well. It's turned chilly.' Willow headed determinedly to the back of the shop to look at bobble hats in startling lime green and pink. Her shadow followed. Morgan was intrigued by her obvious tactics to shake him off.

'I don't think they are really your colour.' The voice was gently teasing, but the phrase unfortunate. Barry had told her too many times what she ought to wear, for Willow to take the comment lying down. She pulled off her green mittens and seized a hat from the counter, pulling it down over her blonde hair. Then looked in the mirror. She burst out laughing. He was right; it really wasn't her colour, or style for that matter. The large bobble danced around on the top of her head like an onion flower in a gale. 'Perhaps you're right at that.'

Morgan grinned at her in the mirror. 'Now this is much more the thing.'

Willow looked at the tam-o'shanter he held out in muted shades of pink and lavender. She took it from him, feeling the soft merino wool warm against her chilly hands. 'Mmm maybe.' It was like nestling a cloud on her head. She looked at her reflection, turning to look from a different angle, and she did like it. She peeked at the price tag and laid it regretfully down. 'But maybe not today.'

Morgan had seen both the looks. He picked it up. 'Let me treat you.'

'No, thank you.' It was more than just the physical cold that had turned her into the ice-maiden now confronting him. Morgan found the change bewildering after the laugh they'd just exchanged. Willow turned away and headed out of the shop.

Morgan shrugged at the male assistant who'd been a silent bystander. They exchanged puzzled glances before Morgan picked up her gloves lying neglected on the counter, and followed her, catching her up as she headed down the street. He caught her arm and then let go as if burned; as she pulled away, almost stepping into the path of a passing car in an effort to evade his hand. Stepping back he held both hands at shoulder height; the gloves dangling forlornly from one of them.

'Whoa. What was that all about? I didn't mean to offend you, Willow.'

Willow, who by this time had calmed down sufficiently to be a bit ashamed of herself, looked at the handsome man standing in front of her and offered an apology. 'Sorry, Morgan. It's just - I don't take gifts from men I don't know.' She raised eyes, with mute apology in them, to his face.

Morgan lowered his hands. 'Hm!' He thought she was too independent by half, but kept the reflection to himself. Most of the women he knew couldn't wait to part him from his cash. 'Would you be offended if I invited you to lunch?' He stretched out a hand to pull her out of the passing foot traffic then dropped the hand as she moved even further away from him. 'I've booked a table up at the hotel for one o' clock.' He glanced at the watch on his wrist. 'Then you can get to know me a bit better.'

Willow stood thinking amid people who detoured round her, and swirling leaves which danced in and out of the gutters with each passing car, until recalled by one particular gust which sent a shower of rain down her neck.

Morgan stood watching her patiently, neither cajoling nor ordering. Patience brought his reward.

She looked at the calm face and nodded. 'I've got to eat. So long as it isn't lamb. I couldn't eat lamb.'

'You a vegetarian then?' For the first time she heard a hint of the Welsh lilt in his voice as surprise coloured his accent.

'No.' Willow looked equally surprised as they began to walk back towards the car park, and then felt the bubble of laughter rise inside her chest. She grinned across at him. 'My landlady offered me lamb from the farm down the road. I'd watched them gambolling in the field.' She offered the explanation and hoped he didn't think she was a complete fool. Then wondered why it mattered.

'I didn't think the law allowed sheep to gamble.' He offered the feeble joke as he looked down at her from his superior height. Morgan was thinking that she was a remarkably pretty girl, when she let down her guard a bit. The smile on her face actually turned her into a little beauty.

Nothing like the high society misses whom he normally invited out to dine. They tended to be all polished manners and make-up. As far as he could tell Willow didn't seem to be wearing make-up at all and, if the exhibition in the shop was anything to go by, her manners could be a bit absent too.

They turned towards the entrance of the hotel, Morgan resisting the temptation to take her arm as they went through the glass doors into the foyer. 'Would you like a drink before we sit down?'

Willow shook her head. 'No, but I do want to go over there.' She pointed with her head in the direction of a sign saying, *Merched.* Then offered a shy grin. 'It's the cold weather,' she said by way of explanation.

Morgan looked at her blankly, then, as the light dawned, said 'Oh! Ah! Yes,' in a rather strained voice. 'I'll, er, see you in the lounge then.'

As Willow headed in a purposeful way towards the toilets he shook his head. The only other woman of his acquaintance who would have dreamed of telling him she wanted the loo was his sister Jane. The fashion plates would have wriggled and refrained.

He walked into the lounge as an elderly waiter, resembling a monk in civvies, entered by another door. As Morgan was taking off his top coat, he beckoned him over. 'I'm not quite ready yet, Charles, but can you set my table for two?' He folded over his coat and looked absently at the mittens still in his hand, stuffing them in his pocket, giving the coat to the waiter who draped it over his arm. Morgan seated himself, facing the doors, to wait for his companion.

'Certainly, sir.'

Morgan had visited before and was known to tip generously, but that wasn't the only motivation. He was always polite to the waiters, and Charles appreciated the courtesy that saw a waiter as a human being.

He glided away on his errand and Morgan sat waiting, reflecting that it was an odd position to find himself in. Pursuing rather than pursued. He stood up as Willow entered and came across. 'Sure you won't have that drink?'

Willow shook her head. 'Nope, I'm driving!'

'Fine, let's go eat then.' They walked companionably into a restaurant area which was quiet and discreet, the tables draped with stiff white damask and set with silver, and far enough apart to allow for conversations to be relatively private.

The aroma of roast beef floated on the air to tantalise the senses, and Willow sniffed enthusiastically 'Mmm!' She sniffed again.

Charles, coming across the expanse of good Axminster to meet them, smiled quietly to himself. Most of Mr Williams' lady friends might sniff, but it was rather a disdainful sniff, not this appreciative variety. He was disposed to look kindly on the young lady, and led her to her seat punctiliously. 'Shall I take your jacket?' He smiled down at the young face turned towards him. Willow shrugged out of the thick cord and handed it over.

'We'll order straight away, Charles.' Morgan hadn't missed the sniff either. While the business of looking at menus was pursued silence reigned. Then the oracle spoke. 'The Beef Wellington is rather good today, sir.'

'Right, Charles, I'll take your word for it.' Morgan looked across at Willow. She had been working her way down the menu with a finger. But now she looked up and said, 'I'll have the same, thank you.'

'No starter, sir?'

'Not for me, Charles. How about you, Willow?'

Willow shook her head. 'No, thanks, I want to fit in a sweet!' She settled back in her seat.

They handed over the menus and, as Charles discreetly retreated, silence reigned. Willow was wondering how she came to be looking across rather nice napery and a little vase of carnations at Morgan Williams when he was supposed to be a misogynist and she had sworn off men - especially rich ones.

Morgan was thinking that she washed up rather well, and that she was beautiful when she lost that guarded look and you shifted all the oil and grease. He wanted to touch, just to see if that skin was as dewy fresh as it looked, but having received two unmistakable 'hands off' signs, refrained. They looked across at each other and both started to speak at once.

'Have ...?'

'I ...'

Morgan waved a hand at her. 'After you.'

'I was just wondering what brought you to Beddgelert today. Did you come to see the progress of the line?'

Morgan was tempted to tell the truth, that he'd followed her from Bryn Y Felin. On balance it didn't seem a good idea just at the moment. He'd been parked up in a lay-by, watching the work and wishing he'd come in his old clothes so that he could join in, when he saw her pull over. He had admired her slim figure from a distance and admitted to himself that his curiosity had been piqued by her refusal to accept a lift on Friday night.

Now he took a sip of water and offered to pour her a drink while he thought out his answer. At her nod he poured and set the jug carefully back down. 'Well, yes and no. I was wondering how they were getting on, but I was doing a little research for the railway archives. I couldn't quite visualise the area the information was talking about, so I thought I'd come and look for myself.'

'Oh!' Willow raised an eyebrow, 'I thought you came from round here originally. You speak Welsh like a native.'

'I am a native. But further across the country, from the Bala area.'

'I've been trying to learn the language,' she confided. 'I'm hopeless.'

Morgan grinned wickedly and said something in Welsh to her. The only word she understood was darling. 'I didn't understand any of that except *'Cariad'*, and I know that's 'darling', for my grandad used to call me that.'

'Then I shall have to be careful. There might be other words you understand and I'd lose my entire mystique.'

'What mystique?' Willow leaned back, allowing herself to relax in his company and letting Charles place a plate of steaming food in front of her. 'Thank you.' She smiled up charmingly at Charles.

'You enjoy that, Miss!' He went round and placed Morgan's food in front of him.

'I'm supposed to have some mystique. Its how I keep the girls interested.'

Willow snorted inelegantly. 'You're a man like other men. You put your trousers on one leg at a time.'

'True, but look at the cut of them.' Morgan mocked his elegant attire with an elegant hand.

Willow looked across at the beautifully cut suit and silk tie on display across the table. 'Well, they're very nice, but hardly suitable for working on an engine.'

'But then I'm not working on the engine. I'm dining with a beautiful young woman.' He both felt and saw her stiffen.

Willow felt her stomach curl away and laid her knife and fork down carefully as the beautiful pastry turned to cardboard in her mouth. What was she thinking about? Hadn't she learnt anything from her association with Barry? She looked up at Morgan to see him watching her curiously.

Laying his own cutlery down he gave her his full attention. Before she could say anything he spoke. 'It's only a compliment, Willow. Men pay them to women, and sometimes they even mean it. It wasn't meant as an insult.'

Willow took a deep breath and sipped her water, clearing her throat of the obstruction caused by nerves and food. 'If I told you you were a handsome man how would you feel, Morgan? It makes me feel rather belittled, as if my only worth was as an ornament on your arm.'

Morgan took his time answering; there were obviously deep waters here, and she deserved an honest answer. 'It would depend whether the one offering the compliment had previously shown me respect as a person or not.'

He picked up his knife and fork and waited for Willow to do the same. As she followed his lead, he continued. 'My sister is a beautiful woman; I'm proud to be seen out with her. And I tell her so. I'm not belittling her, because I know her worth. She works as hard as I do and earns every penny of her salary.' He patted his mouth with the linen napkin.

'It's most unfair to the poor male to accuse him of treating you like a sex symbol and demanding equality one minute, then expressing surprise when we don't open doors for you and pay you compliments.' Morgan tried an aggrieved expression of injured perplexity and won a faint smile.

'I never wanted equality, Morgan. I like having doors opened for me, and Women's Lib has wrecked a lot of lives with its insistence that women can do the same things as men. We might be as good, but we're different. I don't even particularly want to 'earn a salary'. I'd love to have the chance to stay at home and bring up a clutch of children. But that isn't the way of the world now, women have to work. We appreciate men acknowledging what we contribute to the workplace, in the same way they would for any colleague.'

She took a sip of water to moisten a throat suddenly gone dry at the thought of what Morgan's children would be like. Dragging her mind away she looked resolutely at him. 'But all the same I'd rather not have false coin. Because you don't know my worth and I know what I look like.' She gave him a grave look from her clear green eyes. 'Now what archival research are you doing?'

Morgan accepted the change of subject, and if he was disappointed he didn't say so. He would have liked to find out more about this unselfconscious young lady, maybe flirted a little with her, but apparently he wasn't to be admitted into her charmed circle today.

'I've been checking up on the original line down from Caernarfon, trying to find who owned land or lost it when the line went through. We need to know exactly who owns what if we hope to re-lay track on the land, and some of the older families still live on it. But some of the land has been parcelled out. National trust has some. It's interesting, and not a little complicated.'

He paused to cut into a succulent slice of beef. 'One of the problems has been right-of-way access of walkers along the old trackbed.'

'It is difficult isn't it? People have been walking along there for a good few years and enjoying the scenery and safety. Now we come along and remove that access again.'

They continued to talk about the new line as they ate their way through the delicious meal. 'So,' Morgan laid down his knife and fork on the empty plate, 'what would you like for dessert?'

Willow looked with surprise at her plate and ate the last delicious mouthful. He nodded at Charles as the vigilant waiter arrived to clear away. 'Could we have the dessert trolley?'

Willow all but drooled as it was wheeled into view. 'You don't get trolleys in most places. How lovely!' She scanned the desserts on offer. 'I'd love the Black Forest gateau.'

Morgan looked at Charles. 'Make that two and hold the extra cream on mine, please.'

As they began to eat the wonderful concoction Morgan waved his spoon at her. 'So now you know me a little better, do I get a compliment?'

'Why yes, Morgan, I think your...' she paused impishly, 'suit, is beautifully cut.'

'But will you respect it in the morning?' Morgan put down his spoon and chuckled, much to Willow's discomfiture. He grinned at her and she grinned back, the cake disappearing rapidly, then sat back, patting her tummy with a sigh. 'That was delicious and I ate far too much, but I don't regret a mouthful. Friends, Morgan?'

'Friends, Willow.' He offered a hand and they shook solemnly over the remains of their lunch. Both were surprised at the tingle that shot up their arms, and quickly broke the contact, Morgan rubbing his fingers together, puzzled at his reaction; the palm he'd just touched was warm and calloused.

They parted amicably at the car park as the blustery wind whipped around their legs. 'Thank you for my lunch, Morgan. I hope your research is successful.' Morgan opened her door and waited while she fastened her seat belt before slamming it shut. She rolled down the window.

'Drive safely. I'll see you around the yard.' Then she pulled away, leaving Morgan to contemplate the few meagre facts he'd culled from the encounter. Her self-esteem was low, and she didn't have a high opinion of men, especially ones who paid unthinking compliments. She was as intelligent as she was pretty, and had an excellent grasp of the facts and an appreciation of the other person's point of view. Not a lot, but more than he'd known at the start of the meal. One thing he was sure of, however, he would know more. Miss Willow Edwards intrigued him.

GARETH FOUND SOME INFORMATION lying on his desk when he finally sat down on Sunday morning, he didn't class it as intriguing though, more just another factor in the continuing saga of a lost soul. Knowing the ways of teenagers from the behaviour of his youngest brother, however, he waited until after his own lunch before driving into Porthmadog and going to visit Deniol.

Deniol was sitting comfortably ensconced in a deep chair, with Sian on his lap. Sian was reading a romance. Deniol was watching a video of a rugby match with his father. Gareth nodded at the father and smiled as the mother turned off the TV. Deniol scowled at all three adults and Sian ignored everyone, being absorbed in her book.

'Sergeant ap Rhys needs a word with you, Deniol, and you too, Sian.' Sian looked up at mention of her name and gave an absent smile.

'Sorry.'

Deniol's mother, Eirlys, smiled at her. 'I'll make some tea, the sergeant needs a word.'

Alarm flitted over both young faces.

'It's alright. I just need a brief statement about yesterday. I understand you were with a Miss Willow Edwards when she found a young man?' Gareth let the question hang in the air.

Deniol stood up, forcing Sian to stand too, then gripping her hand. 'Of course, sir. It was my fault, Miss Edwards wasn't to blame. I let the man into the cottage.'

Gareth smiled, it was gentle and reassuring. 'No blame at all, I just need a statement for the record.'

'Won't you sit, Sergeant?' Deniol's father, David Myrddin, indicated a chair and everyone settled back down, though the two teenagers still looked anxious. Both now perched on hard chairs, rather like sparrows on overhead lines, ready to fly at the first hint of danger.

Gareth undid his jacket and pulled out his Report Book. 'If I understand Miss Edwards correctly, you've probably saved the young man's life. Now if you can just take me through the events from when you first found him to when he was taken away in the ambulance.' He watched them both relax slightly.

'It was half term last week. Sian and I, we were going for a bike ride, Thursday. We'd gone over the Cob and got to the slope for the works and we saw the hitchhiker, or walker, or whatever he is. He was going round the back of the Works.'

'Lots of they tourists get the path wrong since it's been re-done.' Sian licked dry lips and looked at authority.

Deniol took up the tale. 'Well, we thought we'd just show him the right way, but by the time we got up there he'd disappeared. We left our bikes at the Halt and went to see if we could find him and, like I say, he was going round the back of the works. It can be a bit dangerous if you don't know your way. There's that really deep well. It's fenced but ... and the slate can be lethal when it's wet. So we thought we'd see if we could help and we found him trying the doors.'

'We didn't know if he was trying to steal anything, and we didn't know if we should ring the police, but he didn't look like a thief.' Sian exchanged a look with Deniol as she finished speaking.

Gareth, reading between the lines, could imagine the argument that had happened then.

'We saw him put his bag down and try to settle in a doorway so we went to see could we help.' Sian nodded at Deniol to take over again.

'He wasn't dressed right, and it was coming on to rain, so we tried if we could get him to go into the town, and we offered him a bed. But he didn't understand us. We tried in the English and French too.' Deniol looked a bit defensive.

'I haven't even got any French.' Gareth praised, even as he reassured them. 'I don't think I'd have been able to do any better. So what did you do then?'

'Well, he looked hungry like, so we gave him our sandwiches. He ate them like he was starving, and had all our coffee. I don't think he'd had much to eat for days. Then we got him to follow us up the hill. Den drew him a picture of a bed and a house and a map and we got him to understand we would show him the way.'

That explained the map. Gareth, making notes, smiled grimly to himself. So much for burglars. But then that message from the port authority had come back negative this morning.

'We showed him the way up to the bach and let him in, and we told him we'd come back on Saturday, but I don't think he understood that bit.' Deniol shook his head. 'Anyway, Saturday we thought we'd just go and see had he gone. Take some more food and an extra blanket. Sian went and got a thick jumper and a pair of thick trousers from Oxfam.'

Gareth nodded, these two had been more than generous, he'd make sure they were recompensed. 'And then?'

'Well, he'd fallen and his leg was broken, Miss Edwards said. She said we had to send him to the hospital.'

'How did you meet Miss Edwards?'

'She was walking the path. We didn't know what to do, and Den said we had to get help, but I said we'd all be in trouble about the cottage.' Sian looked at Deniol and then back at Gareth, her look said. 'And we are in trouble aren't we'?'

'I've spoken to the owner's. They agree that you did quite right to let the young man shelter there, and what's more they said they were glad you'd thought to use it.' Gareth smiled reassuringly at both teenagers before casting a glance at the silent David Myrddin.

'It seems to be that you have done right, Deniol. You got the young man to shelter and you gave him something to eat. It might have been better if you'd come to me, but you did what you thought was right.' Deniol's father smiled at the two anxious teens, and then at Gareth.

Eirlys Myrddin came in carrying a tray which her husband rose to take from her. 'You'll take a *panad* before you go, Sergeant?'

Gareth put his notebook away. 'That would be nice.' They all shuffled round a bit and Sian squashed herself in the seat next to Deniol again. They began to discuss the match that had been on the TV when Gareth arrived.

As he got up to go Sian said. 'Truly, we aren't in trouble?'

'No. *Paid a phoeni.*'

4

THE NEXT MORNING FOUND Willow hard at work at six-thirty, cleaning her engine. She'd used the six foot crow bar under the front wheel to get it out of the shed and over the pit in preparation for her driver to come and oil any wheels and bearings, if necessary, underneath. The messy job of rodding out the steam tubes and emptying the soot box had been accomplished to the detriment of her hands and face, so that she could have had a staring role in the *Black and White Minstrel Show*.

Now she sat on top of the water-tank of the engine, polishing the brass dome. Her breath came in little white puffs as she vigorously applied the rags and *Brasso*. Her ears and nose stung in the frosty air and she could feel her toes getting cold in her soft new boots. She stopped for a minute to look at them, wiggling her feet and thinking they had been broken in nicely. She dragged her mind away from the reason she had had to buy them and returned to the job in hand.

Despite the cold that nibbled at her extremities she loved this job on the little railway; aside from the sheer pleasure of working on a steam engine, there were the stolen days when the air was so clear it made the world sparkle. The wonderful scenery that the train travelled through was a definite bonus. This morning, sitting aloft, she could watch the sun creeping over the Moelwyns. The black storm clouds had blown away and only a few wisps of white were decorating the pale-blue dawn sky.

Snowdon had a little white bonnet of snow, but the air was remarkably fresh despite the traffic a few feet away on the road. She sighed with enjoyment. The tide washed high again, hiding the greened sandbanks of the inner and outer estuary. It promised to be a glorious late autumn day such as they rarely got in Britain at this time of the year.

Dai, the foreman, hailed her as she was climbing down the side of the tank. 'Hi, Will, how did you get on the other night? Did you enjoy it?'

Willow stood up, clutching her rags and can, looking at the small dark man as he came up to her. 'It was great fun. The kids deserve to win; they put so much enthusiasm into the acting.' She unselfconsciously rubbed her nose on the back of her hand where an errant itch was, and left a smear behind.

'Were you alright with Morgan? He can be a bit, er...' he paused for thought, pushing back his cap and scratching his sparsely covered head, 'picky about his firemen,' he concluded with the air of a man walking over a floor of mousetraps and expecting any minute to feel the snap of metal on his toes. Women also could be 'picky', as fifty-one years of marriage had shown him.

'No trouble, Dai.' She liked Dai, he was nearing retirement, again, and to her knowledge he'd retired twice already. He tended to look askance at the way some of the younger men treated the female firemen.

'Yeah. Only...' He looked cautiously at her again. 'Well, what with Gavin still on the injured list and, well, I wondered if I could put you on with Morgan again today.' He paused. 'But only if you don't mind working with him?' There was a question and some anxiety in his voice; he would sooner have admitted to having *Saeson* blood than acknowledged that Willow was one of his favourites.

Willow looked up at the side of 'her' engine; she liked the smaller engines with only one firebox and smokestack to worry about, what's more she preferred working with diesel rather than coal, which could be much trickier to stoke with. 'I thought he was using the double today?'

'Bit of a change of plan there, too; the Earl has a slight boiler leak.'

'OK, Dai. If he can cope, I'm sure I can.'

Dai looked relieved and changed the subject. 'Do you want some help with the cleaning?'

'It wouldn't hurt.'

Dai went off to find some willing hands and Willow went into the shed for clean rags, looking up at the high sides of the double boggied engine of the Earl. 'Two domes, and 180 tubes to clean, and coal-fired. At least I haven't got that!'

She was soon hard at work again on her own engine; she had gone round the side of the old sheds, filled her can with a mixture of bearing oil from the small tank and two-stroke petrol from the larger, and now shook the mix to make a degreaser for the paint work. She'd been given a couple of enthusiastic young men whom she had set to work, one aloft to clean the pipe work on the tank, the other to the driver's side to polish the brass levers and spectacle windows on the inside.

When Morgan arrived she was preparing to get the pressure up. He looked at the frenetic activity on and around the engine, the long black coil of tubing trailing across the yard as the compressor started up, going stiff like a cobra sighting a mouse. Willow being there had not come as a surprise this time. Dai had explained that Gavin was, 'Stiff as a kipper after twelve hours of smoke. And the Earl needs a look see, too.'

He tipped his head back and looked up at the young woman who was now busily wiping on and taking off degreaser on the tank top, leaving the paint work shining. 'Morning.' He nodded at her and began to oil the wheels on the far side of the machine as she alternately worked on the cleaning and checked on the pressure. He undid a couple of nuts and checked a filter; he was to have her company again today, was he? Well, they would see how she got on. But he wasn't giving the gossips any food for conversation while they prepared the engine.

He had registered Dai's astonishment when he'd not made any demur about it. He must have some reputation he thought, if the foreman was so apologetic. Or maybe it was the money again, he thought cynically. Which, if he had but known it, was unjustified. Dai cared not a jot for what people had, he was much more concerned that 'his trains' should be driven well, by people who where enjoying themselves.

THE JOURNEY ACROSS TO the station had gone without a hitch. Willow was quiet as she fired the engine. Conversation was difficult at the best of times on the footplate, but the stiff breeze off the sea made it almost impossible today. Besides, she felt slightly embarrassed being in Morgan's company; she wasn't quite sure how to get back to the comfortable companionship of yesterday.

Now she perched aloft on the saddle of the engine, water soaking into the front of her overalls as she struggled with the weight of hose, while she filled up with water. A number of obvious tourists stood around snapping pictures and generally endangering their lives by walking on the track bed to get a

119

better angle. She ignored them and concentrated on her job. She was deep in thought, with her eyes absently fixed on the harbour mouth just visible round the curve of the wall, when she was hailed by one of the guards.

'Hi, Willow, whatya been doing? There's a couple of coppers asking for you in the café.'

'Speeding tickets, John!' She tried a weak grin. 'Tell 'em I'll be a minute or two, and then I'll come and see what they want.'

'Okey dokey!' John disappeared in the direction of the café and Willow finished filling and stowed the hose. She wasn't looking forward to the coming interview. It was silly to feel guilty in the presence of a policeman, but she always did.

She walked along the platform wiping her hands on a rag almost as dirty as the oil she was firing with. Seeing the blue uniforms approaching she lifted a greasy paw in acknowledgement. 'Hi, I'm Willow Edwards. You need to see me?'

'Nothing much to worry about.' The younger of the two spoke, giving her an admiring glance. 'Just to let you know that you'll be required for a formal inquest in two or three days. After the post mortem, we'll be sending you a witness order.'

'Do you have any idea who it was?' Willow directed her inquires to the older and more senior of the men, deliberately angling her body away from that look.

'Not yet, should have some more news later today. We're going the route of teeth first since the body's a bit er...' he trailed away.

The younger man chimed in, drawing her attention back to his face. 'There was some paperwork in the pockets and a wallet, but forensics aren't sure if they'll be able to read anything, what with the river water and the body fluids!'

Willow paled a bit and gulped, 'Thanks for that!'

He looked apologetically at her and muttered, 'Sorry.'

She swung back to the senior officer who directed a look which caused the young man to colour painfully. 'Anyway we'll let you know when you need to attend. OK?'

'Sure.' Willow watched them stroll away along the platform and turned towards the café, intending to get coffee before she found her driver. A tingling consciousness caused her to turn. Morgan was standing a couple of yards away watching her.

'I'm pleased to see it isn't just me that gets the cold shoulder.' He stepped closer to avoid the crowds and watched as the colour stole into her cheeks. 'I was beginning to think I'd done something to offend you, again?' He lifted a satirical eyebrow.

Willow raised slightly apologetic eyes to him, 'Sorry?'

He lifted the other eyebrow in surprise but didn't comment on her apparent lack of understanding. He pulled a rag out of his pocket and went to wipe a smudge on her cheek. Willow couldn't help it, she swayed back to avoid the contact. 'You've come unwashed again.' He offered the clean cloth; if Morgan was surprised at her reaction he tried not to show it. 'What did the *Heddlu* want? Been taking candy from the kids again?' He joked to cover his own confusion. He found it mildly hurtful to be set at a distance by this girl for some reason.

Willow looked at him for a moment or two; she supposed everyone would know soon enough. 'Let's get on the engine.' They turned and walked the length of the platform. Most of the punters were either buying things from the shop or had already boarded the carriages. Willow preceded him onto the footplate and took up the familiar stance.

Morgan looked across at her. 'Is it serious? Can I help?' The fact that he'd addressed more words to her in the last five minutes than the last two hours made her look at him in some surprise. He actually looked concerned. Willow wasn't sure she was comfortable with that either.

'I found a body down in the estuary Friday night, on my way home. They came to tell me when the inquest would be.' She tried for a lighter note. 'It was a sort of 'don't leave town' interview, this morning.'

After one long look, Morgan digested her statement while he pulled on the regulator and allowed the little machine to gather speed and shunt round to the front of the rake. He waited until she had coupled up and was back on board with their coffee, and they were pulling out of the station, before he passed any more comments. Eyes monitoring the platform slipping back under his eyes, he addressed Willow.

'Ah! That would be what all the police activity round the estuary was about. I wondered.' Morgan pointed out a few distant figures in waders, as they trundled along the Cob. 'If you need some support I'll come with you.' He made the offer almost offhandedly but Willow, stealing a look at his face, saw that he was quite serious.

'I'll be fine; I just have to give evidence.' They settled down to the business of driving the train through the scenic views that the Snowdonia National Park presented, all burnished copper leaves and dying bracken, a relatively uneventful journey for the most part. Once, Morgan pointed out the green flash of a wing belonging to a woodpecker just as they were coming out of the tunnel, and on the way back they had to slow down for some sheep on the line.

However, this peaceful state was shattered when they got back from the second and last run of their day. The police were again on the platform. Willow eyed them curiously as the train drew to a halt. Morgan cast her a curious look. 'Friends of yours again?'

'I hope not.' Willow, rapidly checking gauges and preparing to jump down, gave him a wry look. She went between the carriages and unhooked the coupling. She turned to find the same older policeman as that morning at her elbow as she stepped up on the platform. 'Ah, Miss Edwards. We need to have another word.'

'Can it wait until I've put the engine to bed?'

'I'm afraid not. We need you to come with us now.'

Willow looked astonished. 'What is this? I said I'd come to the inquest; I signed the statement the other night.'

'Do you know a Mr Barry Scott?'

Willow paled. 'Look, I broke up with the guy 'cos he was driving me crazy. I don't know what he says I've done but you ought to be investigating him. You lot weren't so keen to stick an oar in when I told you he'd hit me!'

Morgan came to stand beside her. 'Need some help, Willow?'

'No!' She turned away then swung back. 'I have to go with these two. Can you get someone to fire across to the sheds?'

'Sure.' If he was having trouble coping with the rapid events he didn't show it. 'Where are you going?' He looked at the officers as he asked the question. 'I'll fetch you back after whatever they need you for.'

Willow looked at them too.

'We need you to come with us to Caernarfon.'

She looked down at her grubby overalls. 'Can't I at least get changed?'

'Er…' He hesitated.

'Am I under arrest or something? I won't run away, but I do need the loo! I'll just strip off the overalls.' She appealed to their sense of fair play.

'Fine.' He indicated the loos with a wave of the hand. She shot into the toilets and struggled out of her overalls Not that she was a lot cleaner in the jeans and jumper she wore underneath, but at least she didn't feel quite so dirty. Her hands shook as she pulled off the shiny black cap and allowed her hair to fall down.

Going out she handed the clothes to Morgan, who was still standing silently beside the policemen. 'Could you put these in my locker please?' She passed over the key. 'I hope I won't be too long.' She offered a weak smile along with the clothes but it was a poor effort. Morgan in turn offered her a piece of card. 'My mobile. I'll come for you. Unless you'd like me to come to the station when I've finished for the day?'

'Thanks. But I'll be OK.'

Willow followed the senior officer as he led the way through the thinning crowds and climbed into the back of the squad car.

'Sorry about this, Miss.' The sergeant swung round to speak to her as the car left the car park.

Willow didn't think he looked that apologetic. 'That's as maybe, but I don't like being made to look like a criminal in front of my employers. Can't you give me a clue as to what this is all about?'

'The inspector will explain when we get there.'

The rest of the journey was conducted in a mentally, and physically, chilly silence broken only by the drumming of the rain on the roof and the crackle of static from the car radio as they swished their way through the gathering storm towards the coming interview. The whole atmosphere in the car was as evocative as the build up to the release of a few zombies onto an unsuspecting population.

'MY NAME IS DETECTIVE Inspector Jenkins. Miss Edwards, I'm sorry to have dragged you away from your duties. But we need to ask you some questions.'

The speaker appeared to Willow to be a dapper plain clothes man with a wisp of moustache which appeared to be struggling to grow in the shade from his bulbous nose. His eyes were slate grey, set close to his nose, and Willow was put forcibly in mind of a buffalo she'd once seen at a zoo. It had swung its great head in an effort to bring her into sight from both eyes and disconcerted her badly with its movements.

Inspector Jenkins sat opposite her at a metal table, in a small room, with no windows. Willow was grateful that the room was very warm, but rather wished the young constable sitting ready to take notes wasn't quite so hygienically challenged, deodorants had been around for a good few years now. The inspector leaned forward on his wooden chair and it protested squeakily under his weight. The preliminaries were apparently over.

'We need to know about your relationship with Barry Scott.' He fixed eyes like washed pebbles on her face, waiting for her answer unblinkingly.

'He was my fiancé, he was possessive and jealous and he hit me. Your counterparts in London didn't want to know anything about me or him then,' Willow gritted her teeth in a ferocious smile, 'so why do you need to know now? Whatever he says, you'd better check twice, the man's a liar. And a bully.'

'Then you won't be upset when we tell you he's dead. Will you?'

Willow felt her head spin slightly and her skin go clammy. 'Oh God! What happened to him? Was he knocked over or something?'

The detective nodded to the policeman who got up and fetched a glass of water from a small water dispenser. She took it with a word of thanks, then looked round at the continuing silence in the room. 'He was OK when I last saw him.'

The inspector picked up the neglected pen, 'Which would be when?' he paused, 'Exactly?'

Willow frowned. 'Exactly?'

'Exactly, Miss.'

'I don't think I can give you exactly, but it must have been the middle of May of this year. I came across to Wales the last week of May. I gave a week's notice to my lodgings, and packed up and arranged everything here, then came down in the car.'

'Are you sure about that? You haven't seen him since May?'

'Look. What's this all about?'

'We're just trying to establish his movements, over the last week or two.'

'Well, I can't help you there. Look, I'm sorry he's dead, but Barry hasn't exactly left me with fond memories. You still haven't said how he died?'

'All in good time, Miss.' The detective nodded to the young man hovering by the door who went out and came back with a folder, then seated himself next to the detective inspector.

'We have some pictures for you to look at.' The moustache twitched, like a caterpillar sighting a bird, as the inspector spoke, and Willow suppressed a smile. This wasn't really a laughing matter.

Willow nodded with an assumption of calmness and then looked down. The first picture was one of Barry and herself, taken sometime last year when they had first met. It had been in one of the shiny gossip journals and she had had a stunned look on her face. She hadn't known then that he was such a public figure.

'This is Mr Scott and yourself, isn't it?'

Willow looked across the desk. 'Of course it is.' She squashed down her impatience.

'And these?'

The next few photos were a mix of private snapshots Barry had taken and public photos taken by the enterprising press.

'Yes. These were all taken over last year. Look, I'm not denying our relationship, just saying it's over and has been for some time.'

'And it ended acrimoniously?'

Willow felt her stomach sinking. 'Am I going to need a lawyer, Inspector?'

'That's up to you, Miss. At the moment we're just asking a few questions. We understand he made rather a nuisance of himself at your last home?'

'Barry wasn't too happy to end things. But since I wouldn't let him in and I called the police, you should have a record of that anyway.'

'Yes, Miss, we have.'

Willow was getting rather tired of fencing with the enigmatic man in front of her. 'Look, Inspector Jenkins, I haven't seen Barry for nearly six months. I rather hoped he didn't know where I'd gone after the fuss he made at the flat. I didn't wish him dead but I have to admit to relief that he isn't going to hound me anymore. Is that what you need to know?'

She looked across the spread photos. 'Has Barry been murdered and am I a suspect? If so, say so.'

'We do need you to account for your movements, Miss Edwards. Mr Scott appears to have died in suspicious circumstances, and you admit the relationship ended badly.'

'Fine. When do you need to know where I was and what I was doing?'

'Last week.'

'Last week? That's a bit broad, Inspector.' Willow gave him a quizzical look. 'I could have been a bit more accurate if your goons hadn't dragged me over here without the diary currently sitting in my locker over at the sheds.' She watched the young constable colour slightly. 'Well, let me think. This is Monday. Last Tuesday to Friday I was on the trains during the day, Tuesday I had an early night, Wednesday night I went to the pub. The big one on the high street in Ports. Thursday I indulged in the mad social whirl of going to the bingo with my landlady.' She watched the pen scribbling rapidly over the pages as the constable tried to keep up with her, his mousy hair flopping across his forehead as he worked energetically across the page.

'Friday night I was on the trains until just gone eight then I spent the rest of the evening sitting in another police station, one where they at least offered me a cup of tea instead of treating me like a criminal.' The sarcasm went over the down bent head of the constable, finding its mark on Inspector Jenkins's stony face.

'Oh! Er! Would you like a drink, Miss Edwards?' The question was offered in a singularly grudging voice.

'No, Inspector. I love being driven 30 miles after a hard day's work, to sit answering silly questions without proper explanation, in a draughty room without any refreshment.'

The constable looked at her in a horrified manner. 'Shall I get the young lady a cuppa, sir?'

'No, go and tell young Simms to do it, and then come back here.' He watched the boy leave then he turned back to Willow, picking up the biro and holding it poised over the paper. 'Now, Miss, tell me where you were last weekend and this weekend.'

'Last weekend was my first off for several weeks. I went shopping. I caught the train to Pwlleli and wandered round the shops. Oh! Wait, no, it wasn't Saturday it was Thursday I went to Pwlleli for the market; only it's on a Wednesday I discovered when I got there. I've probably got the train tickets somewhere, do you want them?'

'Yes, Miss.'

Willow had offered in a tone of sarcasm. Now she gazed at him in astonishment. Then she shrugged. 'Saturday was the day I went to the museum, in Ports. Sunday I went to Church. The Anglican one up on the hill.'

'And this weekend?'

'I went walking Saturday, over towards Portmerion. And then across the tops. My landlady made me some sandwiches and a flask, she can tell you when I went out and when I got back. But I didn't know I'd need an alibi, Inspector.' Willow squirmed slightly; she felt guilty about not admitting her dealings with the youngsters, but decided that she was in enough trouble without involving anyone else.

The inspector continued to look at her, only removing his gaze to hand the pen back as his young subordinate re-entered the room and seated himself at the table again.

'Sunday, I drove to Beddgelert, stopping on the way to talk to one of the work gangs. Sunday lunch in the hotel, in company with one of the drivers, then back to read papers and put my feet up at my lodgings.'

'Thank you, Miss, if you'd give the constable the name of your landlady and the people you were working with and the driver you dined with, also those tickets, we'll be in touch. We will be contacting them. It's just routine, Miss.'

Willow looked at him with distaste. 'Barry caused me trouble when he was alive and I see he hasn't improved now he's dead. Make sure all these people you're going to contact know its just routine, won't you, Inspector. I don't want to get a bad reputation.'

Inspector Jenkins got to his feet. 'If you'll just wait here until we can get the statement typed up, then you can go, Miss Edwards.' He walked out, leaving the constable shuffling the papers and his feet. He looked directly at her for the first time that evening. 'He's just doing his job, Miss.' He headed towards the door, turning to offer, 'I'll hurry up that tea for you.'

Willow, left in the interview room to mull over the last three quarters of an hour, decided that she still didn't like the police much. And, she thought, I still don't know how Barry died.

Obviously it hadn't been a natural death if they were saying suspicious circumstances and she needed an alibi. Still, she hadn't been near London for months, so it should be OK.

Her musings were interrupted by a very young policeman who looked as though he should still be in school. Simms, she presumed. 'Your tea, Miss, and I found you some digestives.' His Welsh accent was soft and lilting. She smiled at him kindly. It wasn't his fault if he had a bad tempered boss.

She whiled the time away drinking the tea and pondering the cause of Barry's death, it seemed unlikely she was going to be told. She found she was sorry for a life cut short, but had no regret that she had walked away.

A constable came back with a sheaf of papers and presented them with a pen for her signature. Willow carefully read through the typing, evidently this young man was orthographically challenged as well, she cross out a word here and there and corrected spelling all over the page and put her initials against the emendations, before signing her name at the bottom. It looked like the efforts of a pedantic schoolmarm when she'd finished.

'There you are, Constable Davis. I hope you have a nice time checking up on me.'

She watched him colour up again and mentally shrugged; he'd better toughen up soon or he wouldn't last long in his chosen career. She'd seen policemen like this one come into the

A & E department when she was on call; they didn't last if they didn't learn to keep their feelings hidden.

'Can I go now?'

'Yes, Miss Edwards.' He straightened up and tried to look stern, succeeding in looking like a rabbit caught in the headlights. 'We need to ask you to be available for the next few days.'

'Nicely said, Constable. You know where to find me.'

Willow walked away, closing the door of the interview room with a quiet click on his indignant face. It wasn't until she stepped outside into the persistent drizzle that she realised she had only a couple of pounds in her pocket. She supposed she could go back into the station and demand a lift back to the train sheds but pride prevented her. She stood on the pavement debating the options open to her. She could call a taxi and pay at the other end, but that was too expensive and she hadn't got that sort of money in her purse.

She could call the volunteer hostel and hope someone had both a car and petrol in it, to come and get her, but then she'd have to explain how she came to be stranded in the first place. She pulled a face at the thought.

She could call Morgan. He at least knew why she was there, but it went against the grain to be beholden to a man with money; look at the trouble she was in because of Barry. She nibbled at her lip but had only taken a few steps towards the centre of the town when she was forced to stop short, as she found her way blocked by Morgan's body. 'Need a lift?' His hands had shot forward to prevent her from walking into him.

'Morgan!' She looked up at the handsome face; her nostrils filled with the overwhelming scent of aftershave and Morgan's own particular aroma. She pulled back and stood looking at him in surprise, her heart galloping somewhat at the unexpectedness of the encounter. At least that's what she told herself.

The rain was settling on his hair, making it glisten in the lights from the shop windows and turning it into the colour of barley sugar. He had his black cashmere top coat on and the mizzle was turning it wet where it sat snugly across his shoulders, a pair of black leather driving gloves on the hands currently holding her shoulders were preventing her from moving. She gave a slight wiggle and he immediately let her go.

She felt even more scruffy than usual. His sartorial elegance was a sharp contrast to her dirty work clothes. 'Hi, I was just wondering how I was going to get back home.'

'So, the car's over there.' He took her acquiescence for granted and headed towards the Jaguar. Willow hesitated for only a second. Pride was one thing, but common sense another. And look where pride had got her Friday night.

He stood patiently waiting for her to climb in, holding the door open. She looked at the pristine interior somewhat dubiously. 'Come on, in you get.'

Willow scrambled onto the seat, reluctant to lean back but forced by the shape of the bucket seat to relax her body. She gingerly felt the butter-soft leather with a palm, relishing the feel of it, even as she inhaled the new car smell. She watched Morgan efficiently buckle up, mimicking his actions. 'Yes, but this car is brand new and I don't exactly fit the décor!'

Morgan glanced across. 'Forget décor and just enjoy.' He grinned and placed a well shod foot on the accelerator, weaving expertly through the evening traffic.

'I really appreciate the lift back; if you can drop me off at the works I can walk the rest of the way.'

Morgan nodded his head and then concentrated on his driving. The weather was turning nasty with little flurries of hail hitting the windscreen. He stretched out a hand and turned up the heating a notch, then glanced at his passenger. 'Music?'

He waited for a nod and turned on the radio. A spatter of Welsh assailed Willow's ears, followed by something which she took to be the Welsh equivalent of country and western. It was pleasantly relaxing, and between that and the warmth of the car she was almost asleep when he pulled up at the works. She prepared to alight, reluctant to leave the cosy interior, but wasn't quick enough to prevent Morgan from opening her door for her.

'Thanks so much. I'll see you around.'

Without a word, Morgan, displaying the charm and determination which had won him several contracts, helped her out and escorted her down the path to the changing rooms. As they approached the door he stood back. 'Key.' He handed over her locker key which, until that moment she'd forgotten about. 'I'll be out here when you're ready to go.'

Willow looked up at the strong face. 'I can manage, really I can.'

'Possibly, but you don't need to!'

Willow shrugged. It had been a long and trying day. 'Suit yourself.' She knew she sounded ungracious, and she could hear the gently chiding voice of her father reproving her. She mentally apologised to him as she headed into the changing rooms to have a quick shower, change into clean clothes and gather up her belongings.

If she had hoped Morgan would tire of waiting she was disappointed. He was lounging against the window, using his mobile to text someone, as she emerged. He finished and flipped the machine shut, standing erect and holding open the door.

They headed back to the car in silence and, showing the same courtesy, Morgan saw her safely seated and climbed in himself. He pushed the key into the ignition but didn't start the car. 'I'd like to take you back to my place. You need food and I, frankly, need my curiosity satisfied! I'll drive you back to your lodgings if you insist, but I'd much rather not.'

He waited while she absorbed his statement. The silence stretched out. Then Willow's stomach rumbled protestingly.

'I was going to say no, but my stomach doesn't appear to be in agreement. OK, Morgan - your place.' She had time on the short journey to reflect on why she should trust this man in a way she no longer trusted other men.

Having got his own way Morgan started the car without another word and drove rapidly homeward. The gates of Portmerion flashed past Willow's astonished gaze and they drew up with a flourish. 'Wow! I've been meaning to come here all season, but it's so expensive just to come through the gates.'

Morgan smiled at her enthusiasm as she peered round in the gloom. Some of the statues had been illuminated and the central ponds floodlit. He opened his door and ushered her in, taking her coat and showing her into the sitting area. 'I'll just order a meal, steak and chips do? That's a good standby and won't take too long.'

Willow nodded. She felt as though she could eat a horse with the saddle as well. Morgan picked up the phone and, she assumed, ordered, but since the conversation was conducted in Welsh the only words she picked out were 'thanks' and '*sglodion*'. She knew that was chips.

'Have a seat. I'll find some coffee while we wait.'

He threw his coat over the back of a chair near the door and went into the small annex kitchen while Willow sat down in front of the fire. Someone had obviously been in and lit it while Morgan was out, for it was burning quite merrily. She stretched out her hands to the blaze but couldn't quite bring herself to sit back in the dark upholstered chair.

He came back with two steaming mugs on a tray, complete with milk jug and sugar basin. Placing the tray between them on a small table he sat down with a sigh, stretching out his feet to the blaze.

'Drink your coffee and relax, dinner won't be long.'

Nursing his mug between his hands he leaned back and closed his dark blue eyes. Willow gazed, astonished at her host's behaviour but then, mentally shrugging, after taking her own mug and adding sugar, sat back herself, before looking thoughtfully at the man opposite.

Incurably honest, she spoke her thoughts out loud. 'You're older than I thought.'

A grin flickered over his face. 'Middle name's Methuselah!' His eyes remained closed, the lashes fanning out in almost female fashion across the high cheekbones. Willow felt the blush start in her bones and begin to radiate outwards.

'Sorry, that was rude.'

'I'm thirty-six and still have my own hair and teeth.' He briefly displayed an excellent set of teeth in a smile, before his face relaxed into its usual calm look. A soothing silence crept into the room and Willow found she was relaxing back in the peaceful atmosphere. She covertly admired that same hair as it started to dry out in the warmth from the fire; curling around rather large, but well shaped ears. Morgan opened his eyes as a knock on the door heralded dinner. The blue was veiled now as he glanced at her and then away.

The repast was a bit more than plain steak and chips having mushroom sauce, baby carrots and peas and being followed by a Pavlova that made Willow's saliva pool. She finally sat back with a sigh, replete. 'For that sort of meal I'll be happy to satisfy your curiosity.'

Morgan hadn't said anything while the business of eating had been indulged, but now he smiled across. 'You don't have to, if you don't want to. But I would like to know what's going on. Witnesses don't generally get hauled away in quite such a cavalier fashion. Do they suspect your body was foully done to death?'

'I have no idea. They didn't mention the body that I found Friday!'

'*Be*'?' Morgan looked across the dishes at her. 'What did they want you for then? Let's clear this away, now I really do want to know what happened if it wasn't your body they wanted you for.' He grunted and grinned. 'Let me rephrase that. If it wasn't the body you found Friday.' He managed to stop his wayward tongue just in time from saying unless a man was dead he'd definitely want her body. He didn't think that comment would go down very well.

They rapidly piled the dishes onto the draining board and settled back in front of the fire.

Willow looked across at Morgan. 'I think I might be suspected of putting a period to the life of my ex-fiancé, but they weren't very forthcoming. An inspector asked me lots of questions about my relationship and then demanded my whereabouts for the last week.'

Morgan listened in silence while she detailed the interview with Inspector Jenkins. Finally he spoke. 'I knew your face was vaguely familiar, but out of context I hadn't placed you with Barry Scott.'

'Oh!' Willow didn't know if she liked the fact that he could now link her to Barry. It wasn't a connection she was proud of, or wanted others to know about. The papers had, inevitably, labelled her a gold-digger, when they weren't describing her as his trophy.

Morgan was obviously reviewing what he'd read about her and she shifted uncomfortably in her seat as his eyes drifted over her face and figure.

'Well, the papers write a lot of garbage about me as well,' he commented, 'but you can prove your whereabouts for the last week or so, so I should think it will just be routine, as they said.'

'I expect they will ask you if you lunched with me. I'm sorry, Morgan, it hadn't occurred to me until just now, how this will look for you if the papers get hold of the story.' Willow rubbed her hands down her trousers legs and grew warm at the thought, her cheeks flushing with embarrassment.

'I shall tell the police I enjoyed a delightful lunch. And the papers to go and find someone else to hound. Now, this body you found Friday. You were on the trains all day Friday, including your stint with me, so when did you have time to find it?'

'Well, actually, after I left you, on my way down Quarry Lane.'

'What was it, a hit and run?'

Willow absently scratched the back of her head dislodging several long strands of the blond hair she tied back out of the way with a scrunchy, and scattering the pins placed haphazardly in it, onto the carpet. 'Er, no. It was... It was a very dead body, lying just on the side of the estuary. The sergeant at Penrhyn seemed to think it was a walker who'd got trapped by the tide and maybe drowned.'

'So how did you find it?'

Willow told him about stepping out of the way of the teenager's car and onto the body. Morgan kept his inevitable reflections to himself; he'd known he shouldn't have left her to walk home, but short of kidnapping, what choice had he had? He watched as the long silky hair became more dislodged as she talked. She was a very active speaker, hands moving to express her emotions. Perhaps the interview with the police had unnerved her more than she knew; the barriers he'd sensed yesterday weren't so evident today.

'And then of course there was the young man we rescued on Saturday, I didn't like to mention him but I suppose that will have to come out now too.'

Morgan held up a hand to stem the flow. 'What young man, and who's the we? Willow, you lead the most intriguing life.'

Willow blushed. 'Oh dear, I didn't intend to mention that bit.'

'Well, you have now, so tell me about it, you can't just throw leading statements about like that and not explain.'

'Yes, but it's not just me.' Willow was feeling rather embarrassed at letting her mouth run away with her. 'You shouldn't lull me with food and warm fires, Morgan. I forget who I'm talking to.'

'Oh! No, you aren't going to change the subject like that. My sister will tell you I'm the most curious man alive, but I can be trusted with secrets.'

Willow sat silently wondering if she could. After all it wasn't that big a deal. Morgan held his peace. He found, for some strange reason, that he really did want her to trust him.

Finally she started to speak and he felt his heart give a thump of pleasure which he couldn't quite understand. 'I went for a walk Saturday morning.'

'Yeah! I saw you.' Just in time he stopped himself saying how pretty he'd thought she looked. He remembered yesterday's reaction to his compliment.

'Well, I met Deniol and Sian up the hill and they'd found a young man a few days before. He was a foreigner, apparently, and in need of somewhere to stay but wouldn't go back into the town so they let him into one of the holiday cottages.'

'Ah! I begin to see. I've heard Sian on the subject of incomers.' Morgan grinned, revealing a slight gap in the otherwise perfect teeth. 'She'd have Owen Glyndwr resurrected and massing an army to drive out the *Saeson* if it was humanly possible.'

Willow grinned back. 'I love her enthusiasm even if, as one of the despised English, I can't go along with it. Though Deniol did tell me I didn't count!'

'Oh! They're a great pair. Enormous potential that boy has, but diplomacy obviously isn't his strong suit.' He raised a mobile eyebrow. He privately thought she counted a great deal.

'Hmm! Well, anyway, their young *protégé* had fallen and broken a leg, unfortunately or otherwise, while in the confines of the cottage. We got him off to hospital in an ambulance but he's seriously ill and still lacking an identity.

'Meanwhile back at the ranch,' Willow paused and looked across at Morgan, 'yours truly was confessing to B and E and trespassing, to the police down at Penrhyn on Saturday afternoon. I don't think it'll lead to problems for the youngsters, but I am worried about their friend. What I didn't tell them was he could quite easily die.' Willow was serious again; her hair, now totally unfastened, framed her face in a curtain of silky waves which glowed red gold in the firelight.

Morgan felt an unbidden urge to run the mass through his hands and hoped she hadn't noticed the barely perceptible movement towards her; he didn't want her swaying away again.

'I thought you said he'd only broken a leg?'

'Yeah but he might have a clot on the lung from it.'

'I hope you're wrong. Sian has been through enough traumas over the last couple of years.'

Willow looked at him curiously but didn't pursue the obvious knowledge he seemed to have. She had just caught sight of the clock.

'Heavens, Morgan, I must get back! My landlady will be sending out the mountain rescue if I don't turn up soon.'

Morgan too glanced across at the clock, just then the phone rang. With a word of apology he picked up the instrument. '*Cariad*'. There was a wealth of love in the word and Morgan's face, unguarded for a second, lit up. He spoke in Welsh, into the receiver, and then placed a hand over the mouthpiece. 'Excuse me, Willow, this is an international call I've been waiting for. It'll be quicker if I speak Welsh. OK?'

Willow nodded and began to tidy her hair in preparation for leaving. Morgan, absently watching her while he spoke, found he was quite irrationally stirred by her actions. He wanted to reach out and stay the busy hands. He deliberately averted his eyes and fixed them firmly on the opposite wall.

'Yes, darling, Mary told me the Americans were being chauvinist pigs. But I think you're the right woman for the job. Do you need your little brother to come and defend you?'

He listened to the reply, and then said, 'I can come if you want me to. Is there one particular MCP or are they all horrid?'

'Well, I may be your little brother but we're only talking five minutes. And that gives me special knowledge and rights, doesn't it now.'

He listened some more. 'OK, I won't come yet, but if they give you any more problems you can ditch the contract. I won't have you upset.'

He paused, frowning at whatever was being said over the phone, 'No, I'm not upset either.'

He paused again and Willow, watching from the other side of the room, was astonished to see a red mantle on his cheekbones. Maybe his girlfriend was hassling him, she thought, and felt her stomach sink. He was a nice guy and didn't deserve to be harassed on holiday. She also found that she was experiencing a stray twinge of jealousy and wondered where it had come from.

'Yes, I know the twin thing goes both ways,' Morgan continued, 'but I'm not involved with anyone down here.' He smiled absently at Willow, then as he continued to look at her his face became quite still and all trace of emotion left it to leave a still, blank mask.

Willow felt herself blushing again at his continued scrutiny. What on earth had she done now? The man looked like a bad tempered schoolmaster about to reprimand an errant child.

He concluded his conversation in a somewhat abrupt manner it seemed to Willow. As he set the receiver down she reached for her donkey jacket, speaking over her shoulder. 'I'll be on my way. I hope your friend isn't too annoyed with you, Morgan. I must go home anyway.'

Morgan looked first astonished, then puzzled, then a queer smile like a tiger sighting potential prey crossed his face. 'Oh, no, she'll come round. She can't decide if she wants me in New York or not.'

If Willow thought it was odd that such a confident man was willing to be ordered about by a woman she didn't say so. Everyone was entitled to their Achilles heel.

Morgan was now all punctilious politeness as he escorted her out to the car. The short journey was conducted in silence and Willow regretted having said so much to a man who she thought was wishing her somewhere else.

Like a well brought up child she thanked him politely for her meal as they arrived, only to have the words ignored as he got out and came round to escort her to her door. The nets twitched and the door opened with a rapidity that showed her landlady was on the watch. Willow tried in vain to prevent them meeting. As they walked up the path she muttered. 'She's a terrible gossip, Morgan.'

The man appeared to be impervious to the hint. '*Nos da*.' He smiled down on the curlers.

Willow looked at the blush currently spreading over the wrinkled cheeks, and the hand doing its best to hide the plastic rolls currently nestling in Mrs Jones' hair like so many piglets in straw. Morgan appeared to be making another conquest.

'One of the boys popped round to say the *Heddlu* had taken you off to Caernarfon. It'll be about the poor soul you found then.' It wasn't quite a question but the eyes glistened with curiosity. 'I'm pleased that you got back safe. It's about time you found someone to look after you.' She gave his coat and the car sitting on the roadway an assessing glance. 'And he can do it properly, not like those boys down at the hostel!'

Willow felt her cheeks going hot, she wasn't sure which was more embarrassing, her landlady's assumptions about Morgan or the fact that he now knew she didn't apparently have anyone to 'look after her'. God forbid the man should think she was on the lookout for a man, especially a rich one.

Morgan, an interested and slightly amused bystander, suppressed the chuckle. So she hadn't got a boyfriend. Now wasn't that interesting. 'Good night, Willow, thank you for your company. It's been a pleasure dining with you.' He gently laid a hand on her back, unable to resist the lure of the lustrous gold rope hanging neatly once again. He felt her withdrawal but kept the hand in place. He wasn't sure yet if his sister was right, but if she was, Willow had better get used to his touch.

Willow wasn't quite sure what she muttered, she was getting hotter by the second. Her landlady moved to the side and she went past, mortified to hear that lady say, 'She needs feeding up, she does.'

And Morgan's answer, 'Do you think so? She's looks just the right shape to me.'

She hoped to avoid any more comments by heading straight for the stairs, but Mrs Jones had closed the door and was following rapidly in her wake. 'Do you want a drink, *Cariad*? I was worried when you didn't come back, but when the boys said it was the *Heddlu* again I knew they'd make sure you got home alright.'

Willow didn't have the heart to disillusion her. 'Er, yes, I was fine.' She edged further towards the stairs. Mrs Jones hadn't finished, however. 'That was kind then,' she nodded her head at the closed door and departed male, 'to give you a meal. Where did you go then, *Cariad*?'

'Er, Portmerion. I'm really tired. I'll see you in the morning, Mrs Jones. I've got the early run again.' She headed purposefully up the stairs. Mrs Jones stood with a hand on the banister and a speculative look on her kind face, her eyes following the figure of her paying guest.

5

YESTERDAY MIGHT HAVE BEEN a stolen day from summer; today the sky was totally overcast, the clouds massing for the attack on the Snowdon region like the Goths swarming across Europe. Willow shivered as she industriously polished from her own particular eyrie, despite the old grey jumper she was wearing under her boiler-suit. She paused; rag in hand, to listen to a robin in some nearby shrub proclaiming his territory. Huh! Typical male, she thought, smiling at the sweet trill before she turned back to the job in hand.

She didn't know if Morgan would be her driver again. The Earl's boiler was proving troublesome still, but the trains, now that the children were back at school, had been reduced to four a day.

She had had time to reflect overnight on her reactions to Morgan. She had to admit privately that she really rather liked him. He had been kind without making a move on her. The gossips had reported he didn't like women but he hadn't frozen her off. However, she rather hoped she could avoid him. OK, he wasn't like Barry, but he was rich and she didn't want to get involved in that world again.

With real contrariness she was abnormally disappointed when Gavin showed up as her driver five minutes later.

'Hi, Willow, how far have you got?'

Willow smiled warmly down from her lofty perch, in compensation for her disappointment. 'Hi, Gavin, how's the leg?'

Gavin bent to roll up his blue overalls.

'No! I've only just had breakfast!' Willow covered her eyes in mock horror. 'Don't show me, tell me.'

Gavin swung up onto the side of the tank, bringing his pointy chin with its designer stubble into closer proximity, and demonstrating that the leg was much improved as he balanced precariously to push back the cotton cap he wore on his tousled blond locks. 'Oh, its much better. I've only got another couple of days and then I have to get home and get everything ready for the start of term.'

'How much longer have you got to go then?'

'Finals this year. Four years of slog and then I have to find a firm that will take me for the brilliant lawyer that I am, and pay me!'

Willow grinned at him. 'You'll have to wash your face and comb your hair for that job.'

153

'I did wash, that's a foul calumnious imputation.'

'Yeah! You sound like a lawyer. Now I look I can see you washed your neck. I can see the line where you left off.'

'Huh! Base insinuations.'

Willow, a lilt of laughter in her voice, looked his unprepossessing person over. 'Will you still honour us with your presence when you're famous?'

'Why not? Morgan does!' Gavin smiled up at her, humorous challenge on his face. 'What's more I hear you're getting to be quite famous too. What's this about the police and dead bodies? Need a fledgling lawyer do you?' The last was said only half jokingly.

Willow groaned. She'd known the scuttlebutt would finally spread round the yard. She'd just hoped that most of the volunteers would have left before it became more public knowledge. Apparently not. Well, sometimes you had to attack as a form of defence. She prayed she wouldn't blush under the scrutiny of the young man in front of her.

'I refuse to talk about it sitting on top of an engine, Gavin. You'll have to wait for all the gory details till the inquest, like everyone else.'

Gavin grinned cheekily at her. 'Ah, but someone else is in the know. I heard in the pub that our Morgan took you home last night.'

'Fishing, Gavin? Who did you hear that from? The man offered me a ride back from Caernarfon after the police interview. Which was kind of him.'

'Hmm! Not only kind. Unheard of!'

Willow looked down on the young face. 'Leave it, Gavin.' She wiped her hands on the greasy rag currently serving her as cleaning aid, thereby transferring even more oil onto her person.

Gavin would have said more but Dai appeared at that moment, his wiry body wrapped in a thick donkey jacket against the elements. 'Haven't you got the pressure hose on yet, Willow? And why are you hanging around like a blamed monkey in a tree instead of oiling those wheels, Gavin?' Dai came towards them as he spoke.

Willow, hastily shifting, climbed down off the tank, and with a grateful look at Dai, who gave her a long considering one in return, went to start the compressor. When she returned she found him still standing watching Gavin from the marginal warmth of the cab.

'Thanks, Dai.'

Dai nodded at her. 'The Permanent-Way is looking to start tamping over at Tan-y-Bwlch in a couple of weeks. Will you still be here then?'

Willow had been thinking about what she would do when the train season ended. She really needed to find a job soon. She had a bit in the bank from her parent's estate and insurance policies, but while she worked for the FR she was living off her capital. Besides, she wanted to spend some time investigating the possibility of any living relatives. The Permanent Way gang worked a full week, not the odd shifts that the firemen and drivers worked.

'I don't know, Dai. I'll let you know by the end of the week, OK?'

'Yeah, that will be fine. I'll let Owen know you're still deciding.'

'And – er...' Willow found her cheeks going red again, 'I may need to take a bit of time off this week too!'

Dai hopped down with the agility of a sparrow off a branch, then turned a sapient eye upon her. 'Time off, noted, just let me know. If you need any other help you can always come to me. I've been around a while!'

It was the closest that Dai would ever come to admitting he'd heard the gossip and was offering help. Willow was grateful, even while she didn't think she would accept the offer.

Gavin got on with the work of preparing the engine, casting her the odd speculative look but saying nothing. Willow looked at the darkening sky and suggested that they get a move on, to which he vouchsafed only a grunt. He didn't even attempt to reopen the conversation on their way over the Cob to couple up to the rake and take on their load of passengers.

Either Dai had had a word with the nascent lawyer driving for her, or Gavin had taken the hint. She suspected the former. But he might have been concentrating on his driving, the lines had been slippery with leaves and early morning dew and they had had to make copious use of sand as they pulled up the incline at the start of the Deviation. The train wasn't exactly full either; perhaps the cold, damp weather had put people off.

It had seemed a long trip, somewhat complicated by a wild goat who glared belligerently at them in one of the cuttings before trotting slowly along the line in front of them. The wild goats could be rather ferocious and Willow was glad that it neither charged the engine nor became embedded in the wheels.

Willow had been wishing herself somewhere else for much of the journey, though she didn't quite understand her restlessness. Normally she loved working the train. She was relieved to see Porthmadog Harbour station through the glass and think that she could leave the train to someone else to put to bed today.

She took her eyes off their destination long enough to glance across at Gavin as he muttered something rude about the men she could see up ahead. 'What's up, Gavin?'

'God knows, still searching for clues about that body you don't want mentioning!' He nodded forwards where the small figures were becoming rapidly larger. Willow looked down from the top of the Cob at a large group of dark blue clad figures, their orange visi-vests a vibrant contrast to the surrounding slate.

'What on earth are they doing on that side of the Cob? They look like they're digging up the embankment.'

'You're the one in the know!' Evidently Gavin harboured a little bit of resentment. He sounded like a grumpy school boy.

Willow attempted an apology. 'Sorry Gavin, I'm just a bit touchy at the moment.' She offered a morsel of information as a way of placating him. 'I found the body way up near Cemetery Cutting though, not down here.'

'Maybe the coppers are checking to see if the tide has brought any evidence down to the shore.'

'That's the wrong side of the Cob, Gavin!' Willow swept a grubby hand towards the sea, where the police force could be seen toiling away in a most industrious manner, using shovels to rearrange the scenery and shift holes about.

The train steamed noisily into the station and Willow was kept busy calming the little beast down as she finished the first journey of the day. Having filled the tank with water and shunted round on the engine to allow a different arrangement of carriages in the rake, she hopped down and handed over to the young man waiting on the platform.

'There you go, Harry, she's all yours.'

'How's she working?' They both climbed back on the footplate and moved across to the fireman's side.

'Fine. The filter might be a bit clogged, had to use sand, so you'd better make sure to fill that up!'

'Have you heard about Morgan?'

Willow shook her head. 'You may need to keep an eye on that left gauge.' She pointed a grubby finger at the inoffensive gauge, trying to deflect the replacement fireman's scrutiny of her face.

Harry didn't take the hint. 'Yeah, fine, left gauge.'

He fixed his eyes on her as he spilled out his news, hoping for some reaction. 'Morgan was greeted by the police when he came into the station this morning at half ninish. They took him up to the office and spent hours talking to him!' Harry was enjoying himself, his eyes sparkling. 'I thought you might know something since you and he are so tight.'

'I think you've been listening to too much gossip, Harry. When has Morgan Williams been 'tight' with any woman around here? I'm looking to marry a much richer man than him to keep me in the manner I want to become accustomed to,' she said mock serious, and with a total disregard for grammar or truth.

Harry opened his mouth but the rejoinder didn't arrive. An all too familiar nose rapidly followed by the bristling moustache attached to Inspector Jenkins' face, insinuated itself into the cab and into their conversation.

'Ah, Miss Edwards! They told me you should be on this train. I'd like another word with you if it's convenient?'

Willow wondered what the man would do if she said it wasn't convenient. Her lips twitched wryly, but her stomach was churning a bit as she said with a fine show of bravado, 'Certainly, Inspector. Did you bring the thumbscrews this time?'

'Will I need them, Miss Edwards?' He gestured with a large flat palm, inviting her to dismount from the train.

'You all set here, Harry?' Willow surveyed the young fireman eagerly listening to their exchange.

'Yeah! Fine.'

Willow grinned as Gavin came up. 'You two can exchange gossip about me now!' She watched as both of them had the grace to blush slightly under their stubby beards.

She stepped down and saw Morgan, his cool blue eyes impassive, watching her from across the platform. She gave him a casual nod. 'Where would you like to go, Inspector? Back to Caernarfon again?'

'That won't be necessary, Miss; we can go up to the Station Master's Office. I only need a little clarification.'

Willow led the way up the uncarpeted wooden stairs towards the half-glass panelled door. Part of her mind was thinking she'd quite like to boil him until he was clarified, but she suppressed this uncharitable thought, telling herself the man was only doing his job.

A young policewoman opened the door for her and she went towards one of the hard wooden chairs in front of the desk and sat down, pulling off the shiny black cap and dumping it in front of her. At her back the policewoman closed the door and stood just inside, her back to the panelling. The inspector made his way round the desk and sat down in the fat controller's seat.

'Now, Miss Edwards. We just need to check on a few facts from your statement of yesterday!' He clicked his pen and looked at her.

Willow raised an eyebrow but kept her mouth shut; she pulled a dirty rag from her back pocket and began to wipe her equally grubby hands, waiting for him to elaborate.

'In your statement you said that you dined with a driver on Sunday. A Mr Morgan Williams?'

Willow nodded. She wondered what was coming next and feeling her hands turn clammy she gave them an extra wipe then stuffed the cloth away.

'Were you aware that Mr Williams and Barry Scott where business rivals?'

Willow felt her skin turn clammy all over now. If she'd thought about it she might have made the connection. It just hadn't occurred to her. She kept her face as impassive as she could. 'No, Inspector. Mr Williams is just a casual acquaintance who I work with when I'm here. I don't know anything about his personal or business dealings.'

'Hmm.' The tone was sceptical; the look even more so. 'Very well. Now can you give us any reason why Mr Scott would be in Wales if, as you claim, you haven't seen him since May?'

'Barry? In Wales?'

'Yes, Miss Edwards. Are you sure you haven't had any contact with him?'

'No. I told you I finished with him, broke off our engagement. I didn't want anything more to do with the man.'

'And you haven't seen him?'

'No. I said so!'

'And Mr Williams hasn't mentioned his name to you?'

Willow paused, and shifted in the chair. Then she looked the inspector firmly in his bulging eye. 'During the course of a conversation with Mr Williams yesterday, I mentioned the name of my ex-boyfriend. Mr Williams, I believe, said that he hadn't connected me with 'that Barry Scott'. He didn't elaborate but added that the papers loved gossip. Does that answer your question, Inspector Jenkins?'

'And Mr Williams hasn't taken Mr Scott's place in your affections, you say.' It was the sneer on his face that caused Willow to lose her calm.

'I haven't replaced Barry with anyone, Inspector. I've had it big time with rich men who throw their weight around and manage to evade the consequences. I neither want, nor need, a man in my life. I'm coping just fine without one.'

'Has the rich,' he paused, 'Mr Williams, been throwing his weight around then?'

'No, Inspector, he hasn't.'

'I heard you say just now that you were looking for a rich man!' Willow opened her mouth to refute the statement then closed it again.

'Just so, Miss.' The inspector fixed his beady eye on her and smiled slyly.

'That was just talk, Inspector. I have no intention of marrying anyone at the moment. I haven't been asked, for a start.'

They sat looking at each other, Willow bracing herself for the next onslaught, the inspector evidently digesting her statements. He placed his hands tidily in front of his tightly tailored torso, on top of the notes he had been taking.

'Very well, Miss Edwards, that will be all for now. We expect to see you at the inquest tomorrow.' He reached into his inside pocket and pulled out a sheet which he handed over. 'That's the witness order.'

She accepted the folded sheet saying, 'Oh! That makes two inquests this week then.'

'Two?'

'Well, Barry's and the body I found last Friday night.'

The inspector gave her a rather curious look. 'One inquest, Miss Edwards. The body was Barry Scott's.'

THE MEN WHO HAD recently been cursed by Gavin as he chuffed by on the train were being issued with small bottles of Vicks Vapour Rub by Gareth. He was in charge of two new recruits who were looking at him as if he'd lost his marbles. 'Rub some under your nose, lads, you're going to need it.'

He watched as they obey in mystified silence. 'OK, Sarge, what now?'

'Now follow me.' Gareth set off at a ground eating walk down the side of the slope and onto the estuary, heading towards the canvas covering that could be seen in the distance. The two younger men followed him after a quick puzzled look at each other.

When they arrived, slightly out of breath, Gareth motioned them forward, he was breathing easily as if he'd just been for a stroll up the garden path. The young recruits were beginning to think that was just where he was leading them. All they could see was a hole in the estuary barrier. 'I've brought my two recruits, Robin.' He turned to the young policemen. 'Look, don't touch. I will be asking questions later.' Then he stood back slightly as they both gazed at the hole in the embankment. The police were busily making it even bigger.

Robin moved closer and Gareth spoke quietly as both senior men watched the recruits. 'Thanks for letting me bring them down, Rob.'

'We've all got to get our experience where we can.'

'What we got so far?'

'Nothing to do with the murder from Friday, that's for sure. The gun they picked up is First World War vintage. The body looks as if it's been there almost as long.'

Gareth breathed in vapour from his own top lip and was grateful to do so. They could see a partial skeleton being slowly and meticulously revealed by forensics. Photographs and sketches and a group of policemen, clad in white, were at the centre of the scene.

'They should have it out by mid afternoon, Gareth. Then it can go off for the autopsy and maybe the air will be a bit better to work in.'

Gareth grunted agreement. He was thinking of the questions his young recruits needed to answer back at the station. 'Alright, lads. Let's get back and you can tell me what you observed, how you think the corpse got there, and whether we'll solve this crime any day this century.' He waved the young policemen away, and with a brief '*Diolch.*' to Robin, shepherded his charges back up the bank to the top of the Cob and through the railway works. He intended those he trained to be alert and courteous.

WILLOW FOUND HERSELF BEING patted on the cheek by a concerned woman police constable who was very alert, but whose thought weren't in the least kindly towards her current inspector. The inspector wasn't around.

Willow sat up abruptly as she felt her stomach begin to heave. Her head spun and the edges of her vision began to go black again, but she fought off the sensation. She would not faint again, once in a lifetime was plenty.

'OK, luv, shall I get you a drink of water?' It was asked in an accent as broad as the Mersey, and the concern was genuine and pure Liverpudlian.

Willow shook her head. Then the abrupt entrance of Morgan threatened to send her head swimming again. 'What the hell happened here? Did he hurt you, threaten you?' The man was in a towering rage; even she could see that, his glacial gaze resting on the face of the WPC.

Willow gazed at him in astonishment. 'I'm fine, I just fainted. Probably missing lunch, that's all.'

The constable chimed in defensively at the same time with, 'She passed right out and gave her head a nasty crack when she fell on the floor.'

'It isn't all; when that nosy copper comes down saying he needs a nurse for you. Now what's going on?'

The entrance of the 'nosy copper' stopped all conversation. 'I apologise, Miss Edwards. I thought that by now you were aware of the fact that you had found Mr Scott's body near the estuary.' As apologies went it was handsome, especially as Morgan was viewing him like something particularly nasty found on the bottom of his hand stitched Italian shoes.

Willow didn't get much chance to acknowledge it, however. The rapidly filling room was filled to overflowing by the appearance of a first aider in the form of Beryl from the café downstairs. Beryl hadn't grown, she'd been constructed, and her lyrcra was stretched for maximum torque around her twenty stone, she exuded authority and capability wrapped in a pinny.

'Right, let's have a bit of room in here so Willow can breathe. You men get out.'

To his credit the inspector was the first to leave, swiftly followed by Morgan. Morgan might not understand women that well, but he could recognise a woman on the prod when he saw one. Nevertheless he braved her wrath to say, 'I'll be downstairs when you need me, Willow.' as he exited.

'Right, *Cariad*, let's have a look at you.'

The next few minutes were a bit painful, as Beryl prodded the rapidly swelling egg on the side of Willow's temple and had her following a penlight, its size swamped by her meaty paw. 'No sign of concussion that I can see. But that's a nasty bump; you're going to need to take some Panadol for that. And no firing tomorrow. I'll let Dai know.'

'I've got to go to an inquest tomorrow, anyway.'

'Well, if you must; but no rushing around.'

She and the WPC helped Willow to stand between them; neither letting go until they were assured she wasn't going to fall down again. 'If you get to feeling sick, or there's any double vision, it's off to hospital with you. Now come down to the café and I'll get you a *panad* and then get yourself off home.'

They walked, one in front and one behind as if escorting a prisoner, while Willow negotiated the stairs, then led her to a quiet corner of the cafe. Morgan, waiting at the entrance to the office, followed the trio along the platform and into the warm steamy fug of the café and sat down opposite Willow.

'You'll see her home, Morgan.' It was a command.

Morgan nodded, his eyes fixed on Willow's pale face. 'Sure.'

'Right, I'll get that tea.' Beryl, on surprisingly light feet, went off behind the counter for the tea. The WPC, after standing looking at the seated couple for a minute, walked away to find her superior.

'We'll talk when it's a bit more private like.' Morgan's perfect English seemed to have slipped his grasp. They sat quietly, aware that there were a variety of speculative and curious eyes trying to appear as though they weren't looking at the couple in the quiet corner.

Willow nodded, and then winced. She would be quite happy never to talk about the subject again but it seemed to be one of those weeks. The arrival of the tea and a sheet of Panadol tablets gave her somewhere to fix her eyes. Beryl gave her another searching look but, evidently satisfied, went to assume command of her realm behind the cash-in desk like a captain on the bridge, or more like the prow, Willow thought, feeling slightly unhinged.

After she had sat stirring the tea round and round, creating a small whirlpool, but without actually trying to drink it, Morgan leant over and gently removed the spoon from her hand.

'Come on, *Cariad*; let's get you out of the public eye.'

He helped her rise and for once she didn't pull away from the arm around her waist. Morgan escorted her from the café and onto the front forecourt where he had parked the Jaguar. 'In you get.'

Willow was torn between a desire to be away from prying eyes and an equal reluctance to go back to her lodgings and face her landlady.

As they pulled out and moved into the slow queue travelling along the Cob she said in a husky voice, 'Morgan.'

'Yes, *Cariad*?'

'Can we go back to your place for a bit? I know I'm a bit mucky but...' She gulped, suddenly finding herself near to tears. 'I need a bit of privacy.'

'Of course you can.' Morgan opened the window a little so that the fresh air blew in and the noise of the cars passing on the right whooshed by. But, aside from enquiring if she was warm enough, said nothing else during the short journey to Portmerion.

He was still astonished to find how much his emotions had been overset that day. The idea that someone might have hurt Willow had put him in a towering rage. Now the fact that she trusted him enough to ask this favour filled him with astonishment and, yes, he thought, despite the circumstances, a quiet joy.

WORD FILTERED BACK TO Sergeant ap Rhys later that afternoon. So, the inspector had used his usual heavy-handed tactics to convey news, and nearly caused an incident. Would the man never learn? Gareth could take a fair bit of insult from his superiors; generally speaking he went his own way anyway. But when it started to affect the public then something would have to be done.

He would see what happened at the inquest tomorrow. He shrugged. Now where was that report about their mysterious stranger. Ah. He shuffled paper. He'd sent a photocopy out with requests for information, to the Russian churches. Nothing. No, wait a minute.

Gareth gave a silent whistle, as he scanned the brief document signed 'yours in Christ', and giving an Archbishops name in Russian hieroglyphs. So they'd got themselves a Polish gent and a piece of Russian history.

He laid down the paper and rang a police station on Anglesey. 'Clancy, how you doing? Yeah, yeah, I'm still here. Yeah, it's a nice little murder, but I'm not involved. I want to borrow that nice young Polish lad you sent across the other week. Well, because he speaks Polish of course! Why else would I want him?' Gareth grinned as his friend made various rude suggestions that neither his mother nor his girlfriend thought he was *au fait* with.

'Well, I'm sure it can wait a day, I'll set it up at the Bangor station. It's like this...' Gareth began to use cop-speak to fill his friend in on the young man that Deniol and Sian had befriended.

MORGAN USHERED WILLOW INTO the warmth of his cottage and pulled forward a chair to the fire. He was trying to be a friend too, but in truth that wasn't the feeling uppermost in his mind. Not that he was about to share that little gem with Willow. 'I'll make some more tea, shall I?'

Willow sat down and, for the first time since the inspector had appeared on her horizon, began to relax. She closed her eyes and allowed the quiet to flow over her, soft and comforting as a feather duvet.

Morgan, coming soft-footed into the room with the tea, sat down opposite and waited for her to speak. The chair squeaking slightly alerted her to his presence, along with that indefinable scent which was Morgan. When, she wondered, had she become aware of that?

Without opening her eyes she began to talk. 'You know that body I stood in?'

'Mmm.'

'It was Barry!'

'Ah!'

She opened her eyes. 'I didn't recognise him. He was just a body. One I was a bit impatient at finding, because he wasn't pretty, Morgan. I know we all die and all sort of disintegrate.' She raised eyes swimming in tears. 'But you don't like to think of someone you know, like that.'

'Do you still love him then, *Cariad*?' Something she couldn't define lurked in his eyes.

'No. That's what makes it worse. I don't think I ever really loved him! He was a bully and a bastard.'

He passed over a square of Irish linen big enough to masquerade as a small tablecloth. 'Wipe your eyes; you can't fall in love to order. What did the bastard do to you then? Would it help to talk or do you just want to be left in peace?'

'I think I want to talk. Maybe,' She looked across at him and blew her nose vigorously, leaving several oily streaks from her face on the fabric. 'If I talk about him alive, I won't remember him dead, if you follow. Only I don't quite know where to begin.'

'Well, start with Inspector Jenkins. What did he want you for today?'

'He wanted to tell me you and Barry were business rivals. I'm sorry Morgan; I seem to have landed you in a whole lot of trouble.'

'Barry was trouble on two legs. I tried to steer clear of him, but the business world of London can be almost as elite a group as the Welsh one. Sooner or later the police would have made the connection between us. Not that I had any dealings with him. He tried to take over my Dad's firm about five years ago, when we were struggling a bit financially. He was annoyed when we managed to stave off the creditors long enough to get the securities necessary to survive.' He paused to drink tea, looking at the pretty picture she made in the firelight, notwithstanding the tears that had tracked down her cheeks.

'The inspector has all but accused me of fraud and industrial espionage. It's put me in a hell of a difficult position.' Morgan looked angry, and Willow felt guilty again. It seemed she was involving this man in trouble just by the company she'd kept.

She digested the sudden wealth of knowledge about Morgan. She wished there was something she could say to make the situation better. The more that he told her, the worse she felt. And it appeared he'd told her more than he'd told her, or anyone else for all she knew, in the three years she had known him.

She picked up the mug of tea and took a tentative sip. 'I don't know anything about his business, but in his private life he was,' she shuddered, 'difficult, demanding, and arrogant. He seemed to consider me his personal property.' She wrapped her hands around the mug and fixed her eyes on the scene through the window. She could just see the sea in the distance, a grey swirl of water merging into a grey and lowering sky.

'When I agreed to go out with him he was delightful, an apparently caring companion. But as soon as I agreed to an engagement things changed. He told me what to dress in.' She waved the hand still clutching the hanky, endangering the contents of her mug on the way. 'I could understand what he was saying. We come from different worlds, I didn't know what was right always, and I can't stay clean.' For the first time a glimmer of her enchanting smile peeked out as she caught sight of the linen.

Morgan smiled back; pleased to see she was regaining her poise.

'Anyway, I went along with it for a bit. My mother had only been dead a few months and I guess I was looking for a degree of security, which at first he seemed to supply.' She paused. 'It's not exactly a new story, King Cophetua and the beggar maid. How many times have I read it in romances and thought the heroine a bit of a wimp. But this was me.'

She sniffed indignantly, setting down the mug with a clink on the small table between them. 'Well, anyway, one night we'd been to a party. First he shouted at me for not saying the right things to 'people who matter'.' Willow put the phrase in inverted commas with her fingers. 'Then he complained that I'd been making up to other men. Then he hit me.'

Morgan stiffened in his seat, his frown becoming dangerous; he found he wanted to hit the dead Barry very much, for laying hands on Willow.

Willow had closed her eyes and her voice wobbled treacherously. 'That was when I decided enough was enough. I was at his flat. We'd had the usual argument about me staying the night already, and he was a bit drunk anyway, so I called a taxi and left while he was in the bathroom. I don't think he expected me to leave.' The gamine grin was surfacing again, a sparkle of sun through the clouds of gloom in her voice.

Morgan looked across at the young girl, his heart overwhelmed with tenderness, but also exultation. So they argued about staying the night and she didn't. He found that thought filled him with enormous, and very male, pleasure. 'Yes, that sounds like the Barry I knew.' He brushed back his hair and, finding the band holding it loose, pulled his hair free of its confines. 'I wonder just what mischief he was up to here in sunny Wales!' They both laughed, Willow's chuckle sounding a bit soggy at these words, as the rain they'd both been unaware of, made its presence known by rattling against the window in a torrent of ferocity.

'God knows. Maybe he'd tracked me down. He came to my flat once and raised all kinds of mayhem when I wouldn't let him in.' Willow shuddered in retrospect. 'I had to call the police to get him to go away.'

'Oh, he'd love that!'

'Yeah, right! I don't know, Morgan. I definitely haven't seen him since I came down here in May. He was very secretive about his work, telling me not to worry my little head,' she wrinkled her nose in self-disgust, 'and I bought it too. Because it suited me to have a big, strong, rescuer instead of standing on my own two feet.'

'Stop beating yourself up for being vulnerable, Willow. We all need a little support when we're bereaved, and just because Barry Scott took advantage of that isn't your fault.'

Morgan set the mug down with a snap and caused Willow to flinch slightly. As she recovered she became aware that she'd put herself in the same situation again. Relying on someone else, she silently berated herself, when was she going to learn to be independent? The man seated opposite looked quite as annoyed as Barry had.

'And don't flinch like that. I'm not bloody Barry Scott, I don't hit women!' Morgan smiled grimly. 'I might hit on them if they've got a figure like yours though!'

Willow felt she was in imminent danger of fainting for the second time in her life. She held up a hand as if to stop the flow of words.

Morgan was appalled at himself. He'd meant to lead up to things, now he'd probably wrecked the slim chances he might have had. Jane would say he'd bungled it properly, and she would be right. He watched as Willow's skin turned alabaster white, and then flushed red, as the temper he'd only dimly suspected glittered in her eyes.

Willow got to her feet, her body felt cold from the inside outwards, despite the warmth of the fire. 'I think you'd better take me home, Morgan, or shall I get a taxi?' She gave him one fleeting glance from under her eyelashes. 'I don't think we'd better refer to this conversation again. I might have been a rich man's trophy once. I won't be again.' She looked at him defiantly. 'And I won't have any man's pity either.' She busied herself pulling on her fireman's jacket over her overalls.

Morgan also rose. He was furious with both of them. 'I don't feel sorry for you. Oh, Hell!' He all but pulled his hair out by the roots as he thrust his hands through it. 'Look, the next few days are going to be difficult enough once the papers get hold of this new twist. Barry Scott's firm and mine were both after the same American contract. It wasn't public knowledge that we were close to signing the deal. Now it will be. I've the inspector to thank for that piece of information.'

'Then we'd better not give them any more fuel for their front pages, had we? You really don't want to be seen with his 'gold digger'.' She spat the comment bitterly as she headed determinedly towards the door. Morgan had no option but to follow her out into the teeming rain. He opened the passenger door and saw her seated inside the car, wishing there was something he could say to undo the last few minutes of conversation.

He looked across at the still face once he was seated, but decided that he'd said more than enough for one day and now needed a space to remove the foot firmly wedged in his mouth. He pulled away and the journey was taken to the accompaniment of windscreen wipers going at full tilt and the muted roar of a Jaguar being throttled back.

When they arrived at Willow's lodgings Morgan got out and went to open her door, only to find she'd already alighted. 'I'll pick you up tomorrow to take you to the inquest.' Willow shook her head, wincing at the resultant pain flashing across her eyes. 'Don't argue, Willow. We both have to be there, and there'll be even more speculation if you find your own way. Besides you're not fit to be running about on your own just at the moment.'

Willow looked stonily at him. 'Very well.' She had to concede that she felt far from well at the moment.

She turned away and as she went to enter Morgan spoke again. In Welsh. She had no idea what he said. But her landlady, an interested and unobserved spectator, had. She gave a quiet gasp, and looked from one face to the other. Morgan, hearing the intake of breath looked up and addressed her. Then he turned on his heel and got back into his car, and drove away, with a fine display of temper and spinning gravel.

Willow walked through the open door, then curiosity overcame her. 'What was that last comment?'

'He said I wasn't to say, he'd do his own translating when you were ready to hear it!'

'Oh!' Willow looked at the blushing woman before her. 'Well if it's all the same to you I'm going up to bed. I've had a bit of an accident and I've got a headache.'

Mrs Dilys Jones allowed compassion to overcome curiosity. 'Would you like some tea then, *Cariad*?'

'No, I'm fine. I just want to lie down for a bit.'

Willow continued up the stairs, reflecting that if she didn't have another cup of tea until next week she would be happy. As soon as she entered her room she undressed and crawled under the blankets without bothering to wash, closing her eyes determinedly.

Even the entrance of her landlady five minutes later carrying a hot-water bottle didn't cause her to open them. 'Here you are, *Cariad*. This will warm you up.' She bustled about pushing the bottle under the bottom of the covers and then re-tucking them. She went over and drew the curtains on the cold and wet afternoon outside then, with one last speculative look, took her curler decorated head away to think about her lodger.

Willow lay still, allowing the warmth to seep back into her bones and the tears to seep out from under her eyelids.

6

'ALL RISE FOR MR. Wynn!'

The fussy little man who had been rushing around with a pile of clipboards for the last half hour finally seemed to have settled like a hen on a clutch of eggs, his clipboard and papers held guardedly under his hand as he invited the public to stand for the entrance of the coroner.

Willow, tucked away in a pool of quiet, hoisted herself to her feet with reluctance. Despite a good twelve hours' sleep brought about by the triple action of tears, tiredness and Panadol she still felt very tired.

True to his word Morgan had been knocking on the door at what seemed to her like the crack of dawn. At least, she smiled tiredly to herself, it must have been dawn, that blasted cockerel down the road had been crowing, but then it seemed to crow whenever it felt like it. It wasn't exactly a good timekeeper.

She was aware that she was distracting herself with trivia to avoid thinking about the bulk of Morgan now rising up like the bulwark of a ship at the side of her. The business suit in charcoal in which he was dressed, brushed against her hand as he shifted to rise from the more comfortable position in his seat.

She'd dressed in her best black gabardine trousers and a white polo neck jumper. Her hair she'd scooped back with a barrette, since the whole side of her face felt sore. She had put some make-up on but cleaned it off when the mirror had told her what she already suspected. Her face was a bit of a mess; the bruising on her temple a dark patch highlighted by her pale cheeks.

Still, she reflected, who was she trying to impress anyway? Except maybe a judge. She stifled a sigh and waited patiently for the order to sit down again. She'd never been in a courtroom, much less an inquest. She tried to take an interest in her surroundings, but it didn't really match the idea in her mind.

Her father had loved *Perry Mason*, but this was just a plain room with a long table and a sort of high desk at the front, and wooden chairs in serried ranks to the back. Someone she had taken at first to be a typist sat to one side of the room, hands twiddling some small silver knobs on a fairly complicated machine, instead of the typewriter she'd expected. The speakers were angled towards the front of the courtroom, and she could see that he wore headphones.

The front row of chairs had tables in front of them, unprepossessing tables at that. There was a chair set on the opposite side to the man with the headphones, which she assumed was for those giving evidence. And really that was it. No glamour at all.

Everyone shuffled their feet and muttered and then grew silent as a rather plain man came in and went behind the long table and mounted to sit behind the desk. Assuming the seat of Judge. He sat down and took out a large blue spotted handkerchief, blowing his long thin nose with vigour before saying, 'Right, usher, let's get on with it. Hand the papers over.'

The fussy hen handed over his sheaf of A4 and the Coroner cast an eye over them while everyone waited in anticipation for his words of wisdom.

'This inquest is convened to discover the identity, place, time, and how this person came to die. All those who can assist the court in this matter are required to come forward.' Having completed his preamble the Mr Wynn nodded across the room.

'Right. Inspector Jenkins, come up to the front if you please.'

The inspector walked forward full of breakfast and bombast.

'Take a seat and let's hear what you've got to say.'

The usher handed over the Bible. The usual swearing in was rushed through and the inspector, conscious of having every eye fixed on him, swelled a bit more and started his preamble.

'On Friday October 27th the body of a young man was discovered in the Glaslyn Estuary by a young woman. It was in a somewhat macerated condition and the cause of death was determined to b....'

'Just a minute, inspector. Let's stay within our own confines here. The doctor will tell me about the condition of the body and the cause of death.' The man depressed pretension with a finely judged hand. The inspector deflated rather like a pricked balloon, his head sinking, and his shoulders seeming to sag slightly.

Caught with his mouth open, he took a second to remember what he needed to say next. 'In a somewhat macerated condition.' He paused then took up the tale again, seeming to inflate as he took a breath filled with self-importance. 'The local police passed the case on to us as how he came to die was undetermined, and his identity at that time was unknown.'

He scowled across at someone who Willow assumed was the doctor. The man smiled nicely back and Willow warmed to him. 'Upon your instructions we instituted investigations and, following upon this, forensics managed to identify some letters written by the deceased.'

Someone behind Willow whispered to his neighbour, 'Must have been spirit writing.' Willow wasn't the only one to suppress a nervous giggle. She couldn't like the inspector; it was good to hear his pomposity pricked.

'These letters led us to visiting a certain house in London.'

The unknown voice behind suggested, 'One of ill repute if I'm any judge.'

Willow smiled again, but the coroner was speaking. 'What, you personally, Inspector?'

'Er, no, a London detective.'

'Then we'll hear his statement in a minute if it becomes necessary!'

The inspector was feeling put upon. 'I,' he stressed the word and looked aggressively at the coroner, 'after receiving information from our London office, decided to re-interview the young woman who found the body. Her name and photograph had been found in the flat of the deceased. There were also several magazine articles in which the press talked about their relationship.'

Those around Willow muttered inaudibly, and a few from the Ffestiniog gave a muted gasp, and shuffled to get a better look at her. Morgan sat up more fully, thus shielding her a little from their curious eyes. Willow could feel herself growing warm, and resisted the temptation to duck down in the seat. She felt like Alice in Wonderland, her head and hands seemed to be growing larger by the second.

The inspector waited for the buzz to die down a bit. 'I wished to ascertain if she had recognised the deceased when she had found him. Or indeed had had contact with him immediately prior to his demise.'

Willow felt Morgan stiffen next to her and heard him mutter something under his breath. She glanced at his face and saw the mouth fold into a relentless line. She shuddered slightly. She wouldn't want Morgan looking at her like that.

'Very well, Inspector.' The coroner stemmed the flow with an upraised hand. 'We'll hear next from the police who were called to the scene first, before you continue.'

Sergeant Gareth ap Rhys stepped forward and raised his hand for the oath. The coroner waited patiently, then said, 'If you'd just tell us how you were first informed of the body and what your subsequent actions were, Sergeant.'

The coroner nodded at the larger than life figure and the sergeant faced the front of the room, flipping open his day book in his hand. Then he settled his bulk into the chair, looking like everyone's favourite uncle about to read a bedtime story.

'Dispatch called through on the aforementioned night to tell us of a report of a body found down Quarry Lane, Minffordd. They reported that a 'distressed' female had rung in the report. We...'

'Just a minute, Sergeant. Who is 'we'?'

'I was just getting to that,' Sergeant ap Rhys gave the man a look of reproach. 'We, PC Gwyn Davies and I, responded. We found Miss Willow Edwards waiting for us at the side of the road. She indicated the corpse with her torch.'

The sergeant looked across at Willow and gave her a smile of reassurance. 'I arranged for the crime scene to be secured and all the necessary equipment to be sent to the scene, and took the young lady back to the police station to take her statement. I also informed the Coroner's Office at this time, of a death in suspicious circumstances. PC Davies was left to guard the scene and await the team from Caernarfon.' He looked across at Mr. Wynn who was making use of the handkerchief again.

'Do you wish me to read out the statement obtained at that time, sir?'

'No, I have it here. Just give us the bare bones, man.' The coroner stowed his handkerchief away again in a blue pinstriped pocket.

'The witness was returning home on foot, after volunteering on the FR for the day. She stepped out of the way of traffic and subsequently stood on the corpse in the dark. She was naturally in a much shaken condition at the time of the interview. But I have no reason to doubt the veracity of her statement given then.' He looked across at the inspector with a frown on his face. 'She stated that she hadn't recognised the deceased at that time.

'We, in conjunction with Caernarfon, are still following up various leads arising from the statement. We have located the car which passed her, and have statements from the young men driving it. They state they saw her walking in the direction of Minffordd, on Quarry Road, and that she stepped out of their car's way as she had stated.' Gareth smiled grimly. The interview with those young men wasn't one they were going to forget in a hurry.

The sergeant looked across, awaiting further questions. The coroner was flipping over some papers in front of him. He looked up as the silence penetrated. 'Just so, Sergeant. That will be all for now. Would you like to give us your report, Doctor Gwynn?'

The doctor was small and chubby. He bounced across the room like a small cricket ball, clad in rough tweed, and smiled amiably on the crowd of interested onlookers, a pronounced twinkle in his eyes. 'Dr Gwynn,' the coroner nodded for him to begin after the usual formalities.

Dr Gwynn had a surprisingly deep and authoritive voice. 'I conducted the autopsy on the corpse over the weekend. I found it in a badly decomposed state, having been in the water for possibly as long as a week; maybe more. It isn't possible to be too exact about time of death even allowing for stomach contents. I would estimate that death took place seven to ten days before and that it was sometime in the morning when the young man died. His stomach contained the partially digested remains of a standard English breakfast.'

He grinned in a slightly macabre way at the press reporters over on the far side of the room. 'I only have the preliminary entomological information, and I'm not an expert witness in that field. However, I understand that certain larvae found in and on the corpse give an approximate timeline. However, due to immersion it can only be approximate, and the fish had had a nibble too.'

The twinkle had gone now. 'I would challenge Inspector Jenkins to recognise his own mother after that kind of treatment, so I would not have expected the young lady to have recognised the deceased.' He sniffed and looked across at the inspector of police.

'The death was caused by dry-drowning, probably in the estuary, though the small amount of water found in the lung tissue was not of a brackish nature; so not the part of the estuary where I understand the corpse was discovered. The young man was in a reasonably good state of health though the liver showed some signs of alcohol abuse, and there were signs of occasional cocaine inhalation via the nose, though none was present in the system at time of death, as far as I could establish.' He nodded his head as if to reaffirm this to himself as he looked across at Mr. Wynn.

'There was a large contusion on his jaw consistent with someone punching him and several marks around the neck region which might indicate an attempt to throttle. But, as I say, while both might have contributed their mite, neither of these caused death, the Glaslyn did that.' He smiled again, a sunburst in the solemn and dingy room.

'At this stage I would be loathe to state how he came to be in the Glaslyn. I cannot rule out the possibility that someone assisted this unfortunate young man to his death.'

'Thank you, Doctor, that was very clear. Could you perhaps elaborate on the phrase 'dry drowning' for the benefit of those present?'

The Doctor looked across at the assembled population. 'I'm sure everyone has experienced a drink going down the wrong way and subsequently coughing and wheezing afterwards. This is due to laryngospasm, a protective mechanism of the body to prevent fluid filling the lungs. When fluid continues to enter the area the spasm closes off the lungs, preventing both fluid and air reaching them. The subject thereafter dies because neither the fluid, nor air has been able to enter the lungs due to the spasm.'

'Thank you, Doctor. That will be all for now.'

Mr Wynn paused and coughed discreetly into his hand. 'Might I hear from the young lady now?' He peered at the notes under his hand. 'Miss Edwards.'

Willow, getting to her feet, shuffled to the end of the row and walked to the seat next to the table. She held her head up and fixed her gaze on the coroner.

'Now, Miss Edwards, state your full name, address and occupation for the records.'

Willow went through the details until she came to occupation. 'Do you want what I'm doing now or trained as?' She looked across at him.

'Oh, I think both for clarity.' The coroner wiped his nose again.

Willow finished, then tried to relax on the seat while she waited for the questions.

'We have established that you found the body of Barry Scott last Friday night. In your subsequent statement to Inspector Jenkins you have stated that you were unaware of his presence in this area of Wales. Is this correct?'

'Yes, sir.' Her voice came out in a husky whisper and Willow wondered as she looked across at him if she should be saying 'My lord' but he didn't correct her.

'Further, the inspector has established that you had a long term and quite public relationship with Mr Scott but had broken off your engagement when he became abusive?'

Willow nodded.

'You must answer verbally, Miss Edwards'

Willow blushed, but managed to answer, 'Yes.' She was very aware of eyes looking at her and tried to keep her gaze fixed on the long pale face and the voice of the coroner asking the questions in his quiet manner.

'Can you shed any light on why Mr Scott should have been in this corner of Wales if he was not in fact attempting to make contact with you?'

Willow started to shake her head and then managed a clear 'No, I hadn't seen him since he came to my lodgings in London last May. He was very aggressive and verbally abusive then, and I called the police.'

'So you would agree that you had no cause to like the deceased.'

'No.' Willow looked horrified as she suddenly realised the tenor of the questions. 'But I didn't kill him!' There was a buzz round the room which Willow thought was in her head for a moment, and the press section muttered as it awaited further revelations.

Mr Wynn also looked at their antics but refrained from comment until the noise level quieted. 'If the young gentleman who has just used his phone to take a photo wishes to retain it and escape a charge of contempt of court he will put it away immediately. You will not take any photos while I am presiding! It is illegal.' It was said very quietly but with obvious determination.

The youth caught with the phone in his hand went very red. Mr Wynn motioned to him to come down to the front.

He shuffled to the end of the row, his hair reflecting his obviously horrified state as it stood up all over his head in the latest fashion. He came to the front and stood, not daring to look at anyone, his eyes resting on the scuffed trainers on his feet.

'In view of your youth I am issuing you with a severe warning. It is a serious offence to take photos in court. The law might not have caught up with modern technology, but it has caught up with you, sir. If any photographs of these proceedings become available to the press I shall know exactly where to direct the police. Now you may return to your seat or leave the court, and be grateful I don't fine you severely.'

The youth turned and fled as if chased by the devil himself, a swinging door and a puff of dusty cold air marking his rapid exit from the room. The interlude had given Willow time to regain a small portion of her composure but she was still shaking on the wooden seat, a fine trembling passing over her arms and legs.

'No one has accused you of murder, Miss Edwards. This is a Coroner's Court, not a trial.' The coroner offered the comment in a calm voice, and then cast a look of caution at the inspector who had opened his mouth as if to speak.

'That will be all for now.' Willow stood up and, avoiding eye contact with the interested Press, locked eyes with Morgan and walked shakily back across the room.

'Would you like to come forward again, Inspector Jenkins?' He waited patiently for Willow to resume her seat and the inspector to step forward.

'Now, Inspector, have you anything further to add that might assist us in determining how this man came to die?'

'No, I would like an adjournment while we pursue further enquiries both here and in London regarding this man's business dealings and other activities. It has also come to our attention that a business rival of his is present in Wales. We need to establish if there is any connection between both men's presence and Mr Scott's subsequent death.'

'Hmm!' The Coroner raised an eyebrow. 'You really should have declared this knowledge before court commenced. However,' he looked down, pondering, 'is this other man present?'

'Oh yes,' Inspector Jenkins looked smug and nodded his head in Morgan's direction.

'Would you step forward and take the stand Mr...' he looked hopefully at the usher who said, 'Williams,' quietly.

'Mr Williams, come forward and state your full name and residence for the record, please.'

Morgan rose and made his way to the front, a grim look on his face and a hard look in the blue eyes directed at the inspector as the policeman went back to his seat.

'Now, Mr Williams. Inspector Jenkins has stated that you were a business rival of Mr Scott's. First could you tell us what brings you to this area yourself?'

'I'm here in a voluntary capacity working for the FR as a driver.' Morgan gave the brief answer and waited for the next question.

'And have you any business connections in the area?'

'I have several interests in engineering firms around the Gwynedd area. Most are of long standing.'

'Perhaps you could supply that information to the court.'

'Inspector Jenkins already has those details. My holdings are, however, always available for public inspection at Company House.' Morgan's face remained calm. 'Do you wish me to state them again for this inquest?' He laid slight emphasis on the word inquest.

'Er, no. That won't be necessary. Could you, however, state if any of those holdings would have placed you in the position of rival to Mr Scott as the inspector has stated?'

Morgan's firm mouth thinned a little. 'I was proceeding with negotiations with an American firm. The details are confidential. Inspector Jenkins was kind enough to let me know the details of plans that Barry Scott's firm had also submitted to them.' Morgan's voice dripped sarcasm.

'Were you aware of that submission before the inspector told you about it?'

'I wasn't and it placed me in a difficult position as I don't approve or practise insider trading or employ others to spy for me. However, my negotiations have been placed on hold for the time being until this situation is sorted out.'

Mr. Wynn looked across at Morgan while pulling out his handkerchief. 'Very wise.' He looked across at Inspector Jenkins with a frown on his face, which he concealed behind its folds, and then transferred his gaze back to Morgan as he put it away. 'Were you aware of the previous relationship between Miss Edwards and Mr Scott?'

'I became aware of that relationship on Monday when I chanced to work on the same engine as Miss Edwards.'

'Yet the inspector has stated that their relationship was of a public nature?' It was gently said, but the question was unmistakable.

'Nevertheless, I was not aware of it. I don't read magazines. They mostly make up what they don't know and can be a broth of speculation and scandal. I should know; I've been the butt of those speculations myself.' Morgan looked across at the Press and remained impassive as several enterprising young men left; no doubt to check on the speculation and scandal in their own papers. A buzz of comment circled the room.

Mr Wynn eyed them, but as no-one else seemed inclined to leave the room he turned back to Morgan.

'Now Mr Williams, can you shed any light on the reason why Mr Scott might be in North Wales at the present time?'

'No.' Morgan didn't elaborate. He remained impassive as he waited for the next question.

The coroner looked tired all of a sudden. 'Very well, Mr Williams. You may return to you seat.'

Mr. Wynn paused and then addressed those present with all the dignity of his office around him like a cloak, 'At present the finding of this inquest is that Mr Barry Scott met his death by drowning. The cause of death is determined. How he came to be in the Glaslyn, and why, have yet to be determined, so I will state that the case remains open until further information is made available. This case is adjourned for fourteen days.' He banged his gavel neatly and gathered up the papers in front of him.

Inspector Jenkins stood up hastily and his mouth opened to speak, but Mr. Wynn, standing, ignored him and left the room. Inspector Jenkins followed the authoritative figure with a look that would have curdled the milk of human kindness and made yogurt of it. There was a general scraping of chairs and relaxing of the atmosphere at the coroner's exodus. The shuffling of feet and clearing of throats vied with the zipping of coats to signal the end of the session.

Willow, aware that once again she was being scrutinised, this time by the press, felt the colour flood her cheeks and wondered how she was going to escape without more questions. She stood up and Morgan took her hand firmly in his. She wriggled it and tried to pull it away without success. Rather than cause more embarrassment she suppressed the desire to struggle in an undignified manner and left it there.

As the volume of noise rose Morgan smiled grimly to himself and towed her gently along the line of chairs. He stepped into the aisle first and stood, a dam against the flow of people, till she had extricated herself from the last chair, then pushed her gently in front of him towards the doors.

He ignored shouted comments from various members of the Press addressed both to himself and Willow, who was, by now, as pale as she had been red. 'Keep going.' the words were uttered in a soft voice near her left ear. 'Head for the exit but don't go out through the doors.' The hand which had been holding hers was now around her waist, guiding her away from the press of bodies making a beeline for the open air.

With a slick move, she could only afterwards appreciate, he suddenly steered her towards a far door, through it and down a flight of stone steps to the outside. Peace enveloped her like a blanket. The hand around her waist remained firm as Morgan part led; part towed her, towards his car. It wasn't until he was opening the door that she had a chance to protest. She pulled away and stood firm on the pavement.

'Where are you taking me, Morgan?'

'I think it might pay us to go to earth for a few hours. I'll deal with the reporters when I have to, but you, darling, are a little too fragile at the moment for that sort of scrum. Get in the car.' The hand at her back brooked no argument as it urged her forward. Willow was still wondering how to take the darling when she found herself seated and driving away from the courtrooms.

'Yes, but I had plans for this morning.'

'OK, tell me and we'll see if it's safe to fulfil them.' For some reason his reasonableness irritated her.

'I said I had plans, not we. Look, Morgan, I seem to have got you into enough trouble already without you being in my company more than necessary.' She paused for breath. 'What's more I don't care to be told what's safe for me to do. I had enough of that with Barry.'

'But I like being in your company, Willow.' Morgan offered the comment, and a quick glance, as he steered the car round a roundabout. He ignored her comments about Barry; he'd learnt his lesson there. Yesterday he'd nearly lost the little leeway he'd been making with her. He wasn't about to lose anymore when chance had allowed him to be in her company again. 'Now, where would you like to go before I drive us into the Menai Straits?'

Willow glanced out of the car window to see they were heading towards Bangor at a fair speed. She sighed. 'I wanted to go to *Ysbyty Gwynedd*.'

Alarm crossed Morgan's face at a fast trot. 'Aren't you well, *Cariad*? Why didn't you say?' He put his foot down and the car shot forward to the astonishment of a Mini which had been eating their exhaust fumes since they had left the last bypass.

'I'm fine. Slow down for God's sake! I wanted to check up on Sian's stranger.'

Morgan eased back his foot and risked another quick glance at his passenger. 'How had you planned to get there?'

'There are buses, Morgan!' The tone was exasperated.

'Well, now you can travel in comfort, that's an even better place than I'd planned for us.'

Morgan turned off, nodding to a small shop at the side of the road. 'They do a lovely portion of fish and chips there. Do you want to eat before we go and visit this young man of yours?'

'Morgan.' She sighed gustily.

Morgan grinned. 'I do like the way you say my name, *Cariad*.' He kept driving, however, and took the small roundabout into the hospital. 'Ah,' he muttered and turned the car sharply into a parking slot. Willow was left thinking that he was the kind who would find parking just where he needed it, unlike lesser mortals.

Morgan slid his bulk out of the car, coming round to open her door as she struggled with the catch. 'You're going to get cold with just that jacket on,' he swung his heavy cashmere across her shoulders, and snuck an arm round her waist, holding the coat firmly in place.

Willow, enveloped in warm black wool and the scent of Morgan's aftershave, said nothing. In truth he'd taken her breath away with his tactics and his very personal, very male, aroma. She found both very comforting though she wasn't about to admit that to anyone, including herself.

They walked towards reception, Morgan sniffing the air as they went. 'It's going to snow, I can smell it.'

Willow looked up at the clean shaven face surrounded by the mousy brown hair which he'd released from the confines of a piece of leather as soon as they left the courtroom. It was curling riotously against his collar in the damp air and she experienced the unbidden desire to feel it and see if the curls were really as soft as they looked.

Morgan swept her into reception and headed for the window behind which a young lady was perched on a high stool, totally absorbed in her nails. Willow cleared her throat and addressed the girl, while Morgan stood slightly back. She'd found herself momentarily distracted as the arm he'd been holding her by was withdrawn.

'Er, a young man was admitted to Intensive Care on Saturday. With a broken femur. I –er - I wonder if we might go and visit him for a minute.'

The young lady was evidently bored; she glanced up from the nail she was assiduously filing. She had a nasal twang to her Manchurian accent. 'I'm only filling in here.' She looked critically at the nail, and then as Willow continued to stand waiting said, 'Follow the yellow line to the lift and then follow the blue line on the third floor.' She went back to the nail.

Willow muttered, 'Follow the yellow brick road,' to the down bent head and turned to meet the glimmer of laughter in the blue eyes looking into hers.

He took her hand and led her along the corridor towards the lifts. They stood waiting for the whoosh and ping which would signal its arrival. Willow stood absorbing the sounds and smells of the hospital, the low hum of machinery, the curious mixture of bleach and antiseptic mixed with humanity in various stages of pain and duress. She knew she ought to remove the hand holding hers so gently but found she had neither the willpower nor desire.

The lift, when it arrived, ejected one tired doctor with stethoscope worn in the traditional position around the neck, and two ambulance drivers talking rugby. Morgan and Willow waited for the trio to exit and then boarded. Morgan ran a finger down the board and keyed in the floor. Willow, her hands free at last, took the coat from her shoulders and silently handed it back. Morgan doubled it and slung it over his arm then re-possessed himself of her right hand.

'You really must stop holding on to me. I'm not going to run away.'

'But you might, and besides, I like holding on to you.'

Willow rolled her eyes but said nothing. What could she say after all? She'd given him fair warning, and secretly she rather liked holding his hand too.

When they exited and followed the blue line, it brought them to double doors with porthole windows. Willow peered through, 'Do you think we ought to go in?'

She'd hardly said the words when a friendly face appeared at the other side of the door. 'Hello, can I help you? Have you come to see someone?'

Willow looked at the slim young woman dressed in green scrubs standing in front of her. 'I found a young man on Saturday and arranged an ambulance for him. He had a broken femur. The nurse I spoke to on Sunday said he was up here and rather poorly. He hadn't been identified then, but I suppose he has now. We just wondered how he was getting on.'

'Ah!' The nurse looked at the pair sympathetically. 'Would you like to come into this room here?' She indicated a small room furnished with a low settee, and coffee table littered with Styrofoam cups and ancient copies of women's magazines.

She opened the door and stood back for them to enter, closing the door and seating herself on a plastic chair, enclosing them all in silence as she waited for them to sit down. When they had, she looked across at Willow. 'I'm afraid he died, my dear. In the early hours of Tuesday morning. He only regained consciousness briefly. Unfortunately no-one could understand him. The police are looking into his background. It happens sometimes.' She spread her hands and looked sympathetically at them both.

Willow looked stunned. 'I knew he could die, but I suppose I thought since he was in hospital he'd have a fighting chance.'

'Well, he might have had if he hadn't been quite so malnourished. Nothing to fight with I'm afraid.'

Willow swallowed the lump in her throat. 'What will happen now?'

'I'm not sure. The police have discovered his name was Ivan Proponov and that he was probably Polish, but they don't seem to know how or why he came to be in Wales. There must be someone out there who is desperately worried about him, but so far no-one has come forward in response to the police appeals on the TV and radio.'

Willow looked up at Morgan sitting silently beside her. 'I don't quite know what to do now?' It was a plea for help. 'I've got to tell Deniol and Sian.' She turned back to the nurse. 'Two teenagers who helped me get him to help.'

'You tell them the truth, my dear. The young man fought hard, but was too sick to overcome his illness.'

'I knew I should have come in to visit on Sunday.'

'It wouldn't have done any good if you had come in; he was still unresponsive then, and very ill.'

'Yes, but to die so far away from anyone he knew, all alone.' Willow felt her eyes begin to fill and bit her lip in a determined effort not to cry, looking down fixedly at the strap of her bag which she was mangling between her hands in an effort to maintain control.

'Would you like a drink and to sit here for a bit?' The nurse looked at the couple sitting before her.

'No. I'd like to go now please, Morgan.' Willow looked at the silent man beside her, then across at the nurse, as she stood up. 'Thank you,' she said the words thickly round the lump in her throat.

'Right, *Cariad*.' Morgan in turn stood and, fishing in a pocket of the suit, pulled out a card which he handed to the nurse. 'Could you have this card tacked to his notes? I'll see to the burial if no-one else comes forward.'

The nurse also got to her feet. 'I'm sorry I can't be more helpful, my dear.' She patted Willow on the shoulder and stood back as they went out and down the corridor then, with a sigh, she went back into the ward to begin again the never ending tasks of looking after the sick under her care.

GARETH AP RHYS WAS working with the men under his care too. His two trainees had been told to hand in their reports and observations regarding the skeleton found on the foreshore. They stood sweating slightly as he read through the paperwork.

'David. You say that the area was cordoned but fail to give any indication of where the cordon begins and ends. You don't mention how many men are working inside the Cob and how many inside the cordon. You have, however, mentioned the numbers involved, which is good, and you observe that the stone and gravel is being removed to a separate area for further analysis. Good.

'Pete. You write that the corpse has been there for several years.' Gareth looked up at the young peach fuzzed faces and settled on Pete's. 'That might be observation, but it's also conjecture, lad. We deal in facts.' He continued to skim down the page to the next section he had underlined. 'You can't write that a gun was the murder weapon. You haven't seen the autopsy report. No matter what you hear other's saying, you have to have facts. Not gossip in the staffroom.' He smiled at both youngsters. 'Overall a good attempt, however. Off you go.'

Gareth waited for the two youngsters to leave the room and set the reports down on his desk. He quite liked the role of teaching. He rose and went to fetch a mug of tea while he thought about that morning's court proceedings.

He felt that Miss Willow Edwards had stood up to the questioning well. Thinking about the initial interview in the light of these new revelations he thought he could guess why she'd been so hesitant about disclosing her relationship with the deceased. He sat down again and poked the papers so recently critiqued. He'd heard the gossip among the coppers down on the foreshore and, regardless of what he'd just told the two men just departed, sometimes you had to take it into account.

There was definitely something going on between Willow Edwards and Morgan Williams. Even if they didn't know it yet! He sighed, turning to the witness reports he was accumulating regarding the injured Pole Willow had sent to hospital. There was a report of him in Penrhyndeudraeth Spar; a week last Saturday he'd bought a loaf and a bottle of milk. They said he'd thanked them in a heavy accent and paid in cash. The quarrymen up the coast had seen him, but only from a distance. They'd taken him to be a walker and had shaken their heads at the stupidity of walking in the Snowdon range in late October.

He'd also been seen in Porthmadog. Along the High Street, the following Tuesday. The greengrocer, Dai Roberts, who had goods on the pavement, said the man stole an apple but he'd looked so threadbare that Dai hadn't done anything about it. In fact he'd said if the man had asked he'd have given him more. According to the report Dai reckoned that the young man was starving.

The next report was from Deniol and Sian. Gareth shook his head at the final piece of paper found on his desk this afternoon.

So far so good. But they needed to find out how he'd arrived in Wales in the first place. Gareth scribbled a few notes to himself on a block of paper. It looked like the young man had worked his way down from Penrhyn to Porthmadog. The train station there was small and any strangers getting off would have been noticed. He must get them to check at Minffordd too.

Buses. He scowled at the paper. They'd checked the buses when they first had reports about the man. He hadn't arrived that way, or seemingly travelled on one. There was no report of him hitchhiking either. The latest report said he came via train. They needed to start at the other end of the train line then. Pwlleli.

Their Pole was dead. But at least he had a name and a contact for the wife. God help her. He picked up the phone. She would need to be brought over from France for formal identification. He rang the number for his friend Clancy again and waited for the other policeman to pick up the phone.

WILLOW WALKED SILENTLY ALONG the corridor, her head down. She badly wanted to cry and if she'd been on her own would have disappeared into the chapel to have it out in peace, but with the quiet man beside her, she tried to swallow the emotion. Morgan waited until they had entered the lift and they were enclosed in the sterile box, and then pulled her close. 'It's alright, darling. Cry if you want to.'

Willow gulped and pulled away, only to be brought firmly back into his arms. 'It's so silly. I didn't know him at all,' she sniffled. 'I just feel so sad for him, and I think he might have a pregnant girlfriend or wife too. What about her?' She stood in the comforting embrace for the short journey to the ground floor, fighting back tears and gradually becoming aware of other sensations which she sternly repressed.

Morgan led her out and towards his car, an arm securely round her. 'I'm sorry, Morgan, I seem to be forever weeping on you and causing trouble.' She hiccupped and gave a watery sniff. This is neither the time nor the place, she told herself, for the growing attraction her body was feeling towards Morgan.

Morgan fished out one of his beautifully laundered hankies and offered it.

209

'And I'm supposed to be keeping out of your way.' The last was muttered under her breath but not quite quietly enough for Morgan.

'But I don't want you to keep out of my way, darling. Better to face the trouble together, don't you think?'

He opened her door and stuffed her gently into the seat, closing it on her, then walked round and threw his coat in the back before sitting in the driver's seat and starting the engine. He didn't drive away, however, but swung round towards Willow. 'What had you planned to do after your visit? Do you want to go and see Deniol now? By the time we get back to Ports he'll be coming out of school.'

Willow gave a final hiccup and wiped her eyes. 'I don't know, Morgan; I don't know what I had planned. I hadn't really thought beyond the visit.'

Morgan flicked back his shirt sleeve and looked at the slim Swiss timepiece. 'It's nearly one. I know a little pub over on the isle where you can tidy yourself up and we can get something to eat.' He held up a hand. 'I know you don't feel hungry but you need to eat, you'll feel better for it.' He smiled wryly. 'And so will I.'

He bent to fasten his seat belt and took her agreement for granted as she fastened hers.

THEY'D HEADED TOWARDS *Ynys Mon* and the Menai Bridge, the silence companiable in the warm car. Looking back later, Willow was surprised at how much she'd enjoyed the meal, despite the sadness she felt for the death of the young man. They hadn't spoken much. Morgan had found a quiet corner of the restaurant, partly shielded from most of the other tables by potted palms, and pulled out a chair facing the window and the Menai Straits.

With her back to the other customers Willow had managed to pull herself together while Morgan was at the bar. The meal had been typical pub fare, scampi and chips in a basket. Unasked he'd set a glass of cider in front of her, while he drank a bitter lemon. He'd kept the conversation on the mundane while they ate, but over coffee he'd asked again what she wanted to do. Which was why they were heading back towards Porthmadog hoping to be able to talk to Deniol and Sian, and Morgan was coming with her.

She felt slightly guilty at the way she was leaning on him for emotional support. But this didn't feel the same as it had with Barry. Where Barry had dictated Morgan involved her in the decision. She smiled to herself, even when he'd already decided the outcome!

Willow started to give instructions as they approached Porthmadog. 'You turn left after the main railway line, Morgan.'

He glanced across. 'It's OK, I know the way.' Willow opened her mouth, and then quietly closed it again, resisting the temptation to ask how. She merely raised an eyebrow as he swung the car left down the narrow roadway, like a greyhound streaking round the last bend in the track.

They pulled up in front of Deniol's front door just as the young teenagers appeared at the other end of the street.

'Hi, Morgan.' The pair greeted him like two puppies spotting their master. Sian, holding his arm in a two handed hug and looking up, had a big grin on her face. Her blonde locks floated out and settled against the black cashmere. 'Are you coming to visit?'

'Well, just for a few minutes, *Cariad*.' Morgan looked across at Deniol, evidently some sort of message passed between the older man and the youth.

'Where are your manners, Sian?' Deniol nodded at Willow standing a silent observer. Sian looked at Willow and offered a smile of apology. 'I'm sorry, Willow; it's just that Morgan hasn't been to visit us this time. I know we saw him the other night, but that was different. We were all busy.'

Willow looked at the glowing face and wondered how she was going to bear to diminish such happiness with her news. 'That's OK.' She looked slightly desperately at Morgan. He was smiling down at Sian.

'Well, can we come in then?'

Deniol tugged his girlfriend's hand. 'Com'on, Sian. Let's go put the kettle on.' He pulled his house key out of his uniform pocket and opened the street door, leading the way into a front room along the same pattern as Sian's house. Pushing Sian gently in front of him they went off into the kitchen.

Willow looked at Morgan. He was busily divesting himself of his coat and hanging it up in the tiny inglenook where she could see some coat hooks. He came over to her. 'Give me your jacket, darling.' She handed it over meekly, reflecting that the man was quite obviously at home in this little house.

'You've been here before.' It came out as almost an accusation. Morgan just grinned at her.

'Oh, yes.'

Deniol emerged from the back room with a tray of mugs and a tin with shortbread biscuits painted on it. He set the tray down on the glass coffee table in front of the leather settee and smiled shyly across at Willow. 'I was going to come up to the Works tonight to talk to you, Willow. I've been talking to my *Taid* about your letters.' He took a biscuit from the tin.

Willow looked confused. Morgan looked across. ''*Taid*' is 'Grandad' Willow.'

Before she could pass comment, however, Sian came in bearing an empty plate and a sugar basin. 'Deniol, you don't put the tin on the table!'

Deniol just grinned at her and helped himself to shortbread. 'It's a waste of time, Sian. I eat them too fast to need a plate, and Morgan doesn't care.'

Sian looked at him reproachfully. 'He does care, he's a gentleman.'

Morgan exchanged a look with Willow at this exchange, and then doused the sparkle as he turned to Sian. 'Quite right, Sian. The niceties always count.'

He took the offered mug of tea and waited for Willow to receive hers. 'We've got some rather sad news, kids.' He looked across at the smiling faces opposite. 'The young man you rescued has died.' He waited for them to absorb the news. Sian's eyes filled up and she looked almost accusingly at Willow. 'But you said if we got him to hospital he'd be alright.'

Willow swallowed. 'No, dear, I said he had to go or he might die. I hoped we'd got him there in time, but he was too sick to survive the broken leg and the embolus. The clot.'

Deniol swung an arm round his girlfriend's shoulders. 'Well, we did our best.'

He looked across at Willow. His young face suddenly looked considerably more than the fifteen years she knew he was. 'Did the police find out who he was?'

Morgan answered, 'They found out his name. He was called Ivan Proponov and he was probably Polish, but that's all they know at the moment. You two should feel proud of yourselves, without your help he might have died alone and in pain.'

Sian was crying quietly now, big fat tears rolling down her cheeks. 'We didn't know him, and I know it's silly, but I do feel sad for him.' It was said indistinctly from around the tissue Deniol had found for her.

'It's alright, darling; you're allowed to feel sad.' He looked across. 'Thank you for telling us, Morgan, and you too, Willow.'

Morgan sat back against the old leather squabs and drank his tea. As Sian stopped sniffing, Willow gradually relaxed and allowed herself to sit back also. This brought her into rather closer proximity to Morgan's body than she had anticipated and she wriggled away slightly, only to find herself sliding back towards him on the shiny leather.

Despite the gravity of the situation, Morgan smiled. He eased himself sideways so that she was resting against his side. Oh! Yes! There was that tingle again. It seemed more and more sure that his sister was right. He'd got 'trouble' too.

The four of them sat quietly, each absorbed in their own thoughts for several minutes until their reverie was interrupted by a whirlwind in the shape of a small child. She shot into the room, all legs and arms and flying ponytails, to hurl herself into Morgan's lap with a giggle, snuggling her little round person against his chest and pelting him with questions while she patted his face.

The resultant conversation between them was totally incomprehensible to Willow. The child was followed into the house by a woman who could have only been Deniol's mother. 'Gwyneth!' It was said in a slightly despairing tone.

The gap-toothed smile turned towards her mother was angelic. Another torrent of Welsh assailed Willow's ears. Morgan stood up, the little girl clinging to him like a limpet attached to his chest, so that he was forced to hold her up with his free arm while he leaned over to place a kiss on the cheek she offered to him. 'Eirlys, good to see you again.' He spoke English, which apparently got the attention of Gwyneth. She looked from him to her mother in puzzlement.

Morgan looked down at the small enchanting face so near his own. 'We have company Gwyneth. I'd like you to meet Willow. She works with me on the trains.'

Gwyneth gave a wriggle and slid down to stand before Willow. '*Sut da chi*, Willow.' Her English was as good as Deniol's though there was a lisp due to the missing tooth. 'It's nice to meet you. Are you Uncle Morgan's young lady?'

This drew gasps from Eirlys, Deniol and Sian, a muffled 'No!' from Willow, and a 'Hopefully', from Morgan.

Deniol grinned and Eirlys said, 'Gwyneth!' in appalled accents, but it was clear that she was everyone's pet for that was all that was said.

Eirlys turned towards Morgan, 'Sorry, Morgan.' She cast an indulgent look at her child. 'Will you stay for your tea the both of you?'

Morgan shook his head. 'Not today, I'm afraid; we have to be going soon. We just called in to give Deniol some news.' He watched the passing of looks between mother and son as Eirlys sat down in an easy chair. 'He'll fill you in when there aren't any pitchers about.'

'There are lots of pictures on the walls, Uncle Morgan.' Gwyneth looked puzzled as she looked around the room, then she dismissed the subject and moved on to more important matters. 'Will you come to our bonfire, Uncle Morgan? Deniol says I can hold sparkles this year and *Tad*'s fixing a Catherine wheel, and Sian's *Tad* is going to help build a bonfire at the beach.' Gwyneth tugged at a hand for attention.

Morgan turned his attention back to the little interruption who was once again settled on his knee now that he'd reseated himself. 'I won't promise, *Cariad*. I'm not sure what I'll be doing at the weekend. I might have to go back to London early, I have to see someone.'

Willow, an interested listener, sighed and felt her stomach sink a bit. She was inexplicably upset again as she heard him talking. She told herself she was still sad about Ivan's death, and suddenly tired and headachy. It had been a long day.

He hugged the little one in compensation as he looked across at Deniol. 'You take care of this one when she's playing with sparklers.'

The talk turned to general comment about the upcoming Guy Fawkes Night, before Morgan stood up again, setting the little girl on her feet. 'We must be going.' He fished in his pocket and drew out some pound coins. 'Here you go, *Cariad*, for the fireworks, but mind now, I want a promise that you'll do what *Tad* and Deniol say.'

Gwyneth looked up at the serious face. 'I promise, Uncle Morgan.' She added something in Welsh and Morgan bent down and gave her another hug and a kiss on the button nose before going to get his and Willow's coats.

He offered a hug to Sian too. 'I'm sorry he died, Sian, but you were a good friend to the young man. OK?'

Sian offered a sad smile. 'At least in hospital he'd be taken care of.'

Morgan gave another small squeeze. 'Yeah.' and, dropping a kiss on Eirlys' cheek, he swept Willow out into the street and into the car.

Willow sat silently beside Morgan. She wanted to ask so many questions. 'How did he know the families so well? Why had he got to go back to London? When would he be coming back? Would he be coming back? Would she see him again?' But she didn't think she'd got the right to ask any of those. After all, she'd told him he shouldn't have too much to do with her.

She finally settled for politeness. 'Thank you for driving me today, Morgan.' She glanced across and then fixed her eyes back on the estuary passing on her left side. The dusk was making the edges of everything blurred, at least that's what she told herself. 'I appreciated your help, telling Deniol and Sian about Ivan.'

Morgan nodded. 'I enjoyed your company, too, *Cariad*.' He took a hand off the wheel to push his hair back in a habitual gesture she was coming to know well. 'I'm going to take you home now.' He heard the tiny sigh despite the roar of a motor bike overtaking as they passed in the lee of the Cob. 'Not because I don't want to be with you, but because you look tired to death. You need to rest and take something for that headache I see swimming in those pretty green eyes of yours.' He reached out a hand and gave hers a gentle squeeze before putting his hands back on the wheel.

7

THE NEXT DAY FOUND Willow closeted in the office with Dai. 'So I think all things considered it might be best to find a space for me on the P-way. There's bound to be lots of inquisitive people down at the station and we can all do without that kind of publicity.' Willow grimaced. 'Would Owen be happy to have me early?'

Dai cocked his head on one side, thinking, and then rasped a hand over his unshaven chin. 'I think you have the right of it, Willow. I'll give him a ring down at the yard and see what he says.'

A short conversation later Willow found herself hitching a lift down to Minffordd Yard and swinging aboard a carriage behind a small diesel engine. Owen was bald, broad and short; his donkey jacket bulged over his beer gut, his knees, as if struggling under his weight, bowed out. His tiny feet appeared as a delicate afterthought. A chorus of greetings came her way with Owen's voice booming out above them all. He greeted her with real pleasure. 'We're in need of a tea girl today. It's going to be cold up at Tan Y Bwlch. We're going up to mark the fishplates that need replacing or re-bolting down at Plas Halt, when we've got the line to ourselves.'

The engine pulled away and the five men in the carriage shuffled their feet and settled themselves for the journey. The windows soon fogged up in the unheated carriage as the small train climbed higher up the line. Willow was glad of the extra layer of T-shirt and thick socks she'd put on that morning. She had a yellow fluorescent jacket over her donkey jacket and felt a bit like the Michelin man.

The carriage swayed round the curves with a rhythmic clanking she found very soothing. She broke the silence. 'How's the family, Owen?'

The question allowed everyone to relax it seemed, as she was brought up to date with his various progeny and their prowess. The others chipped in with pieces of news, but everyone carefully refrained from asking her why she was working the line when there were still a couple of weeks of firing time left. The engine stopped briefly at Plas Halt and Owen and the driver off-loaded some supplies into the shelter at the station, then they continued on.

Tan Y Bwlch, when they reached it, was deserted, no cars in the car park and the trees bare of leaves. The driver pulled the diesel into a siding out of the way of the passenger trains.

Willow, stepping down first into the stillness, heard the little rill that fed the water tank running in the field to her right and the lone caw of a corbie up the valley. Then the others all piled out and the silence was broken with Paul's chuckle at some joke and the hacking coughs of smokers breathing in fresh, cold air.

Everyone went round to the tool carriage to take what they wanted, leaving the engine to click quietly and the station cat to slink out of the undergrowth and settle herself on the top of the engine and bask in its warmth. They would have to leave their transport at the station while the trains were running and walk back down the line to the halt, checking fishplates on the way.

Willow was amazed at the sheer energy of Owen. He might look fat, but seeing him walk along the line with his tireless gait made her feel incredibly unfit. They started as soon as they passed the points beyond the bridge, checking at every joint between the flatbed rails to make sure there were plates overlapping the joins and that they had their correct complement of nuts and bolts. One of the men worked the opposite side of the line to her, marking with chalk any fishplate that needed work.

Owen and another man were now further down the line. Occasionally Owen would get down on all fours and look along the line. He made her think of a shaggy bear ambling along a forest track; when he stood he looked as if he was sniffing for snow. She smiled at his antics. She'd watched him do it before, but still marvelled at the ability to check if a line was out of true with the naked eye.

By eleven she was starving. She felt the comforting weight of her sandwich box resting against her side in her workbag. 'Hi, Owen,' she had to raise her voice to the distant figure, 'isn't it time for elevenses yet?'

Owen gave her a wave in acknowledgement and Iwan, who was working opposite, said, 'I think the plan is to eat at the Halt.' Willow looked down the track to where the halt was a tiny box in the distance. Before she could pass comment Owen had come back up the line.

'Mark your place, girl, and go and put the kettle on. We'll join you in fifteen.' Willow grinned at him and walked down the line, sniffing at the spicy scent of the leaves and the damp smell of the earth. As she left the others behind the silence closed in, broken only by her boots crunching along the hard shoulder of the ballast. She took a deep breath of the frosty air; for now she would put her worries aside and just enjoy the tenuous peace of the countryside.

The next half hour was very pleasant; she sat listening to the men teasing each other about how little work each was doing, while they smoked their poison of choice. Owen favoured a pipe, his stubby hands filling it with surprising delicacy. Iwan seemed to get through half a dozen home-rolled smokes, his hands busy making one while he smoked the last.

'I noticed there are fewer fishplates this year. That'll be all the 'thermit' welding you did last year, Owen? I'm not very good at physics; won't the global warming thing have you undoing all your work?' Willow looked across at Owen as she relaxed back against a mossy stump, soft as a velvet cushion, at the side of the track.

'There's 'not being good' and there's abysmal, girl. No, we won't have to undo our work - the bottom temperature rises as well, so the expansion of the line is still the same. Why? Did you want to get your flash welding cert this year?'

'Not really.' Willow grinned. 'You should have seen my work in the machine shop last year. My braising looked like whipped cream and I had to see the Doc for arc eye! It was most embarrassing.'

'Well, you are a girl. And, despite all the papers say you can't always do a man's job, as you've discovered. At least not if you're built like a girl, and not a Russian stevedore!' Iwan grinned across at her. 'Remember the 'pogo stick'?'

The men all roared with laughter as Willow started to giggle. 'Oh yeah! Well, I did try, fellas.' She'd made a valiant attempt to use the tamping machine on the ballast the previous winter. It was heavy and she just hadn't enough weight or muscle to control it, so she'd bounced about the track like, as Iwan said, 'A small child on a large pogo stick.'

The laughter died away and the silence crept back until she could hear the birds further down the line and a distant roar of a car engine. It was never really quiet and the illusion of peace was just that, an illusion. Even the men looked rather villainous she thought, like smugglers after a successful night's work.

None of them had shaved and she could see the shadow of beards sparkling with moisture from the damp air, on their faces under the watch-caps. They were chatting about the history of Campbell's Platform now and it gave her an idea. As a pause occurred in the conversation she turned to Owen. 'Owen, do you know where the, 'big crane that wouldn't go under the bridge', used to be kept?'

'Now who on earth have you been talking to, to hear about that, Willow?' Owen looked at her in astonishment, his eyebrows quivering like startled caterpillars. 'I do know as it happens, but it isn't in the tourist books.'

Willow looked a bit embarrassed as conversation stopped and all the men looked at her. 'Well, I've got some old letters from my great-uncle who lived in this area. And he talks about it. Only,' she grinned, 'I only found out what that bit meant last week as they're all in Welsh. He was called Tudor, my uncle.'

'Oh, so you're really a Welsh girl, are you? Well, we might have known, that's why you fit in so well.' Owen smiled at her. 'Now what did it say in this letter?'

Willow wrinkled her nose. 'Well, I can't tell you exactly because the person who translated it didn't read it word for word. But I remember that phrase.'

Owen rubbed his chin and knocked out his pipe. 'I would have thought Morgan would have been able to tell you all about it.' Owen then turned bright red and the silence could be felt as the men looked first at her, then Owen, with something approaching horrified fascination on their faces.

Willow felt herself growing warm and could imagine her face being as red as Owen's. 'It wasn't Morgan.'

'Sorry, *Cariad*.' Owen stood up. 'Iwan, work with Paul. I'll work with Will for a bit.'

Owen turned back to Willow. 'Look girl, we can't help knowing about the inquest, but that was clumsy of me. I didn't mean to upset you.'

'It's alright, Owen; I know there's going to be gossip.' Willow bent her head to attend to the fastening of her bag, and then looked directly at him. 'Circumstances seem to have thrown Morgan Williams and me together, but there isn't anything secret happening.'

Owen turned towards the interested onlookers. 'What you waiting for, Christmas? Move yourselves!' He shooed them away with all the efficiency of a farmwife scattering a flock of chickens. Dismissed, the team began to tramp back up the line, casting the occasional look back at the pair left behind. Willow followed their retreat, then looked at Owen. 'You didn't have to send them away; there isn't anything else in it.'

Owen kept his reflections to himself. He'd heard plenty of gossip and rumour in the pub the night before as those who'd been at the inquest reported back what they had seen and heard. There were comments about her being standoffish, and speculation, too, about her former relationship with Barry Scott.

There'd been quite a few sly nudges and winks when the way Morgan had spirited her away at the end was discussed. She might not think there was anything happening but, if the reports were half-way true, that wasn't what Morgan thought.

'So tell me about this great-uncle of yours.' Owen began walking the line again, chalk in one hand, and small hammer in the other.

Willow walked beside him, watching as he tapped the lines and listened to the sound of the metal. 'My mother died about two years ago, and I just boxed everything up and stored it. I couldn't face sorting things out at the time. But this spring I started on one of the boxes and found some old letters. They were all in Welsh and that old fashioned spidery writing. I know they're from my great uncle Owen 'cos I heard my grandad talking about him sometimes, and that's the signature on them, only I couldn't figure them out. I did think I'd try to learn the language, only it's so difficult.' She grinned across at him as Owen marked a cross on the line, then muttered to himself in that very language.

'Go on, girl. I'm listening.'

'Well,' she marked a cross herself on the fishplate near her, to note it needed two bolts, then stood up, 'last weekend I met two of the kids who were there when we did the run for the school competition, they translated a bit of the letters for me. Only we hadn't got a lot of time. They said that bit about the crane and something about a hurricane and a bit about the cricket.'

Owen gave her a considering look as he stood up straight. 'I know a bit of history but I'm not really into the old stuff. I mainly know what happened after the 1950's when the line restarted. I do know a little bit. There was a hurricane in these parts, back in twenty-seven it was. It took out part of the Cob, and we ran trains from the works for about six months - all told.' Owen stood up, hands on hips, and looked across the line at her. 'You need to go to the archives or better yet ask...' He trailed off, looking embarrassed again.

Willow offered a small smile. 'Morgan?'

'Well, yes, he does know a lot of the history, Will, and he could translate the letters for you.'

'I seem to have got him involved in quite a lot of trouble already, Owen. The letters will keep a while longer.' As she finished speaking Owen moved to the side of the line. 'Up train.' With these mystic words he pulled out his whistle and looked back along the line but the rest of his men were already moving to the side as he blew a loud blast of warning.

Willow skipped nimbly across the rails to join him and backed into the shrubbery at the side. She was fairly confident that no-one would expect to see her or recognise her up here, but pulled her own flat cap down further just in case she wasn't being paranoid.

The single engine and rake of six chuffed by in stately fashion. The driver and fireman gave a wave as they passed but she noticed that the windows were pretty fogged up in the carriages, so didn't think that anyone would get much of a view of her. As the final carriage disappeared up the line she looked down her bulky person. She wouldn't recognise herself in this get up. They'd be lucky to tell what sex she was, never mind who she was, she thought.

MORGAN HADN'T MANAGED TO avoid the publicity quite as easily. He'd decided that the best damage control method was to give a statement to the press and hope that his well chosen log of information on the publicity fire, would keep them away from other little blazes, like his love life.

He'd contacted one of the local newspapers and was pleased to see that the reporting had been fairly accurate as far as his firm and the inquest went. He wasn't so pleased to see the comment and speculation about Willow, complete with grainy photograph of them both. The papers of course had dug up the old stories about Willow's association with Barry. It seemed the reason for the break up of their engagement was news to the press.

He'd set in motion a firm of private investigators to try to discover what exactly Barry had been up to, since Inspector Jenkins seemed to have the intention of fixing him with dirty dealing at the least, and murder at the worst. He had a lot of respect for the judicial system but he didn't think much of some of its members.

So far they'd reported some rather interesting information about Barry Scott. None of it made him think any better of the man, and some of it had him rather worried about Willow. He wasn't sure how much she knew about the man's dealings and needed to check things out, even if his heart said he could trust her. It wasn't just his livelihood that was at stake.

He pulled his suitcases from the bottom of the wardrobe and began to pack the soft brown calf leather with his clothes in a methodical manner. He looked out the window as he finished fastening the straps. At least Portmerion was a haven from the paparazzi.

Morgan fretted about Willow as he continued to put his life as a train driver into bags and clear drawers of his possessions. He'd intended to contact her before he left for London but it was a bit difficult. He'd gone down to the works that morning, only to discover she was up the line. Now he was running out of time. Jane would be flying in from New York this evening and the negotiations with the firm needed either ditching or revising, in view of his knowledge. He could wait until three, but not much longer.

Suddenly he came to a decision. Picking up the phone he punched in the numbers for the works. 'Hi, Dai, it's Morgan here. Yeah, I'm nearly ready for the off. Look, Dai, I need to speak to Willow. Where are the gang working today? Tan Y Bwlch? Fine, I'll go and have a word before I head back home. Thanks a lot. *Wel a chi.*'

Morgan smiled to himself. He felt the bubble of excitement in his chest at the thought of seeing her again. Oh yes, he'd got it bad. He finished up and went out to the car, throwing everything efficiently in the boot and slamming it shut.

He'd settled his bills earlier, so now he got in and turned his car with a flourish, and set off for the mid-way station. He might have to go to London, but Willow was not going to forget him while he was away, he was determined on that.

Just on one o' clock, he pulled in to Tan y Bwlch station, noting the little diesel in the siding on the other side of the lines. Evidently the gang hadn't got back yet for their lunch. He had time. He left his car under the trees and crossed to the white fence and ascended a few steps leading up to the bridge. He looked down the line, waiting for the group he could hear chattering like sparrows, to emerge from round the curve in the line.

Ah yes, there was his girl, wrapped up like a bag lady carting all her worldly goods. And just as grubby. She was busy talking to Owen, her hands moving and every so often pushing back her fringe. Morgan walked down the steps and waited by the side of the line for the group to come up to him.

He saw the minute Willow spotted him. First she blushed, and then she studiously ignored his presence. The rest of them weren't so polite. Owen lifted an arm in greeting. Morgan snaked out a hand and pulled Willow out of the group where she was trying to bury herself. 'Just the girl I want to see.'

The rest of the group did their best not to grin as Willow flushed even more. And she heard Iwan mutter in a high falsetto, 'There's nothing secret happening.' Owen leaned over and gave the young man a sharp smack around the ear. 'What? What?' Willow heard Iwan protesting as the group continued to walk away.

'Come and admire the flowers with me. The parks and gardens have done a fine job in the tubs.' Morgan pulled her along, away from the gang, to the wooden seats and benches at the far side of the café. He was grinning, he'd heard Iwan's comment and he thought he knew what it was all about. At least he hoped he did.

Willow followed willy-nilly, since there didn't seem much help for it. But she did manage a token protest. 'Morgan, I'm working! The gang will give me grief.'

She could have saved her breath. Morgan just kept walking until he was right up against the wall of a stone parapet, round the side of the café. He swung Willow round so that she had her back to the empty café and was facing the lake dimly seen through the trees and woods in the distance, and then stood close behind her.

He looked around. This little section was nicely secluded and free of the prying eyes of the gang. Then he put his arms round her waist and pulled her back close against him. His heavy topcoat flapped open in the light breeze and she leaned against his business suit. Oh, yes, he'd got it bad he thought, he'd never have let Jane mess his suit up!

Content for the moment with that fragile contact, he started to speak while he looked out over the Welsh hills. 'I've got to go back to London today. Between the inspector's information about my rival, Barry, and his business, and needing to talk to Jane, I must head away soon.'

Willow chanced a quick look at him over her shoulder, then looked away. When he'd spoken about Jane there had been such tenderness in his voice she suddenly felt incredibly jealous. She tried for a stealthy withdrawal of her person but Morgan only held her more firmly against him.

'What with one thing and another we haven't had much chance to talk, *Cariad*, and we haven't got much time now. But I'm coming back here soon, and then we can get to know each other without dead bodies and policemen tripping us up at every turn. I really want to get to know you, Willow.' Morgan swung her round to face him. 'But what I want even more is to kiss you.'

Willow gaped at him in astonishment, then fixed her eyes on the open neck of his white silk shirt. She could see little blonde curls in the vee and found the sight strangely erotic. He pulled her even closer, locking both arms around her waist so that they stood with the length of their bodies touching.

Morgan watched her carefully. He moved a hand up and took off the cotton cap, brushing the golden hair back from her face and running a possessive hand down the soft cheek until he was cupping her face. 'You really are a beautiful girl under all that dirt.' The hat fell unheeded onto a nearby picnic table.

Willow found herself enveloped in warm velvet as Morgan swooped down for the kiss he could no longer resist. He felt bubbles of excitement explode inside his stomach; yes, this was what he'd been waiting for, needing. As Willow uttered a faint groan he pulled her even closer and deepened the kiss, changing the angle and nudging her lips open, running his tongue against the hot softness.

Willow stood, slightly dazed, as he eased back and rested his cheek against her hair. It seemed her body had a will of its own when it came to Morgan Williams. She discovered she was breathing rather fast, and made a valiant effort to slow the tempo down. However, that didn't seem to be doing much for the upheaval in her stomach, or the caterpillars parading up and down her spine.

'It's probably just as well we're in a public place and you've got more clothes on than my aunt Bessie. Because,' he moved and looked at the green eyes with their stunned expression, 'I might forget to take things slowly.' He grinned beguilingly at her.

Willow opened her mouth, attempted to speak, and came out with a, 'Tha,' coughed and tried again, 'This is taking things slowly!'

'Oh yes!' He smoothed back the errant curls blowing against his fingers and rubbed a thumb over the rosy cheek. 'Now this is speeding things up.' He bent swiftly and captured her lips again, feeling his heart go from naught to a hundred in a blink, as one of Willow's hands crept up, to just touch the curls in the nape of his neck.

He stifled the groan of frustration as his hands encountered the heavy donkey jacket firmly buttoned against the weather. Definitely too many clothes on, was his only coherent thought for the next few minutes. Willow, aware of the pounding of her own heart, and the sea surge of noise in her ears as she dealt with her body's arousal, caught the sound of Morgan's groan.

With a final hard kiss Morgan swung her around again to face the open woods. He snuggled her back against him resting his chin on the top of her soft hair. He gazed out, seeing the bare branches of the trees and the distant vista, he could even see a line of smoke as the up train made its way through them, then heard the hauntingly eerie noise as the whistle signalled Plas Halt. He mentally charted its progress but then dismissed the sight, and sound, for the feel of the girl in his arms.

She was aware of his rapid breathing as he fought for a measure of control. 'You go to my head, woman. Not to mention other areas.' He chuckled quietly in her ear, and nuzzled and sniffed against the pulse he could see beating at the side of the slender neck, setting a kiss on it. 'You smell of violets under the diesel. How nice.' He sniffed again.

Then, when he was sure he had firm control of himself he swung her round to face him again. 'Willow, darling, I have to go, but I need you to know that I'm probably falling in love with you.' He felt her instant withdrawal and held her hands firmly in his, pulling them up to his chest.

'Look at me, darling. I know you've had a rough ride where Barry was concerned, so we'll go at your pace, but I believe you have some feelings for me, otherwise I wouldn't be standing here now, would I?' He gave her a little shake and waited for the huge, brilliant green eyes to focus on him.

Willow stood looking at him. She wasn't that much of a coward that she would deny the reaction of her body to herself, but she was scared enough not to acknowledge those same feelings to him. 'Morgan,' she paused, 'I don't know quite what to say.' A glimmer of humour peeked out. "*This is so sudden, Mr Rochester*', might be appropriate. Maybe you need to remember who we both are. Barry found I didn't fit into his world, and that's your world too.'

Her hands curled around his in direct contradiction to the statement, as she tried to hold on physically to that which mentally she was pushing away. She stopped speaking as he tightened his hold on the hands he had been gripping so lightly. He bent and kissed her fists. 'Well, at least Barry had the sense to realise what a gem he'd got and wanted to hold on to you. Even if he was a total bastard in other ways.'

Willow looked up at a mouth suddenly gone grim. 'Do you know why he was in Wales then?'

Morgan looked down at her, ignoring the question. 'I have to go. I'm going to collect several speeding tickets as it is, if I'm not careful.' He grimaced as he pulled her closer and bent his head for what he told himself was a quick kiss goodbye.

Several minutes later Willow raised a head which seemed to be empty of all rational thought, to hear him muttering in Welsh as he planted feather-light kisses across the bridge of her admittedly grubby nose. She opened her eyes as she felt the cool air blow between them and looked at the strong face in front of her.

'I said, I think we're both in trouble, darling. I intend to be around in your future, Willow, and I'm coming back as soon as I can.' Morgan kissed the nose one final time and released his hold, sliding a hand down to grasp her left hand. 'Walk me to my car, *Cariad*?'

At her nod, he started to walk back along the stone parapet and round the corner of the café. Sometime in the last few minutes both up and down trains had pulled into the station. Locked in each others arms they had been oblivious to the groups of tourists who had alighted. Now they simultaneously became aware that they had been observed.

A group of tourists, all gabbling in what Willow vaguely recognised as German, surged around, then passed them, on their way to the shop in search of guide books and ice cream. One particular burgher offered them a wink as he strolled past, his hand firmly holding a child who skipped along chattering ten to the dozen like a mynah bird on speed. Morgan offered his own wink back, but Willow was now so flustered she daren't meet anyone's eyes.

She knew the driver and fireman from the down train and the quick glance she'd spared them had revealed some very speculative looks. She felt as though her face was glowing like the fire door of the boiler.

Morgan approached his car, fishing in his pocket for the car key and releasing the locks as he drew near. 'Damn, but I'm going to miss you.' He stopped on the driver's side and turned towards Willow who up until then had failed to get any words passed the large lump in her throat. 'Say you'll miss me too, I need something to keep me going, *Cariad*.' He ran a gentle thumb over a cheek gone pale again.

'Morgan.' She looked up at the serious blue eyes gazing into hers and swallowed. 'Don't you think you're going a bit fast? You've only been speaking to me for a week.'

'And look what I've missed! My life was so peaceful before I started,' he hesitated and slanted her a sly grin, his fair eyebrows raised in irony, 'speaking to you, darling.'

He leaned in and gave her a gentle hug. 'Have you still got my phone number?' At her blank look he sighed. 'Give me your mobile.' Willow looked mystified but fished in the recesses of her jacket and brought out the slim silver machine. He took it and carefully programmed in his own number. 'You can ring me anytime you want. Miss me, *Cariad*. Please.' He put the machine back in her hand and wrapped her fingers around it.

He got in the car and Willow stood back as he revved the engine and reversed out of the slot, scoring the gravel as he shot down the slope and left the station. Willow stood a moment watching the dust settle and the sparrows start to chirrup up in the nearby trees, then turned and walked over to the gate next to the waiting room, surprised to find the station once more deserted, the last carriage just disappearing round the right-hand curve towards Portmadog, and the dust settling. She stared fixedly at a plastic bag drifting between the lines, giving an air of desolation after the last few minutes bustle. She was achingly aware of just how desolate she felt too, set adrift and blowing in the wind.

Owen watched her approach across the lines with a certain amount of sympathy; he was very much in love with his own wife. 'You've still got time for a *panad* before we go back down the line, Will.' He waved the battered enamel teapot before her and patted the grassy bank where the men were lounging. 'Reception's not that good here.'

Willow looked down at him absently for a second or two then, as what he'd said registered, shook her head absently, and put the phone away, taking the offered mug from his hand and accepting the smile in the same absent manner. Owen didn't remove his kindly eyes from her face but as Iwan opened his mouth spoke warningly to him without turning round '*Cau dy geg,* Iwan.' Iwan shut his mouth with a snap, as instructed.

The older men shrugged and got out their smokes, settling back against the fence of the Signals and Telecommunications stores for a few minutes before they went back to work. Willow glanced at her serviceable watch and was astonished to find that the whole time with Morgan had only lasted fifteen minutes.

As Willow lowered herself to the grassy sward next to Owen and nursed her mug between her hands he asked, 'Did you talk to Morgan about the crane then, Will?' Owen might keep the others at bay, but he had his own sly sense of humour as well.

'Er, no, we didn't get round to talking about the past.' She was rapidly recovering from being kissed senseless. 'But from one or two things he did say I'm going to have to learn Welsh fairly quickly in the future.'

Owen grinned his pixie grin at her and, for her ears only, said, 'I'll bet you are.'

THE REST OF THE DAY was fairly uneventful. Owen kept her as his partner, thereby circumventing any prying and teasing from the others. They kept to general topics as they worked and, as the inevitable rain closed in along with the dusk, the gang called it a day at just gone three and headed back down the line, rattling along in the old coach behind the diesel engine.

Since Owen was driving on the trip home he'd signalled Willow to climb aboard the diesel. The noise and the need to wear large ear defenders made conversation almost impossible. Willow hopped off and on to change the staff and swing the bob weight points as they came down into Minffordd yard, and then, as he halted the train and the blessed silence descended, turned towards her protector. 'Thanks for looking after me today, Owen. I appreciated the chance to hide, but you can't stand as my shield all the time.'

'No, Will, but it does no harm to have someone in your corner at times. The lads don't mean any harm, you know.' He smiled across at her as they heard the doors slide back in the carriage behind them with a solid thunk, then the resounding crunch of steel toed boots jumping onto hard limestone gravel.

'Do you want to come up the line tomorrow?'

'I don't think so somehow, I've got some things I need to do.' She gave him a lopsided smile. 'And I've got some thinking to do too.'

Owen risked a look, then looked away, fiddling with the engine brake. 'Don't think too hard, Will, most men aren't like...' he trailed away for a moment. 'What I mean is, Morgan's one of the good ones, see?'

'Yeah, but I don't want to make the same mistake twice.' It was the closest Willow had come to admitting anyone into her confidence and was accepted as such.

'OK then, Will, I'll see you around.'

Willow scrambled down on the other side and, slinging her bag over her shoulder, turned into the wet and wind, and headed out the gates. She set off for home along the main road. She wasn't at work the following day; there were more volunteers than places now that the timetable had been reduced for the season. She could actually stop firing at this stage without inconveniencing Dai that much, she thought.

But what was she going to do with herself? Originally she'd planned to work in the machine shop until Christmas. There were Welsh classes starting again in January. She might try to get into one of those. They were full time. But having managed to get a bit of one letter translated she didn't want to wait to find out more until she could read them for herself. Deep in thought she didn't hear the car which pulled up just behind her until she felt a hand on her arm.

Being touched unexpectedly caused a reaction Sergeant ap Rhys wasn't expecting. His six foot odd frame moved back sufficiently quickly to avoid the back kick, which was just as well, Willow thought, as she swung round to check on her potential attacker; she really didn't want to be on a charge for assaulting a police officer.

'Whoa there, Miss Edwards!' He stood with both hands raised in a sign of peace. 'I thought it was you as I passed. I stopped to offer you a lift, it's teeming down out here.'

Willow looked up at the dark sky and the rain coming down in buckets, creating haloes round the street lamps. She'd been so wrapped up in her own thoughts she hadn't noticed. Now she blinked the rain out of her eyes and smiled at the sergeant who was standing, dripping patiently, on the sidewalk as he observed her.

'I hadn't noticed.'

'Well, get in the car before I have to arrest myself for illegal parking, and I'll give you a lift; before we're both soaked to the skin.'

Willow walked round, climbed in the squad car, and fastened her seat belt as the friendly young police sergeant put the car into gear.

'I was glad to see you making your escape yesterday with Morgan Williams. The Press can be a bit, er... persistent at times.' He risked a glance across to his passenger then focused his attention back on the wet roadway.

'I've got a bit of news for you, if you're interested.'

'Oh!' Willow slewed round in the seat. 'About what Barry was doing here?'

'No, about your young Pole.' The sergeant tsked at a driver who didn't dip his headlights. 'Fool.' This addressed to the rapidly disappearing motorist, but he continued to drive sedately along. 'We've traced him back to Pwlleli so far, and we now know he had a train ticket for the nineteenth of last month, for the special steam train that runs on the main line on Thursdays. We don't know if he was on it yet, but it seems likely.'

Willow opened her mouth then closed it again before saying, 'How odd! I was in Pwlleli that day.'

'Were you? That is odd.' The sergeant pursed his lips then, dismissing that for the moment, went on, 'We've found his wife. It turns out the photo was of her.'

The sergeant continued, 'She's in France at the moment. The French police are dealing with her; she doesn't speak any English, and very little French. But we're sending over one of our Polish community officers to sort things out. He's going to bring her over to identify her husband. It seems this couple hadn't realised they could enter the country legitimately through EU rules. Thought they needed to smuggle themselves in. He paid someone just about all the money they had saved to get himself over here. Could have taken the ferry for a pittance.' The sergeant sighed at the folly of people.

'Oh, how sad.' Willow grimaced. 'How did you find her?'

'You remember the notepad in his rucksack?'

Willow nodded.

'Well, it was a letter to his wife, telling her all about how he'd been met off a fishing boat by someone and taken by train. He didn't say where, but he did say the place wasn't England. Poor soul must have been very confused landing in the heart of Wales!' He shook his head sadly.

'That's how we tracked her down. He said he'd had a falling out with the man who brought him in, but not to worry. Then there was a bit about how she was to look after herself and the baby and that he'd send her the money as soon as he found work. We've got a nice Polish lad working over on Ynys Mon who just happened to be visiting his girl in Caernarfon when they were trying to decipher the letter.'

'What will happen to her now?'

'I don't know, *Cariad*. She obviously has no money, and the poor wee thing is struggling with the French police and their justice system. She fell apart when they told her he'd died. Apparently she has no family in France, or anywhere else for that matter.' He obviously had a low opinion of any police force which wasn't British, by the expression on his face. 'Maybe she'll be forced to go back to Poland.'

He stopped the car and Willow looked out, surprised to find herself outside her lodgings. 'You can let those two teenagers know about him if you want. Tell them they helped him, even if he did die.'

'I already did. We went to the hospital yesterday to visit and the nurse told us he'd died and his name.' Willow offered a sad smile. 'Sian was upset.'

'She would be. But Deniol will look after her alright.'

Willow unfastened her belt. 'Thanks for the news, Sergeant, and the lift. Mrs Jones will be wondering if she wants me as a houseguest. I always seem to be coming home in police cars just lately.'

'Don't you worry about Dilys Jones, she was my dinner lady at school, and she's got a marshmallow heart under that marshmallow figure.' They grinned at each other and Willow got out and went up the short path to the door, watched by the sergeant. He gave a wave as she turned, having opened the door, then drove off with a quiet toot of his horn.

8

HE'D ONLY JUST MADE it to the airport on Thursday evening. Morgan had driven fast and efficiently across Wales and out into England via Oswestry the previous evening. Traffic had been light on the motorways but even so he had concentrated on his driving, doing his best to put his worries about work and women to the side.

He was looking forward to seeing his sister; they had been inseparable as small children, and even now liked to be in frequent contact. Working for the family firm had made that possible. Even when one or other was away on business they made time for each other over the phone.

The airport seemed to be busier than usual, if one could have degrees of busyness with several million people milling about. A keen observer, he spotted several photographers from the big dailies and concluded that someone famous was entering or leaving the country. He turned his back on them and went over to the barriers. He stood patiently waiting for Jane to come through the checkout.

Where he was fair with their father's deep blue eyes, she was a dark, Welsh Celt. Dark auburn hair swung about a heart-shaped face in a pageboy bob. Big gold hoops swung from her ears as she turned her head, looking for his familiar face. The deep brown eyes surveyed the teaming throng and then lit up her whole person as she caught sight of Morgan. He felt the familiar leap of joy when she beamed across the hordes at him. The reward for his journey was trapped in that smile.

She all but threw herself into his arms as she emerged from passport control, clinging tightly to him, grinning, and planting kisses on the cheek nearest to her as he hugged back.

'So you missed me then?' Morgan allowed her slim body to sink back, allowing her stockinged feet to touch the floor again.

'Nah! I would have kissed the floor if you hadn't been here, I'm just grateful to be out of that plane and on the ground again.' She tipped her head back, smiling up at him, pleasure beaming from her face as she continued to hug him round the waist, her shoes clutched in one hand.

He twitched slightly as mile-high heels dug into his kidneys. 'They aren't called stilettos for nothing, darling!' He gently drew her hands round to the front.

Jane grinned up at him, then hopped on one foot as she replaced first one shoe then the other, clinging to his arm in the meantime with a death grip.

'Why do you wear those things?'

Standing erect she looked him in the face. 'Because you stole all the height genes.' She turned with him to walk towards the luggage collection area. 'But I got the better deal - I got the looks!' The handsome pair turned into the large echoing hall with its faint smell of rubber and noisy creaking belts, attracting attention by their obvious delight in each other, even in that emotion-charged place.

'OK, where's the luggage? I've got a Pickford's van outside ready.' Jane gave him a light punch, and then had the grace to look slightly abashed as they went over to the carousel, and she started to remove bags. When they got to the third he raised an eyebrow, by the time they were removing a fifth and a box he was grinning all over his face. 'Have we got any money left in the firm, or have you spent it all?'

She cast a wicked smile back up at him, poking out her tongue before returning her attention to the slowly revolving belt. 'There was a sale on at Macy's and I had to do some Christmas shopping as well.' This was said absently as she gazed rather anxiously at bags passing before her, like the Queen reviewing her guards.

Morgan pretended to give a long suffering sigh, but he wasn't really cross. He stood with an arm round her shoulders enjoying the physical contact. He was slightly surprised to have his photograph taken by an enterprising young man hung with cameras like a Japanese tourist. The boy gave him a cheeky grin. Morgan pointed across to a small mob on the other side of the hall where a political personage was holding forth. 'I think you got the wrong guy. He's the famous one.' The young man just winked and wandered away to the swirling mass of humanity.

Jane looked up as he spoke, then dismissed his comment as she snagged what proved to be the final item, a dress bag, from the conveyer. 'That's the lot.'

'*Diolch Byth!*' He loaded the various suitcases onto a trolley and began to push them towards the exit. Jane, an arm firmly tucked through his, walked alongside him. She didn't speak but he could feel the faint vibration of tension in the arm holding his so warmly. He waited until everything, including his sister, was safely stowed away in the car then turned towards her. 'Give. You're all but bursting with news. It wouldn't be the MCP, would it?'

Jane blushed but nodded. 'I might have known I couldn't keep a secret from you. But oh, Morgan, he makes me happy!'

Morgan squeezed her hands. 'I'm glad for you, *Cariad*.' He turned the plain gold band on her left hand round.

'You're sure?'

'Oh! Yes! I'm very sure. He isn't Michael, and there'll always be a corner that belongs to Michael, but he understands that. After Michael died I thought I'd never love like that again, but I do, so much!'

Morgan leaned over and kissed the scented cheek, brushing back the hair and looking deep into her eyes. 'Well, I might have some news for you too, but I'm not so sure I'm going to win the lady. She has grave doubts about me.'

Jane was immediately indignant. She surveyed her elegant brother, noting for the first time the strain lines around his eyes. 'Well, she's a fool if she doesn't love you.'

'Oh, I think she loves me, she just isn't sure she wants anything to do with me, and I don't blame her at the moment.' Morgan gave the hands a final squeeze and released her. 'Let's go home and you can tell me all about your male chauvinist pig!' Jane accepted his unspoken desire to keep his thoughts to himself for now. He swung round and belted up, starting the car.

'He's not really a male chauvinist, Morgan, or maybe he is.' She paused, eyeing her brother. 'Actually he's a lot like you; he likes to have his own way too.' She wrinkled her nose. 'Maybe it comes of being in charge of digs and things.'

'What? He runs a boarding house?' Morgan raised an eyebrow.

'Not those sorts of digs,' she gave him a light punch, 'archaeological digs, and you knew what I meant. I bet you've already got your tame sleuth looking him over!'

Morgan just grinned at her. 'Well, darling, you are my favourite sister.'

'I'm your only sister.' She shifted and dropped a light kiss on his cheek. 'Thank you for caring.'

Morgan changed the subject. 'I've arranged a meal to be ready at my flat. I thought you'd want to eat and drop after the flight and get over your jet-lag. OK? Or do you want to go to your own place straight away?'

'No, your place is fine.' Jane settled back in her seat, allowing Morgan to concentrate on his driving as the big red buses lumbered by them. They swung round Piccadilly towards Green Park, to the accompaniment of horns from a less than impressed taxi driver. Jane looked out at a London dressed in its finery for the upcoming season, but couldn't find it in her heart to regret the imminent move to the States that she contemplated.

She looked across at her brother. Becoming conscious of her gaze Morgan turned and offered her a brief smile. 'Alright, *Cariad*, soon be home.'

'I'm going to miss you so much, Morgan.'

'Don't look so sad, darling. It's just across the pond, and you can always tell him about the fascinating archaeology in this country. It's much more interesting than American stuff, I'm sure.'

She grinned at him. 'Don't be so insular. He's studying early Inca remains just now.'

'Oh, well! That's South American.'

'Morgan!' she'd shifted in her seat so that she could rest her head on his shoulder as he drove the short distance to the home he'd inherited from their parents.

They'd eaten a light meal, prepared by his housekeeper, in the small dining room at the front of the house, talking very little. Jane was tired and so was Morgan. She smiled sleepily at him. 'I'm going to have a bath and crawl into bed. Business in the morning, Morgan?'

'Yeah, that's fine, *Cariad*. Sleep well.' He made his way to the spacious library at the back, its smell compounded of books and beeswax. Morgan settled down in one of the comfortable old chairs in front of the gas fire and allowed himself to dream a little.

Much later, on his way to his own bed, he put his head round Jane's half closed bedroom door to say good night. He found her asleep with the light on, her reading glasses resting crookedly on her nose. He tiptoed in and took the glasses off, setting them on the bedside table. He gently prised the book from her hand, glancing at the title. Perhaps not his choice of reading material, he thought. He had no desire to dwell on the decomposition of bodies, no matter how ancient.

Jane muttered something in a slurred voice and he gently place a kiss on her forehead, brushing the soft hair away. 'Go back to sleep, *Cariad*.' A faint smile turned up her lips for an instant, then she relaxed in sleep again.

WILLOW AWOKE ON FRIDAY morning, conscious that during a restless night she had come to a variety of decisions. The first was that she would go and see Dai and cease volunteering for the rest of the season. The second; that she would concentrate her energy on discovering what exactly her great-uncle had been doing, and where he had gone in 1927.

Hearing about the young Polish girl and her lack of relatives made Willow determined to track down any family she might have, and to get to know them. She wasn't sure where she would start, but the letters were obviously her best clue.

Accordingly she'd headed down to Boston Lodge works at a time when she estimated that Dai could spare her a few uninterrupted minutes.

'Hi, Dai.' She hailed the wiry little man as he headed into the machine shop from the engine sheds. His overalls were liberally sprinkled with shards of swarf, so she assumed he'd been busy filing something down.

He swung round at her voice and gave her a come ahead sign. 'I thought you might want to see me today.' By mutual consent they walked in a companionable manner through the machine shop, awash with the smell of bearing oil and hot metal, towards the door leading to the long low building that held the staff room.

The place was deserted, too soon for the morning break and too late for the engine crews. The long low windows down one side looked out on the blank stone walls and rotting doors of the old forge.

The room was set with Formica-topped tables and battered steel-framed chairs. Several of the tables had much tea-stained and dog-eared copies of railway magazines on them. Tucked into the corner next to the sink a small table held the paraphernalia of tea and coffee making. Dai headed for this.

'Take a seat. What will you drink?' He held up a plastic cup.

Willow looked across as she shuffled herself behind a wooden table, with her back to the window. 'I'll have hot chocolate, Dai, with sugar.' She shrugged her green jacket off and laid it on the bench at her side, then pulled down the sleeves of the thick blue jumper she'd put on for warmth that morning.

Dai came across holding two cups, and set them carefully down on the table before sitting facing her.

'I suppose you've come to tell me you aren't going to work for us anymore this season and that I've got to rearrange my roster... again.' He grumbled, but the twinkle in his eye said he wasn't really mad at her. 'Between you, and Morgan finishing early, I've got more crossings than the GWR on that roster.'

Willow sipped carefully at the scalding and muddy brew. 'Well, since I don't think the Great Western Railway exists now, that can't be many.'

'Much you know! Once you've put a railway onto the ground, it will exist for ever. Even if they take up the lines you can still see where it was. Railways have that sort of impact on the land and the people.' Dai sipped his own version of the murky liquid they served up in the canteen and sighed for the past glory of the railways.

'Anyway, Will, I'll be sorry to see you go, but I understand. What with all the publicity and everything. We're running down now until the Christmas specials anyway, so don't worry about it. Will you work for the Permanent-Way gang?'

'No, I don't think so. I've got other plans for the rest of this year and I'm not sure how much longer I can manage without a cash job.'

'I could maybe get you on the payroll in a temporary capacity,' Dai offered. 'Or even sub you a bit if you're stuck.' He offered the last tentatively.

'No, Dai, I'm not that stuck. I can manage at least until Christmas without going bankrupt.' She reached across the table and just touched the hand resting next to the cup. 'But thanks anyway.' The wrinkled face looked back with concern for her. Willow knew that he wasn't well paid himself, being well past retirement age.

They went on to talk in a general way about the engines and rolling stock and Dai's plans for the coming season, then Willow left him submerged in a sea of grimy paperwork spread across the table, also in imminent danger of being submerged in coffee. She walked up to the Halt through the cold grey daylight. It was nearing lunch time and she thought she might see what she could find out at the local museum across in Porthmadog. She never actually got there though.

The sun was doing its best to break through the clouds, and the path across to Portmerion enticed her. She crossed the line and started to walk up the rocky path, breathing deeply as the path climbed steeply upwards. The air smelt fresh and frosty with just a hint of *odour de* sheep. Little rivulets ran down the path in narrow channels between the stones, and formed the odd puddle which reflected back the grey sky above.

When she reached the first curve in the path she stopped to breathe and turned to look back across the vista spread before her, like a banquet for the discerning traveller. Now that she'd left the works behind, she could see across the estuary and up the Glaslyn to Snowdon. A farm on the far side was miniature, and the cattle mere dots as they foraged down by the side of the briny water. The other way she could see the tide creeping in and the long greeny-grey line that marked the barrier that the Cob formed against the sea.

She picked out the white tent the police had erected on the seaward side. There were orange and yellow jackets flashing in the brief glimpses of sunlight as police apparently fossicked about among the stones of the Cob. 'What on earth are they looking for now.' She spoke out loud as she watched their antics. 'I suppose they're looking for more clues. It must be interesting.' She watched for a minute or two longer before becoming aware of the fine shivers of her body. 'Well I'm either cold or scared, whichever it is I think I'd better start walking again.'

She sighed as she stood a moment longer looking over the scenery. She would like to stay in the area but she would need a job, and there was no need of a radiographer at the local hospital. She could look for shop work, but most work in the area was seasonal and needed at least a rudimentary acquaintance with the Welsh language, no matter what the government said about equal opportunities.

If she was honest she would like to get married and have a clutch of children and just be a homemaker. She thought of the brief interlude with Morgan yesterday. It was a lovely dream, to make her own family and not worry about being alone. Sighing deeply she moved on up the hill.

The way led through a narrow path lined on either side with brambles, dying now as the winter set in. She trampled hazel nuts underfoot and, looking up, spotted a pair of squirrels racing across the overpass of trees and skittering up the far side of a trunk. Finally she emerged in the car park of Portmerion. She looked around, almost expecting to see the now familiar green jaguar, but the place was deserted, not even a coach load of tourists to be seen.

Well, today would do as well as any other to look around the place. Not yet would she admit to herself that perhaps she had gone there because that was where she'd spent time with Morgan. She mooched her way round the brightly painted houses and into the few shops that were open, admiring the work of Clough Ellis and his foresight in saving the wonderful old buildings and erecting them here in this little cove in Wales.

She found herself picking things up and putting them down again like a nervous shoplifter. She noticed she was being eyed like one too, and decided to take herself off to the stone ship on the shore and sit down with her feet dangling over the edge of the stone promontory.

She eventually admitted to herself that the main reason she was sitting on this extremely cold piece of rock getting the seat of her jeans damp was to connect with Morgan, hoping to make some sort of sense of his comments of yesterday, in the place she knew he'd stayed.

She watched the waves licking against the shore line and creating a lazy slop against the stone frigate, till it almost seemed as if the sea could shift even that obstacle. That's what he was doing, she thought, and so subtly, undermining her will before she knew it.

As the tide began lapping the edge of the shore like a thirsty dog, she realised that her hands were nearly as frozen as her butt and wondered absently where she'd left her mitts. She also came to the realisation that she was starving again. I can't be in love, she thought to herself. I'm too hungry all the time. She decided that she would have to go home. She hadn't reached any decisions at all, but the peace and quiet of the place had helped to settle her somewhat. Scrambling to her feet and dusting the sand off, she wandered up through the tunnel towards the centre of the town and the brightly painted buildings.

She turned towards the heady aroma of frying chips, like a wolf scenting an elk. Having bought a burger she meandered back up through the town towards the exit, munching as she went. Having polished the lot off in record time, she pulled a rather squashed bar of chocolate out of her pocket and broke a piece off as she left the village behind.

On the trip back across the promontory she came to the conclusion that it might be as well to seek out Deniol and Sian and tell them what Sergeant ap Rhys had told her. It would at least be a distraction from her own miserable company.

She managed to reach the Halt in time to catch a train across the Cob and saw that the police were apparently still hard at work, digging away the embankment. The tent they had rigged acted as a sort of barrier to prevent the general public from approaching too close, but the bird's eye view from the train spoilt their preventative measures somewhat. She said as much to the guard.

'You can see right over their shoulder, but it still doesn't let you know what they're up to.'

The guard, a young lady with acne and an attitude, grunted. 'They've been at it for four days. The management have been down and looked, and then I saw some of the big guns going down there, but no-body seems to have a clue what they're looking for.' She checked out the side window to mark their progress and spread her legs slightly as the van rocked over the points.

'They've dug quite a sizable hole in the side now. You can't see it from here, but they seem to be tunnelling underneath the Cob.'

'Good grief. I wonder if they think it's something to do with Barry, or if they're searching for something else.' Willow coloured at the look tossed her way.

The guard remarked, 'I'd think you'd know about that!' causing her to flush even more painfully.

A thick silence reigned for the rest of the journey. Willow, hopping out at the station, left the girl to her duties and headed swiftly away from the train in the hopes of evading any press lingering in the vicinity.

THE LITTLE TWO UP two down was deserted when Willow arrived there. She'd forgotten about school, and now stood forlornly looking at the brass fox's head that served as door knocker on the front door, wondering if her mind was turning to mush. However, as she turned away a small figure rushed up and offered for kissing a face ringed by a woollen bonnet.

Gwyneth, bubbling over and rosy cheeked, greeted Willow with all the enthusiasm of a five-year old, and cracked the small icy shield that Willow had been unconsciously building around her heart for protection.

'*Sut da chi*, Willow'

'Hello, poppet, '*Sut da chi*' to you too.'

'No, you say '*sut wyt ti*' to a child, like the French *tu* and *vous*.' The voice that spoke was husky, and the hand that was being offered showed the brown stains of the habitual smoker. 'I'm Deniol's grandfather and you must be Willow. I've heard a lot about you from this young lady. She says,' he eyed the rope of hair hanging over Willow's shoulder and entangling itself in her shoulder bag, 'that you've got hair like Rapunzel, and she wants hers to grow that long.'

Willow looked down at the young girl currently holding her hand, jiggling from side to side and smiling up at her. 'I rather thought I'd been overlooked for the charms of Uncle Morgan.'

She exchanged a shy smile with the elderly man twinkling down at her. He was slightly stooped and very thin, but still managed to top six foot to her five three.

'Were you looking for Deniol? He's still in school, but you're welcome to step in for a *panad*?' He gestured towards the front door.

Willow felt a small tug from a slightly sticky hand. 'Please. *Taid*'s bought chocolate marshmallows.'

Evidently this was meant as a huge incentive to staying.

'Thank you, darling, that would be nice.'

'My name's Evan.' He opened the door as he spoke and the young child skipped ahead, struggling to take off her coat and handing it to Willow to hang in the little alcove. She might be everyone's darling but the child was obviously either neat, or well trained. Seating herself on a small box Gwyneth undid the buckles of her shoes, small pink tongue tip protruding as she struggled with the stiff leather. Having placed the shoes side by side she whisked away and came back with slippers shaped like bunnies.

Evan took Willow's jacket and hung it next to his own in the alcove. He was dressed in a heavy dark suit under the raincoat, and Willow gazed with some awe and a quick jolt as she saw his watch chain draped across from one waistcoat pocket to the other. She had just such a watch and chain in her possession. It had belonged to her grandfather and she had loved playing with it as a child. She responded to the memory rather than the man, smiling up at him without her usual reserve as she sat down on the settee. Gwyneth came over and stood next to her, suddenly shy and looking mutely at Willow for a moment. 'Can I sit on your knee?'

'Of course you can, *Cariad*.' Willow managed to get the unfamiliar Welsh endearment out as she smiled at the child, but her mind insisted on going back to the last time she was on this settee. Gwyneth scrambled up and her warm solid weight offered an unforeseen comfort. Willow shifted slightly, accommodating the small personage.

'So where have you been today? I thought you would be at school too.'

'I gotted to go to the dentist this morning in Bangor and *Taid* said if I was good I could go to the swings this afternoon with him. Cause I already read my book in class.'

Evan came in and smiled down at Willow, then addressed his imp of a grandchild. 'Go and fetch the plate of chocolate marshmallows, *Cariad*. Carry them carefully mind, and don't touch the teapot.' This last was said with a warning shake of the head.

'Don't let her pester you.' He watched the child skip through the door to the kitchen.

He turned at Gwyneth's re-entrance, watching her as she carefully carried the plate over and set it on the coffee table between the chairs. Then she scrambled back up onto the settee and snuggled back down on Willow's lap. Evan sighed, but he didn't say anything, just went out and returned with a tray of tea things.

Gwyneth slid off Willow's knee unasked, and settled on the settee, burying her nose in a glass of milk.

Evan settled behind the teapot. 'I do a little babysitting for Eirlys now, but I looked after Gwyneth when Deniol's brother died and they went to stay at Morgan's place to be near him, so we're close, see.'

Willow didn't see at all, but didn't like to ask and appear rude.

Evan evidently took her knowledge for granted. 'He's a grand chap is Morgan.'

Willow felt as though the world was conspiring to keep Morgan in her thoughts. She said 'Mm, yes.' and studiously drank her tea. She could feel Evan's enquiring look and blushed faintly.

He evidently decided not to pursue that topic. As he poured more tea he said, 'Deniol says you've got some letters that talk about the old crane that was stored up at Boston Lodge in the thirties.'

'Well, I don't know where it was stored and I'm afraid I haven't got the letter with me, but it's probably the same crane. It's about the same time as the letters.'

'Well, I remember being taken by my *Tad* to watch them doing some sea wall repairs with the crane in ...' he brushed back his sparse grey hair with one hand and offered the plate of biscuits with the other, '... '39 I think it was. It was a white elephant for the railway, except when the visitors came to gape at it. Great big thing it was, nearly as big as this room the operating platform, and almost as tall as the house. I've got a picture in an old railway magazine somewhere; I'll find it for you.' He smiled kindly at Willow. She could hear the echo of her grandad talking and felt warm inside.

'That would be great. Do you know anything about a hurricane at Beddgelert as well?' She looked eagerly across at the fatherly figure.

'Well, not from personal experience, but now you mention it I do remember hearing my parents talk about summat of the sort. Stopped the train it did, or was that an eclipse?' He frowned in an effort to recall childhood memories. 'Wait now.' This to the sticky face presented to him. He did a bit more frowning while he carefully wiped Gwyneth's face with his handkerchief. 'There you go, *Cariad*, all clean.'

Gwyneth gave him a gap toothed smile and sat back quietly, resting against Willow's side. Willow found she was hugging the small body to her as Gwyneth snuggled closer. Evan watched with an indulgent eye.

'Why don't you have a wee nap while Willow and I talk, then we'll go to the swings.'

'*Iawn, Taid.*'

She obediently closed her eyes, and within minutes was dozing, comfortably tucked under Willow's arm.

'She's still a baby really.' He smiled fondly at his granddaughter. 'Now then where were we? No. It was the eclipse I was thinking of. My Dad was on a train from Bangor going down to London and they stopped the train to watch. They even smoked the carriage windows to make it safe.' He grinned at her, shaking his head. 'Can't see British Rail doing that these days, can you?'

Willow smiled back at him. 'Nope. Sometimes I wonder if they're going to stop for the passengers.'

'But that doesn't help you with your hurricane. I'll ask around for you if you want, but it would be better if you could show me the letter.' He quizzically raised an eyebrow. 'I'm not wanting to pry; Deniol said they were from a relative. Have you relatives round here then?'

Willow smiled sadly at him. 'Well, that's the trouble. I don't seem to have relatives anywhere. I was rather hoping the letters might help me find some around here, because they've all died off in England.'

'*Bechod.* I'll see what the over sixties club can remember between them, when I go tonight. They remember more about the past than what they did last week. For that matter so do I.' He gave a small chuckle.

Willow chuckled too. 'That's what my grandad used to say.' The smile faded from her face and Evan caught sight of the sadness that she still felt.

'From round here your grandad, you say?'

Willow put the empty cup back on the saucer and shook her head as he lifted the teapot. 'Well, I know they came from this area, but as far as I know they moved away when my father was little. My grandad spoke Welsh and so did my grandmother, though I can't remember her, but my mother was English.'

They both looked at Gwyneth as she stirred against Willow and opened sleepy eyes.

'Hello, *Cariad,* awake then. Ready to go to the swings?'

'I need to put on my play shoes, *Taid*.'

'Off you go then.'

The small figure scampered away up the stairs and was heard making soft thumps in the room above.

Willow stood up, 'It's been a real pleasure talking to you, Evan. I have appreciated all your help and the trip down memory lane. I'll certainly bring the letters, if you really would like to read them; they're all I've got left since my mother died in hospital a couple of years ago. I would like to find someone of my own.'

'*Taid*, I've gotted a knot,' the whirligig of a child stood in the doorway dangling a trainer from one hand; the other trainer was on a sock clad foot.

Evan stood too, smiling across at the girl in front of him. 'My dear, it will be a pleasure. I need something to keep the brain ticking over these days, and what better way than delving into the past?' Then he turned to his granddaughter. 'I have a knot, *Cariad*, not gotted.'

'OK, *Taid*. But I still can't undo it.' She grinned at him and offered the shoe for inspection. While Evan battled with the knot, Gwyneth looked at Willow. There was a curious expression on her face for a fleeting minute. One more suited to an adult. It disappeared as Willow spoke. 'Thank you for inviting me in for a drink, Gwyneth. I enjoyed your company.'

Gwyneth gave her the gap toothed grin that was her signature. 'That's OK. Do you have to go back to the train now?'

Willow shook her head, the hair swaying gently with the movement, so that the little girl reached up a tentative hand and stroked it. 'No, sweetheart, but I have to get home. But I'll see you again I'm sure. Your *Taid*,' she paused over the word, 'is going to help me do some research.'

Gwyneth obviously had no idea what research was, but if it meant that she got to see more of Willow she was quite happy about it and said so.

WILLOW WASN'T THE ONLY one to have come to some decisions overnight. Morgan knew that he needed to set his business affairs in order before he could head back to Wales. But he was determined to do so with as much speed as possible. However, he assumed that Jane would be going back to New York as soon as she could. He recognised the symptoms; after all, he was suffering from the same complaint, a desperate desire to be near the loved one.

While Willow had been eating burgers as she walked the Welsh sea shore, Morgan had been holding a business lunch with his chief executives in the main board room of his offices in London.

'Gentlemen and ladies.' He collected the attention of the five men present and nodded at Jane and Mary. 'Are we all in agreement?'

'It's a shame to give up the contract, not to mention the money, but I'm behind you, Morgan.' Hamish smiled grimly, pushing his rimless glasses higher on the bridge of his nose and looking across the polished oak, like a Prior dealing with a wayward monk, an impression heightened by the rim of hair which edged the dome of his head like a circle of grass round the remains of a volcano. 'I don't want any involvement in something Barry Scott's been dabbling in. Yon man had a nasty way with him.'

Hamish had been with the firm from the beginning. He'd acted as deputy to Morgan's father and when he was offered a partnership, declined with the comment that he didn't want that much responsibility. However, he might just as well have taken it, his word carried the same authority and assurance as Morgan's did.

'You say the man was down in Wales when he died. Do you think he was spying on your businesses there?'

'The PI I set to investigate says not; Scott hasn't been round the firms we have any interest in. They haven't taken on any new staff, and you know they're all small firms down there. Anyone fresh would be immediately noticed, not to mention confounded by the Welsh language.' He grinned at Jane. They had been talking quietly in Welsh when Hamish had arrived for the meeting and Hamish had hugged Jane, then told her to 'talk in English for God's sake' so that he could hear the gossip too!

'He was in the same area as me,' Morgan continued, 'and from what the PI said, he'd been up in Pwlleli when I was through for the meeting with the Jones'. We'll check over the books and make sure everything is watertight before we sign any papers with anyone.'

'Now,' he looked across at Jane, smiling into her dancing eyes, 'Jane is going to go back to America.' Several of the senior men looked at each other, then across at him in surprise. The youngest member, Paul, opened his mouth then shut it again. He was an executive because he could think on his feet and Morgan had recognised his potential. He waited with the others for Morgan to explain.

'Jane is going to be married, gentlemen. And for my sins, it seems I'm going to have an American brother-in-law. No, he doesn't work for that firm, Hamish, so don't get your hopes up. He's an archaeologist.' He raised a quizzical eyebrow at his sister. 'God knows what she sees in him when she could be working for me, but there you go.' He turned to Hamish while the board united in offering Jane their congratulations.

'There's going to be a vacant partnership, Hamish. Jane wants to resign and have babies.' He raised a brow. Hamish shook his head.

'I don't think so, lad. I'm too old and always was. But,' he nodded across at Paul offering a hand and some comment that was causing Jane to blush slightly, 'he's young, aye, but he's damn good and I think the others would back your vote.'

Morgan looked surprised, then thoughtful. 'I need someone I can trust, Hamish, and I need them now. I have to get back to Wales. He's only been with us eighteen months.'

Hamish looked at Morgan curiously, head cocked on one side. 'Like that is it?' He watched the faint flush mantle Morgan's cheekbones. 'If you didn't trust him you wouldn't have voted him on to the board six months ago, and gone off last month to play at trains, lad.'

'Aye,' Morgan mimicked the faint lowland accent, 'it's like that. And you're right as usual. I'll give it a bit more thought, but I can't say the idea is entirely a new one.' His lips twitched wryly.

He turned away as one of the men asked some question about the firm and then smiled as he caught sight of his sister's face across the room. She was glowing, partly from the attention and compliments, but he could see she was alive with love.

He'd hardly dared to hope that she would find such happiness after her husband died of leukaemia in a hard fought, but short, battle three years ago. Now she had, he rejoiced for her, but a small part of him was, he realised, jealous that their relationship would be forever changed, which was stupid, he thought. He was changing it himself.

He fingered a rather crumpled handkerchief in his suit pocket and smiled to himself. He in turn was under observation; Jane's attention had been caught by that secret smile. Being a twin he wouldn't have been astonished to discover that Jane was suffering from the same twinges and coming to the same conclusions. They always had been able to hear each others thoughts.

The business lunch over, the members of the firm fled like homing pigeons to their own offices to sort out paper work. Jane went home to catch up on some sleep and Hamish and Morgan conferred over work. They finally sat back with dual sighs of relief, and picked up their cooling coffee mugs. 'So what's she like then, lad? Pretty of course, but what else?'

Morgan smiled across at the lined face. 'Well yes, beautiful in her own way, and shy and adorable, and scared, and she's going to be mine, Hamish.'

'So what's the problem?'

'She was Barry Scott's girlfriend before I met her.'

'Ah!'

'Yeah! Ah!' And being Scott, he exploited her a bit, and slapped her a bit, and threw his money in her face a bit. Which means she's not sure she wants anything to do with me and my money.' He smiled wryly. 'And before you say it, I know that's not my usual problem!'

'What does Jane say?'

'Jane says the woman must be a fool if she thinks I'm anything like Scott, and if she's that big a fool she doesn't deserve me.'

'Aye well, Jane can be a wee bit partisan at times.'

They smiled at each other.

'So what will you do now?'

'With your agreement, Hamish, I'm going to dump the whole lot back in your lap and head back to Wales, Sunday or Monday. I'll have a talk with the members of the board and then, depending on how they feel, offer the partnership to Paul. You can groom him in his new role while I'm away.'

'Huh! Thanks for that.' Hamish smiled a trifle sourly at Morgan. 'All this love around here is addling the Williams brains, if you think that young man will be groomed.' He held up a hand to stem the words he could see forming on Morgan's lips. 'And before you say it I will. You wouldn't have voted him on the board six months ago, if he didn't have that very quality.'

They laughed as they stood up, both satisfied that they understood each other well enough. Hamish headed out the door, grinning to himself. It looked like he might get those proxy grandchildren after all! He closed the door quietly and exchanged a conspiratorial wink with Mary, seated efficiently at her large and overflowing desk.

Morgan waited until the door closed, then reached out a hand for the phone. He didn't know where Willow would be but he wanted to hear her voice. He shook his head. He was obviously losing his mind, but he needed to be reassured that she was still thinking about him. As he tapped in the numbers he muttered to himself, 'I knew I should have written it down,' but the number rang reassuringly. Unfortunately it kept on ringing, and then cut to voice mail.

'Hi, *Cariad*, just checking that you're alright. I'll be in touch later.' Morgan replaced the receiver with a sigh, and then pulled the next pile of paperwork towards him. The sooner he got it out of the way the sooner he could get back to her.

9

IT HAD BEEN A quiet weekend for Willow so far. Saturday she'd stayed close to home, washing her hair in a leisurely fashion then going out to allow the wind to finish the job of drying it for her. She'd walked along the back lane towards Penrhyn, listening to the birds and the trees sighing for the summer.

She was lonely she admitted, if only to herself. It was strange to realise that just over a week ago she'd been firing the engine for the teenagers. Her biggest problem was how she was going to find out about her erstwhile relative of these parts. That problem appeared to have been buried under a ton of other problems. Not least what she was going to do about Morgan, and how she could prevent the inspector locking her up for murdering her ex!

Reality surfaced here, and she addressed an indifferent sheep who had her head stuck through the fencing and was nibbling on the grass verge. 'Of course he can't lock me up. I didn't murder the man, and I don't know what he was doing around here. Morgan's a different problem, though.'

The sheep continued to kneel and nibble without deigning to take any notice. She had her own problems, like how she was going to remove her head from this gap when she'd eaten her fill of this tasty grass.

'Yeah, that's what I did, stuck my head where I shouldn't, to try if the grass was greener, and look where it got me.' The sheep gave a wiggle and managed to get up on all four hoofs, she had stopped eating in favour of escape from this mad human who kept talking to her.

Willow went forward, intending to give a hand, but the sheep suddenly gave a twitch and loosed the hold that the fence had on her. She pulled away and, with a little whisk of her tail, trotted away across the field.

'Yeah, well, it's easy for you to say,' Willow muttered as she watched the animals moving around. 'I'm a human.' She turned and headed back towards home.

SUNDAY HAD BEEN PEACEFUL too, until her landlady had returned from Chapel with the Sunday papers. Dilys Jones was bursting with news; her chest heaving, causing the slightly exotic ruffled blouse she was wearing to strain and flap like sails in a gale.

'My dear, they've found another body in the estuary.' She'd barely got through the door before she started talking to Willow. 'It's all in the Sunday papers! Just fancy, two bodies in less than two weeks.'

Willow, startled from her comfortable half doze next to the Raeburn, shot the cat and her book off her knee, in some confusion at this sudden entrance. Mrs Jones continued to chatter as she trotted around the kitchen filling and switching on the kettle, opening cupboards and putting biscuits on a plate.

'Fair bowled me over seeing our Cob in a Sunday paper. Here, look!' She thrust the paper which she'd been carrying around under her arm into Willow's hand, and went across to the side to get mugs for the tea. A rather muffled, 'Page five,' came from the depths of the fridge whither she had gone to fetch the milk jug.

Willow obediently turned the pages until she came to a picture of the police screen she'd seen on Friday, shielding part of the Cob.

Dilys Jones came over bearing the big blue teapot and still wearing her hat. She looked as though she'd got a particularly active bird of paradise perching on her hair. 'I've not read more than the headlines coming home. Read what it says, Willow, I haven't got my glasses on.' Willow obediently spread the broadsheet out and began to read aloud, while her landlady poured tea and finally came to rest on the wooden chair opposite.

'The police, while undertaking investigations into the death of well known playboy and entrepreneur Mr Barry Scott, discovered a World War One weapon on the foreshore. Mr Scott's body was discovered by his ex-girlfriend, Miss Willow Edwards, last week. The body had been in the Llyn for at least a week according to the coroner's inquest. Mr Scott had been staying in Pwlleli. His car was taken away for forensic investigation from outside the hotel where he had engaged rooms for several days. Police would not say if they had further information as to why he was in the area, or how his corpse came to be found further down the coast at Porthmadog.'

Willow looked up, round eyed, at an equally surprised Dilys Jones. 'I didn't know they'd found his car. That wasn't mentioned at the inquest!'

She turned back to the paper, running her finger down the print until she found the new paragraph. "The fierce winds over the past week have eroded part of the famous Cob which divides the Estuary from the sea. This was built by'...' Willow paused, muttering to herself. 'There's a bit of a history lesson about the MP William Madocks and his grand plan, including a potted history of the railway here.'

'Well, skip that bit. Get to the bit about the body the headline talks about.'

'OK.' Willow obligingly scanned down the page. 'Here we go. 'Subsequent to the finding of the weapon, a Colt 45, which we understand is WW1 American issue, a smell was noted which caused the police to investigate further. Police located a toolbox which had previously been buried in the side of the Cob wall and had become exposed due to the action of wind and waves upon the edifice. This is not the first time the Cob has been undermined. In 1927 a previous storm breached the Cob and caused serious damage to the foundations in this area'.'

Willow looked up. 'Wow!'

'What do they say about the body though?'

Willow took up the tale again. 'They say, 'A badly decomposed body was found in the box, much of it skeletonised but having some adipocere attached to the limbs and part of the face'. Oh! Yuck!' Willow pulled a face.

'What's that then, that adipo stuff?'

Willow swallowed a sip of tea to moisten her dry throat, 'Sometimes when bodies are buried the fat turns to a sort of wax instead of rotting away. Especially if the body isn't underground but is in an enclosed space.' She felt slightly sick remembering the state of Barry's body the previous week, but swallowed and turned back to the news-sheet fascinated, despite herself, by the gory details.

'The body was removed on Tuesday for further investigation and an autopsy. A police spokesman stated that the body was male. This was determined by the clothing that remained. Age was difficult to establish at present. The cause of death was as yet undetermined, but given the circumstances foul play was strongly suspected. When pressed, the Police stated that some marks had been found on the body which might help in establishing its identity.''

Willow looked at her landlady. 'Well, at least the inspector can't say I'm involved in this murder! I wonder what they meant by marks?'

'Nasty piece of work that inspector, I'll give him a piece of my mind if he comes calling here with his insinuations.' Mrs Jones hadn't taken to the reports of the inquest, in the papers; she had taken it as a personal affront that anyone could think her lodger could be capable of anything as horrible as a murder, and said so at great length to anyone she could get to listen.

Dilys Jones looked at the earnest face across from her and reached out a hand to the one holding down the paper. 'Don't you fret, *Cariad*. You wait till I see that Gareth ap Rhys, allowing that Inspector to carry on that way.'

Willow looked startled, but then gently withdrew the hand. 'It's not Sergeant Rhys' fault. He was just doing his job, and he can't be blamed for the Inspector's bad manners.'

'Well, he ought to be able to do something.' The feathers waved up and down as her landlady nodded her head vigorously.

'What else does it say, *Cariad*?' She continued nodding her head, rather like a nodding dog in the back of a car window, as Willow read the account so far.

'They think they can date the burial to the storm damage of '27.' She looked up at the face peering short-sightedly down at the print under her hand. 'Its funny you know, I've been trying to find out about that storm for a week now, and no-one much seemed to know anything about it. Now this reporter has ferreted out a heap of information for me.'

'What did you want to know about the storm then? My Mam told me all about it. It was just after the general strike and they had lots of incomers looking for work in the town. She ran a B and B too, and she got lodgers aplenty. She said she was so grateful, because times were so hard, but the storm gave a lot of people around here extra work.'

Willow gazed at the kindly face, lost for words; here she'd been staying with the woman for months and never thought to ask her about the letters. Maybe because it had seemed a bit too much like letting down her defences, but she could have found out so much if she'd only trusted the woman.

She opened her mouth and then closed it again while she marshalled her thoughts, and Mrs Jones poured more tea and lit a cigarette, waiting curiously for her to speak.

'I seem to have been saying this all this week, but my relatives come from this area. Since my mother died a couple of

284

years ago I've been trying to find any remaining relatives that might live round here. I haven't got many clues, just some letters addressed to my Granddad from his elder brother.'

Coming to a decision she stood up, pushing back her chair. 'Maybe you'd like to see them. I'll go and fetch them, shall I?'

Dilys, revealing a set of teeth that were a credit to the national health, smiled broadly. 'I'll make us a fresh pot of tea, *Cariad*. I do like mysteries.'

She headed towards the sink to fill the kettle as Willow went up the stairs to fetch the plastic folder containing letters and other documents that she'd found in the shoe box after her mother's death.

Coming down with them in her hand she halted on the second step as the knocker banged. She hurried through to the kitchen, a distinct reluctance to open the door, and a feeling of dread pursuing her. She paused just inside the kitchen door as she heard the knocker bang again. Dilys Jones was just seating herself. She squinted over the smoke floating up from her newly lighted cigarette and rose, like a surprised pheasant in the heather, emitting a squawk of annoyance. 'That better not be any journalists come to bother you.'

She marched out of the room, a ferocious glint in her eye and her hat at a slightly crooked angle. She returned beaming. 'Here's your young man, *Cariad*!'

To say that Willow was dumfounded would be gross a misrepresentation of the facts. She gazed at the apparition that was Morgan with a stunned look on her face. Morgan smiled grimly across the cosy kitchen. He noted both the look and the fact that she was reading the same paper he had been privileged to receive with his early morning cup of tea.

As her brain began to function again Willow saw that he was dressed very casually for him; indigo jeans and a wheat coloured Aran jumper were revealed under a heavy casual jacket of dark blue. His hair was loose and curled riotously around his ears. He also didn't appear to have shaved. This in itself was enough to leave her wondering.

'Hi, *Cariad*.' He nodded at Willow, then looked at Mrs Jones. 'Any tea left in that pot?'

Dilys Jones, alerted to the fact that she had been staring at the couple with unabashed curiosity, now edged round his bulk and went to the cupboard to get another mug and fill it from the teapot, as Morgan sauntered, apparently serenely, forward and pulled out a chair, seating himself casually and possessing himself of one of Willow's slack hands as they lay on the table top.

'I thought I'd come back for the Guy Fawkes party at Deniol's tonight and I needed a partner to take.' He offered a lopsided smile, belied by the cautious look in the deep blue eyes partly veiled by his lashes.

Willow was regaining her wits and trying to surreptitiously remove her hand from the light grip. 'Have you come from London? You must have set out awfully early to be here now. It's only,' she glanced at her watch, 'a quarter to twelve.'

Woman-like she was beginning to realise that she was dressed in an old pair of jeans which looked as though they had been bought too small and shrunk in the wash. Her body was outlined in a jumper that, while clean, was faded to an indifferent shade of green, and her hair was hanging round her head like a veil. She thought she looked even scruffier than usual. She looked at the rather stern profile and realised why she had been so lonely. Apparently you didn't necessarily need to lose your appetite to be in love after all. What on earth was she going to do about that, she thought.

Reflecting on the frustration of his meeting with her on Thursday, Morgan thought she looked gorgeous. He smiled beatifically at her then sipped at the hot brew, while he freshened the pictures he'd carried in his mind against the beauty in front of his face.

He set the mug down carefully, reaching for the other hand with which Willow had been vainly trying to tidy her hair and pull her jumper down at the same time; she'd only succeeded in drawing his attention to her rather nice bust. She became aware of that fact when he removed his gaze from her face to see what she was doing and then looked back at her with a definite, and possessive, male glint in his eye.

Willow felt herself growing warm and blushing to the roots of her hair. Morgan thought she was adorable. 'I set out fairly early, yes, but then it's a nice day for a drive through the Welsh countryside.'

Since the wind was howling in the chimney and it was shaping up to be a typical fifth of November, with small spatters of rain hitting the window pane, this was patently untrue, but being delivered in a voice bland enough to paper walls, the two women accepted the statement, for the time being.

Dilys had been watching the pair of them and now she broke her silence. 'Willow was just telling me her relatives come from 'round this area, Mr Williams. She's searching for them.' She paused to stub out her cigarette in the ashtray in the centre of the table, then got up to empty it into the bin under the sink. She swung round, 'We've been reading about the body in the Cob too. Did you see the story, Mr Williams?'

Morgan looked across at the shrewd old face. 'Oh! Yes, I saw it at breakfast, it's very interesting.'

He didn't want the women dwelling on the newspaper just at the moment. He looked at the plastic folder that Willow had dropped on the table at his entrance. 'What were you doing then?' He nudged a blunt finger against the plastic and drew Willow's attention back to him. She had been busy speculating on his presence. Had he come to tell her he had changed his mind, despite what he said on Thursday?

Willow, recalled to the present, looked across at his smiling face. 'Oh! I was going to show Mrs Jones some letters I'd got. They're all in Welsh. I don't know much about them except that they were written by my great-uncle Tudor. There's a picture of him too.'

She pulled open the folder and carefully removed the faded documents. Setting aside the hand written notepaper she unfolded a piece of newspaper. It had obviously been cut out of an old Daily, and the creases deep across the middle showed it had been treasured and preserved with care. Unfolding it tenderly Willow revealed half a dozen young men, standing in old fashioned waistcoats and round necked shirts, sleeves rolled up to the elbows and with shovels standing at port arms over their shoulders, the flat caps as much as the background an indication of the period in which the photo had been taken. The background was obviously the railway station at Porthmadog. Morgan could see a few sailing masts in the background.

'I don't know when or why it was taken.' Willow smoothed the paper with a delicate hand. 'But the names are underneath and that one,' she indicated one robust specimen with her finger, 'is my great-uncle. The one with the watch chain. There are names underneath, but he looks just like early photos of my Granddad anyway.'

Morgan reached out a hand. 'Can I look?'

Taking her agreement for granted he picked up the flimsy paper delicately between finger and thumb. He looked closely at the picture, comparing the young man's profile with the one so close to him. 'You favour him around the eyes and mouth a little.' He focused on the newsprint, turning it over. The back was advertising a film. 'Well, that ought to give us a clue.'

He scanned the fine script, translating the Welsh as he read it out aloud to the two women. 'Come and see the brand new talky at Caernarfon Odeon. Just released. We are privileged to have one of the first copies of this brand new film with the spoken word. Al Jolson sings and dances with verve.' He turned the paper over and laid it carefully down so that the eager young men were once more on display.

'Unfortunately the date and time have been trimmed away. But we could look to find out the release date of 'The Jazz Singer'. That might help us find the newspaper this was printed in, Willow.'

Willow nodded eagerly. 'Deniol looked at a couple of the letters for me last week when we ...' she broke off, sliding a glance at Dilys, an avid listener, gave a slight cough and continued, 'er, when we had a little time together. But he couldn't follow some of the Welsh. He said it was old fashioned.'

Morgan picked up the letter she offered him, beginning to read the curly script as she continued to speak. 'That's got the earliest date on it; Deniol said there was something about Australia.'

'Is there, *Cariad*? Well, let me start at the top. It's obviously in reply to a previous letter. He hopes their Mam is finally over the flu. *And the P.O. for ten shillings,*' Morgan looked up 'I suppose he means postal order,' he turned back to the page, '*is for Mam, even though she will be getting the new government pension now*. Which he seems mighty pleased about.'

'Would that help us find her records, Morgan?'

'Well, it might. I don't know what the new pension was,' he said cautiously. 'Then he goes on, '*The silver threepenny bit stuck on the back is for Hywel.*"

He turned to the back page of the letter, discovering a blob of candle wax. 'I wonder what he spent it on? Would that be your grandfather then, *Cariad*?'

'Yes, he was quite a bit younger than great-uncle Tudor; my granddad was born in 1916. Great-uncle Tudor fought in the Great War. I know that.'

'Well, there might have been an age gap but they were evidently close. This bit is about a football match they'd both been to, at Wembley, with a guy called Seamus, to watch the Welsh win.' Morgan looked up with a huge smile on his face. 'Do you know what that would have been? The first time we beat the English on their own turf. The Welsh won the cup final. My God,' he breathed deeply, 'this is pure gold. A letter from someone who was actually there!'

Willow looked in fascination at the glow on his face. 'Er, yeah!' She tried to sound enthusiastic, but football wasn't her game and ancient football held even less interest. She obviously didn't succeed very well.

Morgan, recalled to his senses by the slightly dry tone, just grinned at her. 'But that gives us a date, *Cariad*. All good Welshmen know when we won the cup. St George's Day, 1927, which made the winning all the sweeter.' He looked back at the paper. 'Anyway Tudor and Seamus had taken your granddad to the game, and now Seamus is back in Ireland. But he hopes to join Tudor again, working on the dock.'

Willow picked up the newspaper picture. 'There's a Seamus Donovan standing next to my great uncle on this picture. Don't they look young?' Morgan looked at the flimsy sheet she held, and the pointing finger indicating another moustached man. He appeared to be dark haired in the grainy photo and had gaiters on his lower trouser legs.

'Well they can't have been that young if he fought in the War.' Morgan gently laid aside the photo. He turned over the first page and scanned down the next. 'Most of the rest is just general news about what he's doing, he had found lodgings at the Minffordd Workhouse and some job, dry stone walling at one of the local farms. They were paying him twenty five shillings a week. That's er... ' Morgan gazed into space a moment.

Mrs Jones, who had remained remarkably silent, suddenly said, 'One pound five shillings, about one pound twenty-five pence.' She nodded across the table. 'And he was sending some home to his Mam. He must have been a nice boy.'

Morgan and Willow exchanged amused glances; they had almost forgotten her presence in their pursuit of the information in the letter. Morgan smiled. 'Quite right.'

Dilys moved in her seat. 'I must get on; the joint will be done to charcoal. Will you stop and eat, Mr Williams?' She pushed back her chair and stood looking across the table at him. He looked across at Willow asking silently what she wanted to do.

Willow smiled across then, at his nod, turned to Mrs Jones. 'We'd love that but we'd really love to carry on with this.'

'Well, you'd better take it into the front room. You don't want grease and such on those letters.'

Morgan gathered up the letters and Willow picked up the folder. 'We'll let you know what we find out.' She all but skipped out of the room, the Sunday newspaper lying forgotten on the table. Dilys gathered it up and stowed it in the newspaper rack next to her knitting, beside the Raeburn. Then she turned to the far more important business of getting lunch ready.

Willow led the way into the small front sitting room. Every flat surface had photographs, from snapshots to portrait size. They displayed Mrs Jones' progeny as they had progressed from infancy to marriage and children of their own.

Morgan gazed in some awe at the display. 'How many children has she got?' He whispered it, looking back over his shoulder at the open door.

'I don't know. I've never managed to count. They seem to come in all shapes and sizes, and I can't seem to get the names straight in my mind long enough to separate them out.' She giggled at his face.

Morgan turned from shutting the door and just stood looking at the enchanting and very sexy picture she made standing amid the very latest in leather three piece suites.

He advanced purposefully towards her, dropping the letters on the settee, and made a quick grab which elicited a faint squeak, before he was kissing her somewhat desperately. 'God, I missed you!' He lifted his head and held her tightly, his cheek resting against her hair. Willow, slightly breathless, clung on just as tightly; she was a bit afraid if she let go she might fall over.

Morgan looked down at her, and then abruptly sat down, pulling her onto his knee. Willow uttered another tiny squeak. 'Morgan, what are you doing?'

Morgan, ignoring this, pulled her more firmly onto his knee.

'What if Mrs Jones comes in?'

'Well, with this number of children she'll know exactly what I'm doing. I'm making love to you.' He then proceeded to demonstrate that Mrs Dilys Jones wasn't the only one to have mastered the practical aspects of lovemaking. Willow emerged from his embrace several minutes later, her heart pounding, and very short of breath.

Morgan settled back and looked at her dishevelled state somewhat smugly. She looked very... he searched for the right word and decided 'loved' would have to do for now. He stroked down the long honey-gold hair, feeling its silky softness sliding over his palm. 'You do know I love you, don't you, darling?'

Willow, who had been trying to get her brain back in gear, found her thoughts promptly scattered in a burst of rainbow sparks as Morgan claimed her lips, the warm soft mouth devastating in its demand for a response which, try as she might, she couldn't resist giving back.

Morgan found that one kiss was never going to be enough and one touch far too many. He wanted her to the point it would soon become apparent to them both if she didn't get off his lap. He found he was almost incapable of thinking in English any more, and that he was muttering words of endearment in his mother tongue as he planted small kisses across her jaw-line and down her white throat.

Willow wasn't in any better case. She felt incapable of saying anything at all. She felt she ought not to be allowing him to hold her in quite such an intimate way, but didn't know how to stop him, or even if she wanted to stop him.

Morgan made a determined effort to pull himself together, sitting up and planting a butterfly kiss on her nose. He reluctantly removed his hands from the warm flesh above her waist, before straightening the green jumper. 'Nevertheless, I'm not going to give lessons.'

'Eh?' Willow gave him a very puzzled look.

'I'm not giving lessons on how to make love, to Mrs Jones. Let her figure it out for herself.' He gently slid Willow onto the settee next to him. 'If we don't stop now, *Cariad,* I might find myself seriously embarrassed.' He grinned at her, but couldn't resist kissing her again. 'Enough! I'm beginning to feel quite drunk.' He looked at her flushed face. 'What's more I ought to have shaved.' He ran a gentle finger across her cheekbone, 'I've marked you.'

'It's alright, I don't mind.' Her voice was slightly husky. But the luminescent eyes spoke clearly for her. She couldn't quite bring herself to say those three magic words, just in case it was all a dream, but Morgan reading the expression felt satisfied, for now.

He moved slightly, trying to ease the fit of his jeans, and became aware of a crackling of paper. 'Whoops! I've sat on the letters.'

He stood up and picked them up, carefully smoothing out the new creases that his weight had put into them.

'I think we'd better look at these some more, it's probably safer for now.' He looked at her lovingly, and then turned determinedly to the task in hand; sorting out the closely written sheets, putting them into chronological order, then put an arm around her shoulders and pulled her close while he started to read the next epistle aloud to her.

'You know, as a snapshot of world events in Wales after the war these are fascinating.' He laid down the third letter. 'Your great uncle seems to have been interested in people all over the world though, and determined that his little brother should share that interest. This is the letter that talks about Australia and the new town of Canberra and how they had built the town especially in the middle of the outback just for that purpose. He'd evidently met some Aussies for he says... ' Morgan turned over the last page,

> "*I thought them splendid chaps in the trenches, so brave when facing the bloody Jerries, so I suppose building a town in the middle of the desert just so that they can have their own parliament is all of a piece with their character.*"

Morgan grinned. 'He's not very politically correct, but then we hadn't learnt that particular idiosyncrasy back then. He continues:

> *'Can you imagine the kangaroos, Hywel, bouncing around outside the windows with the black fellas, while inside they decide if it's alright to knock down the slums in Sydney. I'm going to see that someday, Hywel, and I'll take you with me.''*

Morgan paused. 'Do you know if he did go?'

Willow shook her head. 'I don't know, but if he did he didn't take my Granddad with him. My Granddad never left the shores of Britain. He was a train driver same as my great-granddad, and he acted as a fire watcher in the Second World War, didn't even get called up to go to France.'

Morgan bent over the next letter. 'Well, your great-uncle went back to France. This one makes sad reading. He's writing from Ypres at the opening of the Menin Gate.

> *''It was a stupid war, so many of my mates' names are on this gate. It doesn't seem right, Mam, that this is all they get for being killed and tortured and maimed for their country.*

"Seamus is very bitter about the way the Irish have been treated, even if King George has changed his title and they have an Irish Free State now. Seamus doesn't think it will make much difference. If I never use a gun again I'll be happy, but Seamus still wants revenge. He's with me now. He came across from Ireland and he's full of the talk about the Oath of Allegiance. I think he might be working for the IRA; it's the only thing we can't agree on.

"I know some of your friends wonder why I'm alive and their sons aren't but I thank God I am. At least we can give Hywel a better life. If nothing better comes from it than that I shall be happy, Mam."

Willow looked at Morgan as he continued to read. Would Morgan have fought in the stupid war, and would he have thought it stupid?

Morgan leaned over and kissed the soft cheek, 'He must have loved his brother a lot, darling.' He laid aside the letter and turned, taking her in his arms again and indulging them both in a long and very satisfying kiss. This interlude was interrupted by Mrs Jones rattling the door knob in a very ostentatious manner before entering.

Morgan kept his arm firmly round the now blushing Willow as he smiled across at her landlady.

'Would you like to come to your lunch then?'

The hat had gone, back to its box on the top shelf of the wardrobe presumably; the hair was confined in a brown net, *a la* Ena Sharples, but the pinny was the Sunday one, not the all encompassing paisley of mid week, but a pretty shade of blue with lace around the edges. The twin-set and fake pearls proclaimed that this was a day of, as near rest, as she could make it.

Morgan stood up, bringing Willow up with him. 'We'll be right through, Mrs Jones. Thank you.'

The meal was delicious, a nice joint of pork, the crackling scored and crispy, flavoured with Welsh honey, the roast potatoes fluffy and the sticky toffee pudding fit to make an aesthete drool. Little had been said while the business of eating was going on.

However, now that Mrs Jones had cleared away the dishes and set the teapot back on the table she looked over at the pair and with a decided twinkle and asked, 'Did you manage to discover where your great-uncle went, then?' She paused and arched an eyebrow. 'Or were you too busy?' Her lips twitched as she observed the grin on Morgan's face, and the flush on Willow's.

Morgan, however, rescued Willow from embarrassment by drawing the landlady's fire and telling her what they had discovered. 'We haven't finished yet, but he was definitely living in this area in 1927.'

'Well that's good, Willow. I'll let you get on with it while I do the dishes.' She made to stand but Morgan waved her back.

'Oh, we'll wash up. After that delicious meal you deserve a sit down.' He and Willow stood up and Willow began to fill the sink with water while Dilys Jones beamed all over her face at the compliment and went to sit next to the stove.

She picked up the cat and sat down, drawing out the paper and opening it to the crossword. 'Drat, I've forgotten my glasses again.' She stuffed the paper back into the rack and pulled out the knitting. 'I don't need glasses for this,' she remarked, waving a piece of knitting which was apparently being accomplished using a couple of pieces of dowelling.

'Megan said she wanted a sloppy jumper for Christmas with the new fluffy wool they've got in the Penrhyn shop. It's knitting up really quickly.' To the accompaniment of soft clicks they washed up and, before they had finished, the even softer sibilant hiss of an elderly lady enjoying a post-prandial nap.

The pair stole away to the other room, gathering up the letters and putting them away carefully in the folder. Morgan drew Willow close, his arms wrapped round her waist as he looked down at her. 'So, *Cariad*, will you come and celebrate Guy

Fawkes Night? They're having a bonfire down on the shore near the station. You can renew your acquaintance with Gwyneth.'

Willow smiled up, tipping her head back to look into his eyes. 'Yes, I'll come, but I've already renewed my acquaintance with that imp.'

'Have you now? Tell me more.' Willow thought she saw just a shadow of reserve cross over his face, then decided she must have been mistaken as he smiled down at her.

'Well, I went into town, because Deniol had said he would help me translate the letters, and I got there too early. But Gwyneth and her Grandfather, Evan - do you know him?' At Morgan's nod she carried on as they left the room. 'Well, Evan was with Gwyneth and they invited me in for a *panad*.'

They peeped in the kitchen door, but Dilys Jones was still sleeping contentedly beside the Raeburn. The cat gave them a slit eyed look but didn't move from his place on her knee. 'Shall we leave a note? I need to find some accommodation.'

Willow scrabbled in the folder for the notebook she'd been making jottings in and Morgan wrote quickly in his bold firm hand. 'Gone to a bonfire celebration. Back later.' He signed a quick MW and they tiptoed out again.

'Let's take the letters with us. We're bound to see Deniol tonight. He was really interested, and Evan said he'd ask at the over sixties club on Friday night for me. To see if he could find out more about the Big Crane.'

'Oh, your great-uncle talks about the crane does he?' Morgan swung her hand with his as they walked towards his car in the damp November mist. It had a least stopped raining, but the wind was bitter and as they settled into their seats Morgan turned up the heating.

With a quick word of apology he pulled out his mobile and flicked it open. It was evidently pre-programmed as he didn't put in any numbers; he just waited for an answer and then spoke into the little machine.

'Can I book for several nights, please?' He paused then, listening to the reply; the news was presumably good since he gave his details before saying, 'I hope to be there later this evening. Right, thank you.' He flipped it shut. 'Well at least I have a bed to sleep in tonight.'

Willow, an interested listener, was digesting the fact that he'd said several nights. She wasn't sure how she felt about that, he seemed to be forever nudging her equilibrium so that her emotions teetered like a top on an uneven surface, never sure if she was going to stop, or just fall off into despair and lose herself.

Morgan turned the key and the big car purred into life as he picked up their previous conversation. 'Do you know what he said about the crane?'

'No. Deniol read a bit about it not going under a bridge, and Evan said he thought he knew which crane it was, and if he was right he had a photo of it in a magazine.'

Morgan shot her a quick look. 'Now that I'd like to see. If it's what I think it was, it was one of Colonel Stevens's mad ideas.'

'What? The Colonel that used to run the Ffestiniog?'

'Yeah. That's the man. He was Managing Director, and good at his job, but he didn't always consult the board or the men before he did things. One of the things he did was buy this great big monster of a crane. He was going to send it up the line to help with the loading at the Glaslyn slate wharves but it wouldn't go under Rhiw Plas Bridge. So then he ordered the track lowered under the bridge, but that's solid rock under there so he got an impolite, no.' Morgan chuckled, and Willow laughed with him.

'Anyway the upshot was this great big unwieldy thing, which couldn't do the job it was intended for, was literally put out to grass up there at Boston Lodge.' He nodded up at the works as they swept past in the dusk that was closing in.

'I believe they sold it to a slate quarry sometime during the Second World War. Probably at a financial loss, but it was no real loss to the railway.' Morgan swung the Jaguar across the traffic as they came off the Cob and headed down a side street. 'We'll put the car in the main car park out of the way, and walk. If that's OK with you?'

He took her agreement for granted, parking at the back of the main town and getting out, coming round and opening

Willow's door. He took a hand and swung her round, buttoning up her heavy jacket as if she was a small child as she stood before him. Then he cupped her face in his two hands, his breath warm against her face in the frosty air. 'I love you. You won't forget will you?' He kissed her.

Willow responded unthinkingly, allowing him to deepen the kiss, her hands going around his shoulders, unconsciously playing with the hair curling over her fingers.

'You are so beautiful.' Morgan rested his forehead against hers.

Willow said nothing. She was in way over her head, and achingly aware that every time they kissed she was admitting to Morgan the feelings she hadn't managed to put into words.

Morgan smiled softly down at her. 'Come on, let's go and find some sparklers to contribute to the celebration.' He took a hand and they walked towards the town centre to see if they could find a paper shop open on this wet Sunday afternoon.

Twenty minutes later Morgan was burdened with a huge box which he carted in both hands towards Deniol's house. 'You knock, *Cariad*; my hands are a bit full.' He grinned at himself, while he stated the obvious.

'Well, you would buy half the shop.'

'It isn't half the shop, it's just our contribution. And anyway, the poor man would have been left with surplus stock tomorrow.'

Willow snorted, 'Huh! Says you!'

The door swung open to reveal a surprised Eirlys. 'Morgan, *sut wyt ti.*' She looked kindly at Willow. 'Hello, Willow.'

'Gwyneth invited us to the bonfire, so here we are.' He winked down at the small child who had come to stand next to her mother. Gwyneth stretched out a hand and took hold of Willow's. 'You came.' There was no doubt of her welcome.

Eirlys opened the door wide and Morgan manoeuvred his way through with the box. 'Take it through to the kitchen, Morgan. David's in there conferring with Evan and Deniol.'

Morgan disappeared and Willow was left marooned on the mat while Gwyneth swung from her arm like a pendulum.

'Gwyneth,' Eirlys spoke to the child, 'let go and let Willow take off her coat. You'd like a *panad* to warm you up, Willow?'

Willow nodded, smiling shyly. Then Gwyneth was towing her to the coat hooks as Eirlys disappeared into the back room too.

'I'm pleased you camed, Willow. Deniol got me a whole packet of sparklers, and *Taid* bought me a new hat to keep my ears warm.' She showed off the blue hat which had a rope of plaited wool coming from the crown and a bell attached to the bottom of the rope. This was duly admired before Gwyneth took her hand and led her towards the settee.

Willow sat down and Gwyneth climbed up, snuggling down on her lap. 'I'm glad Uncle Morgan camed too, are you?'

Willow looked down at the smiling face. 'Oh yes, darling.'

'I've got a photo of him to mind me when he's not here.' She wriggled down and went over to the bureau, coming back with a nice portrait-sized photo of Morgan standing with two young boys and holding a toddler of about three. 'That's me and Deniol and Twm.' The little finger gentle, brushed the photo.

Willow, looking, saw sadly that Twm was bald. She'd seen too many other young children with the signs of chemo to make the mistake of thinking he was making a fashion statement.

Gwyneth carefully put the photo back and settled back on Willow's knee.

'I love Uncle Morgan. We stayed in his house in London this summer. I went to see the Queen's house too. Hers is even bigger than Uncle Morgan's and she's got sodyers outside her gate. It was nice at Uncle Morgan's; his housekeeper's got a cat. Do you like cats, Willow?'

Willow nodded. 'My landlady's got a cat. It's called Fluffy.' While part of her mind was talking about cats, another part was wondering about the artless revelations of her little friend.

Morgan came back in at this, perhaps judicious, moment, bearing two mugs of tea. 'Hey, are you stealing my kisses, Willow?' He looked down at the pair sitting on the settee and placed the mugs on an occasional table. Gwyneth immediately got off Willow's knee and stood next to him offering a rosy face for kisses. 'I got lots of kisses; but you have to share Uncle Morgan.'

Morgan bent down and scooped the little girl up, planting kisses across her face and tickling her as he swung round to sit down next to Willow. 'Has Willow got to share too?'

'Yes.'

Morgan leant across and stole a quick kiss from Willow's lips before she realised his intentions. 'Mmm and very nice they are too.'

His eyes twinkled as he looked across Gwyneth's head at Willow.

He stretched out a hand for the mug as Gwyneth settled into his lap. 'Sit still, *Cariad*. You don't want to get burnt.'

Willow looked at the pair and tried not to think how he'd look with a child of theirs. She would have been astonished to know that his thoughts were running along the same lines, except that he was imagining it and found his heart was running at top speed at the thought.

'Evan will be through in a minute. I was telling him about the letters. He says he's found the photograph of the crane, but no-one at the club remembers any more than he does about it.'

The small room was suddenly crowded with people as grandfather, father and son all came in, talking rapidly in Welsh.

It appeared to be a heated argument. They all stopped waving their arms about long enough to acknowledge the presence of Willow, before starting again and involving Morgan in their dispute.

Morgan answered something lazily, as he sat cuddling the little girl, and then turned to Willow. 'They can't agree on the venue. There's a bonfire down on Porthmadog beach but there'll be another one at Black Rocks.' He slanted a quick glance at Gwyneth, then an oblique warning glance from the trio to Willow and back. 'I would like to go to Black Rocks. I think there'll be a lot of people around the Cob, in view of the papers this morning.' He smiled a trifle bleakly at the men.

They stopped speaking, looking first at Willow and then at him like spectators at a tennis match. 'Hmm you could be right, Morgan.' Evan caught on quicker than the other two, and said softly to him in Welsh, 'They've taken the corpse away to Liverpool General.'

Gwyneth looked from her granddad to Morgan, speaking in Welsh. She spoke in that language too. 'Taid, what's a corpse?'

Morgan shook his head, glanced at Evan in a slightly horror-stricken way and then answered the small girl honestly. 'Someone who's died, darling. But it's alright, they've taken him away to the hospital, but Willow's my girlfriend, and I want to look after her, and she doesn't like corpses.'

'OK, Uncle Morgan.' Gwyneth nodded soberly, then smiled up into his face. 'I don't either.'

While Willow was trying to follow the play, Eirlys came back in. 'Don't be rude, *Tad*, Morgan, - Willow doesn't speak the Welsh, yet.'

LATER THAT NIGHT, AFTER she was tucked up in her bed, Willow made the resolution that she would speak Welsh very soon. Everyone had spoken English after Eirlys' quiet rebuke, but there had been an undercurrent of emotions and unspoken things that she didn't have the key to.

They had had toast and fruit cake and Gwyneth had dipped her toast in an egg. Then they had all gone down to the beach and joined a crowd of families enjoying the bonfire. It had been rather different from the bonfires that Willow remembered from her childhood.

The juxtaposition of the waves steadily stealing up the beach, with its repetition of stones rattling as the surf pulled them, protesting, ever deeper into the water, and the crackle of the driftwood as it burned and gave off the occasional blue flame when it hit a pocket of salty wood, was a bit surreal.

Morgan had devoted himself to the little girl and helped her with her sparklers. They'd watched the rockets shooting up to join the drift of sparks in the clear frosty sky. The rocks had glowed an unearthly red in the reflected glory of the bonfire and Willow had sniffed the mixture of cordite and smoke and thoroughly enjoyed herself.

Gwyneth had 'Oohed' and 'Aahed' at Catherine wheels and finally fallen asleep on her grandfather's shoulder, worn out by the sights, with a thumb securely in her mouth. Morgan and Willow had driven Evan and the little girl home, and seen her settled in her bed, before coming down stairs again to drink tea and await the arrival of the rest of the family.

Evan, coming back through with a tray of mugs, smiled slyly at the pair sitting on the settee. Morgan had contrived to get an arm round Willow's waist and pulled her close for a quick kiss. Willow found herself blushing under the combined look from their eyes.

'Isn't she pretty?' Morgan stroked a cheek and sat back. '*Diolch.*' He accepted the mug as Evan grinned at the pair of them. Willow looked anywhere but at Deniol's grandfather as she accepted her mug.

'Have you brought the letters with you, Willow?' Evan took pity on Willow and changed the subject.

Willow set down her mug and fished for her shoulder bag at her feet. 'Oh! Yes, here you go. It's this one that talks about the crane, I think.'

The two men bent over the fine script, reading out bits from different letters to each other. Willow noticed the same glow come into Evan's eyes at the mention of the Cup final.

'I thought all you Welshmen were rugby men.'

'Oh we are, *Cariad*, except when we're football men.' Morgan grinned at her.

'This Seamus who keeps cropping up sounds a bit of a rebel.' remarked Evan.

Willow pulled out the newspaper cutting and showed him the picture of the young men. He peered at it short-sightedly then got up and, pulling open a bureau, searched in the top, coming back with a magnifying glass. 'Well, and he looks a rebel too.'

'Which one is your great uncle Tudor then, Willow?' She pointed him out and Evan held the glass over it, making the picture separate into individual dots before he got the focus right. 'Yes, I can see the resemblance now.' He passed both glass and picture to Morgan. After a few minutes of study Morgan looked at Willow. 'Yeah, I can see the resemblance too. I think it's the moustache and the tattoo on the left arm that do it.'

Willow punched the arm nearest to her as they all laughed, then the door swung open and the family returned, bringing with them a whiff of sulphur and Sian, who had gone to the bonfire in their company.

The rest of the evening had been spent in reminiscing by Evan, and questions fired at him from the two youngsters. Altogether a lovely time, thought Willow sleepily.

10

Gareth ap Rhys hadn't had such a good time celebrating his Guy Fawkes Night, but he had spent time in the enjoyable pursuit of writing a letter. He smiled to himself as he settled with pen and paper. Why, he pondered as he inscribed his girl's name, did writing to someone bring them so much closer? Then he smiled and acknowledged that bringing Claire closer wasn't a problem, missing her was.

'Dearest darling Claire, I miss you, I just wanted to tell you. This has been such a sad week. Not just the weather, which is horrible. But the cases I've had to deal with. Two in particular last week, reminded me of how lucky I am to have you as my girl.

'The first was a young man, who was found drowned in the estuary. We don't know yet how he came to be there, but the inspector, who never tell's yours truly much, is determined that it's going to be accidental. Either that or he's going to pin the crime on the nearest subject, whether they did it or not. And that's before the PM or anything else. Your dad never does that,

jumping to conclusions. They've found out a little about the man now. He wasn't a very nice man, he beat up his girlfriend, and she either can't, or doesn't know how, to feel sorry that he's dead. It must be terrible not to be missed except in a negative way.'

Gareth paused here to read back what he'd written. He frowned, putting in a few commas and full stops. Then just sat, holding the pen, and looking blankly outside at the pouring rain.

He could hear his youngest brother through the wall of their small house. It sounded as though he was simultaneously sawing through a log of wood and running a marathon. Gareth grinned. His brother was practising for the following year's clog-dancing competition at the Eisteddfod.

Gareth transferred his attention to the teeming rain again for a moment, picturing Claire. He'd come back to Gwynedd to serve his year in uniform, before starting out as a detective sergeant. Back in Cumbria, where Claire lived, the promotion would have taken a lot longer, but it was hard being apart. He hadn't been sure if he was in love with her when he left, now he was certain he was. However, he had yet to declare himself. He wanted her to have the opportunity to stretch her wings a bit before he offered marriage. And marriage it would have to be, he was sure of that too, now.

He picked up the pen which he had laid down, and started to write again. *'The other case was also a young man. He'd come to this country to find work and a new life for himself and his wife. And then he had an accident and died. His wife was heartbroken. She's expecting his baby soon. They'd pooled all their money to get him into this country, the only thing they kept was a Russian triptych, a relic of her great-grand parents. I've taken a photo for you to show to Bob McInnis. I know he's interested in those sort of things.*

'It was partly through the triptych that we traced him back to his village in Poland. His wife doesn't speak French or English. We were at a bit of a stand trying to understand where she came from, but there's a Polish community over on the Llyn so we managed to get someone to talk to her. The police here have brought her over to identify the body, and we brought in a priest for her. We've had the triptych identified too. A Russian bishop from the Orthodox Church got terribly excited. Apparently she goes back to minor royalty over in Europe.

'The British have given her a visa for the time being, and she's staying with the group of Pole's out on Ynys Mon. Her husband was loved and will be missed so much. So you see why I said it was sad, both men dead, one not missed at all, the other missed beyond bearing.

'Which brings me to why you get an extra letter this week. I have decided that I'm coming back to Cumbria as soon as I've completed my year. The Super said she would find me a job. I might have to stay in uniform a bit longer. But I'd rather do that than be here and missing you so much.'

Gareth paused again. He didn't want to declare himself in a letter. He started a new sentence. He could set her thinking with a question though.

'Would you mind if I came back without the promotion?'

He shook his head at the words on the page, told himself he was a coward, and signed it *'love Gareth',* before folding it and the photo into an envelope, and then stood holding it. He hadn't said what he wanted to, but found he couldn't express himself in English. And didn't that tell him how he really felt, he thought. He'd post it on his way to work. He was on duty tonight. He was making sure the population didn't set fire to themselves with fireworks or worse, invade the crime scene down on the foreshore. He tapped the envelope against his hand. He could have told her about their grisly find, then he shrugged, he'd save it for next week's epistle. He shoved the letter in his pocket and went clattering down the stairs to begin the late shift.

As he drove to work he was busy thinking about the next letter; wondering what he should tell Claire, and picturing her face. He wasn't that distracted that he wasn't thinking about work though. His way took him through the town of Porthmadog, on the A487. He pulled up as he approached the main British rail line at the far end of the town. Getting out of the car he followed the rail line with his eyes, before climbing back in and setting off again. He'd had an idea the day before and wondered if it fitted the facts.

It was a very long winded way to get to Penrhyn. Gareth continued on his circular route, passing through Tremadog and popping his letter in the box at the junction, before turning towards the head of the estuary. He was taking the same route that Willow had taken the previous Sunday. He pulled up on a 'B' road that crossed the Afon Glaslyn wending its way turbulently to the sea from Beddgelert.

Standing on the roadway he gazed across the muddy water to the far side where it bordered Quarry Road. He looked at the railway bridge which ran between the 'B' road he was currently on and Quarry road. 'It's an idea, especially if they were on the viewing platform. I'll have a word with Robin when I get in. Not much good speaking to Jenkins. If he knows it comes from me he'll dismiss it out of hand.'

Gareth nodded to himself and got back into the car. He shivered slightly and started the engine, before turning up the heating. He sat thinking for a minute, bringing back the words of the pathologist at the inquest. Dry drowning sounded pretty horrible to him. He looked again at the water tumbling and rushing along the riverbed. It was deeper here than further down where the railway line crossed, but it was still rough enough if you got caught in it, and couldn't swim for some reason. Didn't that doctor say Scott had been in a fight?

Yes, he'd have a word with Robin.

THE NEXT MORNING SERGEANT Gareth ap Rhys appeared on the doorstep of Dilys Jones' bed and breakfast shortly after nine o'clock. Dilys opened the door to him as Willow was coming down the stairs. 'What have you come for now, Gareth? Can't you leave the poor girl alone? Isn't it bad enough that her name's in the papers and that Inspector's accusing her of murder?'

Sergeant ap Rhys, opening and closing his mouth like a stranded cod, glared at her. Then they both became aware of Willow, and shifted effortlessly into English.

'I was just telling him to leave you in peace.'

'And if you'd let me get a word in I would have told you we've got some news which Miss Edwards might like to hear. Only we need to go down to the station first.' He sounded faintly exasperated.

'Huh.' Mrs Jones wasn't very impressed. 'Well, mind you don't go upsetting her or her *Cariad* will have words with you.'

The sergeant looked at Willow in surprise. '*Cariad*?' Morgan must be a fast worker, Gareth thought, though his thoughts didn't, thankfully, stray to a face schooled to impassivity.

Willow blushed. 'Mrs Jones, you mustn't say things like that. We, er, we haven't talked about, er, that sort of thing!' She trailed away; feeling herself going hot as the other couple looked at her.

319

'Well, he was kissing you like he needs to talk about that sort of thing!'

Gareth gave an embarrassed cough. He looked at the two women for a moment, then said, 'As I was saying, if Miss Edwards could come down to the station it would be most helpful.' He coughed again. 'You don't happen to know where we can contact Mr Williams, do you.' Then felt himself redden slightly at the unconscious betrayal of knowledge, and hoped the other two weren't as quick on the uptake.

Before Willow could get any words out Mrs Jones was off again, ''Course she does, that's what I was just saying. He'll come and look after you, Willow; you get him down to the station, before you answer any impertinent questions from the likes of this.' She spun round on the unfortunate sergeant. 'And you behave! I mind when you had a snotty nose and scabby knees, Gareth ap Rhys, so you needn't come all officious with me.'

Willow, seeing school playground wars restarting in front of her, hurriedly lifted her coat from the hook. 'I'll come with you now, Sergeant.' And led the way outside.

She could hear Dilys Jones firing a stream of Welsh at his back as the sergeant walked up the path in front of her, his shoulders hunched against the torrent. He seemed relieved to get in the squad car.

They settled in and Willow volunteered, 'Mr Williams is staying at Castell Deudraeth. I have his mobile number if that would help.'

'No. It's alright, Miss, I'll get them to phone from the station to the hotel. It would actually be helpful if we could interview you together.'

'You're being very mysterious, Sergeant.'

The policeman just smiled grimly at her, then said, 'All will become clear, Miss Edwards.'

When they arrived he showed her into a quiet room off the main office and offered a *panad*. Willow, even more mystified, shook her head. 'I'll just go and contact Mr Williams, and then when the Inspector gets here we can make a start.' With these mysterious and somewhat frightening words he went out, closing the door quietly behind him.

Willow, left to wonder what was going on, looked around the room. It had a couple of easy chairs and a low table. A blank TV was tucked underneath a window whose outlook appeared to be a field full of cows. There was a small counter to one side with the paraphernalia for making drinks, with a small fridge underneath.

Well, she thought, if I'm under arrest this is a very comfy cell, but it looks more like the rest room for the station staff. She sat back trying to calm the slightly sick feeling, and the frogs that jumped in her stomach, which she associated with any visit to the police now.

Morgan, when he arrived very shortly afterwards, looked both surprised and puzzled to find her there. 'Hello, darling. What's going on? A sergeant rang to say I was wanted down at the Penrhyn station right away.' He came over and gave her a hug. 'Here, what have they been saying? You're trembling like a leaf!' He turned to confront Gareth, his mouth grim.

'The Inspector will explain everything, sir. *Paid a phoeni*. Would you both like to come into the main interview room?'

Morgan walked towards the door, holding tightly to Willow's hand. 'Don't worry, darling, I won't let them bully you.'

The Inspector was seated at the scarred desk in the room Willow had been in previously.

Sergeant ap Rhys pulled out a chair for Willow, indicated another for Morgan opposite the Inspector, and sat down himself at the side of the table.

The Inspector looked at him pointedly. 'I don't think we'll need your presence, Officer.'

Gareth ap Rhys smiled sweetly at him and hitched his chair closer to the desk. He wasn't being told to get out of his own station.

After a moment the Inspector turned his shoulder away.

'Right,' He addressed Morgan across the table. 'we just have one or two things to clear up.'

He pulled out a card which Morgan could see from across the table was one of his own. 'Could you perhaps tell me why your card was found in the notes of an illegal immigrant, Mr Williams?'

'*Be*'!' Whatever Morgan had been expecting it wasn't this. 'What?'

'This card was found attached to the personal notes of a Mr Ivan Proponov at *Ysbyty Gwynedd*. Have you any idea how it came to be there?'

'Certainly, Inspector.' Morgan had regained an outward calm. 'I gave it to the intensive care nurse when Miss Edwards and I went to visit Mr Proponov last week. He had unfortunately died. As there didn't appear to be any next of kin, I offered to attend to the funeral arrangements.'

'And why did you do that, sir? Was he a special friend of yours?' The moustache bristled and the Inspector's nose twitched as if scenting prey.

'I have never met the man, but Miss Edwards had found him in difficult circumstances and arranged his admittance to hospital.'

The Sergeant spoke up. 'If some of your lot up there read the notes sent from the small stations, you would have found all this out a lot earlier!'

323

'Thank you, Sergeant. We are, in fact, aware that Miss Edwards assisted the man.

'Now, Miss Edwards, would you like to tell me your connection to the unfortunate young man? How did you become involved with him? Did Mr Scott ask for your help?'

Willow's hand, which had been tightly clasped on her jeans clad legs, moved restlessly as her mouth dropped open.

'What's Barry got to do with Ivan?'

The Sergeant opened his mouth but was forestalled by Inspector Jenkins. 'It came to our attention that Ivan Proponov had Mr Scott's mobile phone number among his personal effects.'

'Did it, Inspector? How did it come to your attention?' Morgan dropped the question into the silence like a stone into a pool; Willow could feel the ripples of tension swirling in her stomach. What had she got Morgan into now?

The Inspector stared at Morgan, obviously not wanting to answer the question. Gareth gave a slightly chilly laugh and his grey eyes looked at the Inspector with enough ice to counter any fears polar bears had of starving. 'I sent those effects through to the main office a week last Saturday, with a list of the contents, and a suggestion that someone try and see if the numbers in the wallet matched a phone number. Too busy chasing murder suspects to bother about missing persons, were you? And if you'd read the report sent through this Sunday...'

'Missing persons isn't my department!' Inspector Jenkins snapped, reddening slightly. 'I can't oversee the everyday running of the station.'

'Anyway!' He swung back to Willow. 'Do you deny knowing that Mr Scott was involved with this Romanian fellow?'

Morgan took a grip on the hand nearest to him. 'She actually doesn't have to answer your questions, Inspector. And Mr Proponov was Polish.'

'It's alright.' Willow returned the warm handclasp. 'I have no idea what Barry was doing down here in Wales as I've already stated, Inspector. I didn't even know he was down here, and I certainly deny any knowledge of his involvement with Romanians, or any other nationality that might be hanging about.'

'Was he involved with other nationalities, Miss?'

Willow looked at him a bit blankly.

'You said any other nationalities that might be hanging about, Miss. Was he involved with any other nationalities?' The Inspector waited patiently while she sorted out his words.

Willow shook her head. 'I have no idea, Inspector. It was just a phrase.'

The Inspector paused, looking at the pair in front of him. He made a pretence of consulting his notes. Then turned back to

Morgan. 'Can you tell me what you were doing on the nineteenth of last month, sir?'

Morgan raised an eyebrow, and then pulled out a small oblong diary. He'd been expecting this question ever since his own PI had let him know Scott had been in Pwlleli. He flipped the pages then swung the book across the table tapping the relevant entry. 'As you can see, I was visiting a firm near Pwlleli. We were discussing my sponsorship of some young lads on work experience. I spent the entire day with them including a working lunch with the MD who is an old school friend of mine.'

Jenkins pursed his lips. 'This man would no doubt back up your story, sir.'

Morgan's lips tightened at the implied slur but he kept his temper. 'He would confirm, as would several of his board, who are not old school friends,' he lay emphasis on the negative, 'that I was present. I believe I left Pwlleli somewhere about four that afternoon, Inspector. Do I need an alibi for any other days?' The question was asked gently, but Willow shivered at the hint of steel in his voice.

The inspector, feeling rather like a particularly revolting grub on a pin, finally managed to tear his eyes away from Morgan's, which could now have cured all known fears of global warming by themselves. 'No, sir. We will have to check, as a matter of routine you understand.'

He hunched a shoulder and looked directly at Willow.

'Now, Miss, what were you doing that day?'

Willow looked at him blankly for a minute. 'I haven't a clue, Inspector.' She bent and retrieved her handbag. As she looked into its depths Gareth said, 'As a matter of fact you...' only to have the Inspector hold up a hand.

'Let the young lady answer for herself, Sergeant.'

Willow, attention caught by the byplay, looked at the two men curiously, then said, 'I think it's one of the days you asked me about before, Inspector Jenkins.' She looked at the page. Her diary, unlike Morgan's, was a recording of events rather than appointments.

Following Morgan's lead she turned the book round and offered it. 'Here you go. I was in Pwlleli too. How odd!' She smiled at Morgan. 'You can see I went to the market, only it wasn't on, so I went to the *Merched Y Wawr* sale in the church hall.' All the men winced at her mangling of the unfamiliar words.

She turned to Morgan. 'It seemed to be a sort of WI for Welsh women. They were really nice. I had coffee and *bara brith.*' She essayed a feeble grin at him. 'I can't say those words either.'

She turned back to Inspector Jenkins. 'In fact I gave the railway tickets to your constable; you can see when I arrived and left by them. I was going to go on the 'Special' at Porthmadog but I missed it. I saw the viewing platform on the guard's van just disappearing round the curve as I got to the station.'

Morgan looked at Jenkins. 'What is all this about, Inspector? I take it you've tracked down some of Barry Scott's movements, since yesterday's papers reported his car as found in Pwlleli. And you think either one, or both, of us had something to do with his disappearance.' He sighed deeply in exasperation. 'We are trying to co-operate, Inspector, but you do seem to like your little mysteries. Now either tell us what you want to know or we shall go, and you can deal with our lawyers.'

Gareth coughed, his hand hiding a smile.

'Very well, Mr Williams. We have traced Mr Scott to the railway station in Pwlleli where he boarded a BR train to Porthmadog. We also have witnesses who state that Ivan Proponov and he sat together on that train, and indulged in what appeared to be an acrimonious argument.'

Willow, listening attentively, said wonderingly, 'I didn't know Barry spoke Polish.'

'One witness said they appeared to be talking German.' He raised an eyebrow at Willow.

'Oh well, that explains it. Barry spoke that rather well. He often went away to Europe on business trips.'

'That's as maybe.' The Inspector looked confused for a minute, then went on, 'Anyway they got off at Porthmadog and boarded the special steam train that runs on Thursdays. The one you now tell me you missed, Miss Edwards.' He paused as Morgan uttered a small grunt. 'Yes, Mr Williams?'

Gareth also muttered.

Morgan's lips twitched. He'd heard the sergeant's muttered, 'I told you that'. Before he said, 'I was just thinking that that line runs over the Glaslyn, and anything falling off the train would be carried by the river down to the shoreline. Unless it got snagged in one of the deeper pools along Quarry Road.' He looked significantly at Inspector Jenkins.

The inspector looked back blandly, 'Yes sir, it's a theory we are exploring.'

Gareth grunted again, and Morgan caught an odd expression on his face before it went suitably blank and official again. He thought maybe the sergeant might have been the source of that theory too. Ap Rhys struck him as being a whole lot brighter than Jenkins.

Inspector Jenkins was continuing his tale. 'Ivan Proponov was seen to get off the train at Minffordd that day, but not Mr Scott. Mr Proponov was later seen walking along the road towards Penrhyn, but we can only track him back as far as the Boston Lodge works, a week later.'

Gareth kept an impassive face, so the slimy Inspector had read his reports, and it seemed, was bent on taking the credit.

'Now, Mr Williams, your name turns up in his effects, an illegal emigrant. We have further evidence for believing that Mr Scott was involved in bringing in members of non EU countries for large sums of money, then either demanding more or placing them in sweat shops. And you were in Pwlleli at the same time.'

Morgan looked as though he was going to take a swing at the senior man. His eyes glacial, he pushed back his chair and stood up, towering over the two police officers, which was a neat trick, given the size of Gareth ap Rhys. 'Are you accusing me of being involved in that filthy trade, of exploiting poor beggars who are desperate to make a better life over here?' He took a deep breath. 'Because, Inspector,' he paused significantly, 'you are about to find yourself hauled through the courts on a charge of malicious slander.'

Sergeant Gareth ap Rhys stood up, his face going white with held back temper, and placing a placating hand on Morgan's arm. Morgan ignored it, his eyes implacably fixed on the Inspector.

'I'm just doing my job, sir.' Inspector Jenkins remained seated with no hint of apology. A faint red line mantled his high cheekbones, and his eyes seemed to bulge slightly more, but these were the only symptoms of agitation he showed as he continued to look at Morgan while he spoke. 'I have to establish that you and Miss Edwards had no knowledge of trafficking in illegal immigrants and also that you were not involved in the death of Mr Scott.'

Willow was feeling decidedly sick. It was all her fault that Morgan was caught up in this debacle. If she hadn't dragged him off to *Ysbyty Gwynedd* he wouldn't have any connection to Ivan or Barry.

She sat, feeling cold and miserable, not daring to look at any of the men.

Morgan continued to stand, looking down at Inspector Jenkins. 'And have you now established that, Inspector? It appears that the relevant day was the nineteenth. I was in meetings, Miss Edwards was certainly in Pwlleli, but I don't think the combined *Merched y Wawr* of the town is bribeable.' A small corner of Willow's mind absently noted the correct pronunciation as she sat mutely on the hard wooden chair.

'Neither of us has been in Barry Scott's company for months. I wouldn't touch the man, or his business, with a bargepole. And I don't believe Miss Edwards would either, since he threatened her with violence.'

The Inspector inclined his head. 'You would both certainly appear to have alibis for the time when we have established Mr Scott died. However, you have to admit that it is rather a coincidence that you were all present in Pwlleli on that day.'

'Coincidences do happen, Inspector.' Morgan relaxed very slightly at the grudging admission that neither he nor Willow were likely to be charged with murder in the near future. He sat down, again taking Willow's cold hand and holding it firmly in his own.

'As to the dirty trade he was dealing with, I would have thought it was more the job of Interpol than you, Inspector, and I shall be contacting them. They can ask me for any information they might need. You needn't be troubled any longer.' He spoke gently as he stood up again, pulling Willow up with him. 'We'll be going now, Inspector.' He turned to Gareth. 'Thank you, Sergeant. If you should require either of us, you know where we are both staying at present.'

Ignoring the senior man he towed Willow out of the room and quietly waited for the young constable to let them out. The young man, after one look at his sergeant, opened the door and ushered them courteously outside. He didn't go back into the room, he'd caught the look on his sergeant face, and he didn't want to be around when that tightly held temper finally exploded.

WILLOW FELT AS THOUGH someone had taken away her heart and left a small cold stone in its place. It appeared as though the man she'd been going to marry was an even nastier specimen than she'd imagined. Morgan was walking her briskly towards his car, not realising that she was slowing as she realised exactly what Barry Scott had been up to, and how it was impacting on Morgan.

She stopped in the middle of the car-park. 'I think I'd better go home.'

'Well alright, *Cariad,* but it'll be quicker if you go in the car!' He raised a quizzical eyebrow as he came to a halt.

'No. I mean, I want to go home.'

Morgan said patiently. 'Yes, *Cariad.*'

Willow realised she wasn't making much sense. She looked at Morgan's face; when had it become so special to her, and how was she going to cope without him? She struggled to gather her wandering wits. She felt as though she was in a little bubble insulated from all feelings.

'Morgan, take me back to Mrs Jones, please. I need a bit of time to sort myself out.'

'Of course, *Cariad.*' He took an icy cold hand and drew her close, his arm going round her as he helped her into the car.

Willow remained silent on the short trip back to her landlady's house. She raised a smile as they stopped outside, but it was a poor effort. Without looking at him she spoke, 'Don't come in with me. I need a bit of thinking time. OK?'

Morgan was a bit nonplussed. 'Well alright, but don't think too hard. You weren't involved in Scott's business, dirty or otherwise. Don't let him hurt you anymore, darling.' He leaned over and turned her head, giving her a gentle salute on her mouth.

Willow wasn't worried about Barry Scott hurting her, she was worried about him hurting Morgan through her, and the more she discovered about Morgan the more she couldn't bear that to happen.

Morgan opened the car door and walked her up the path to the house; he was a bit puzzled but thought it was just the shock of all the revelations over the past hour that had distressed her. 'I'm going into Ports to talk to Evan Davies. Give me a ring, *Cariad.*'

He drove away while she was climbing the stairs, and was crossing the Toll as she began to fill her bags. It was as well she was interrupted before she had finished, by a landlady who had finally managed to find her reading glasses and looked at the Sunday papers. Now she entered Willow's room with barely a knock, thrusting the colour supplement under her nose. 'Here read this, I was never so...'

Willow, obliged to take the paper being held in a shaking hand in front of her face, took the open pages and looked as commanded.

'It's one of those 'seen about town' items.' Mrs Jones pointed. There before Willow's startled gaze was Morgan and a stunning auburn haired woman. He was holding her tightly and the camera had caught, not just the fact that she was kissing him, but that her wedding ring was glinting in the airport lights. The caption simply read, 'Whose wife is millionaire Morgan Williams kissing now?' There was another smaller photo of them standing, he with his arm round her while they waited at the baggage carousel. The obvious love between them was clear for the world to see.

Willow sat down slowly on the bed. Her legs had turned to jelly and she shook her head as if to clear away the fog. Mrs Jones was speaking to her, but it sounded rather like a fly buzzing in her ear. She couldn't manage to get a coherent word past her lips; events seemed to be piling on top of one another rather too rapidly for her to cope with.

First there had been Inspector Jenkins all but accusing her of murder and human trafficking. Then poor Morgan being dragged into it, likewise accused, and his integrity questioned, because she'd taken him to see Ivan. Now it appeared that he was not only involved with a beautiful married woman, but the worst part as far as Willow was concerned - that he was a millionaire. He had far more money than Barry, and look at the trouble that had caused.

She finally looked at the palpitating landlady. 'I think I'd like to be alone for a bit, Mrs Jones.'

Mrs Jones, reluctantly leaving, wondered what she should do. The poor girl looked ill.

MORGAN, ON HIS WAY TO see Evan, was wondering whether he had been wise to leave Willow alone. He drove along deep in thought. She had obviously been distressed by the interview with the Inspector, but he couldn't see why she should be so upset. Unless she was still in love with Barry. He shook his head. God help him, he wasn't sure what he'd do if that was the case.

He pulled into Harbour Station, parking his car and, after a quick word with the attendant, went off down the main street. Evan hadn't expected Willow to be there last night, so he hadn't brought his magazine with him. Now Morgan had come to have a look at the picture of the crane.

The two men had settled down to coffee and a good gossip when the knock on the door caused Evan to get up with a word of apology. 'It's Sergeant ap Rhys to see you, Morgan.'

Morgan grimaced; what the hell did the man want now? And, anyway, how did they track him down?

'Sergeant.' His greeting was on the chilly side.

The Sergeant, who had been wishing the Inspector in Hades for several hours, cursed him again under his breath.

'Mr Williams. I saw your car at the station and they said you were here.'

Well, that explained how they'd found him. 'More enquiries, Sergeant?'

'Well, not to say enquires; more information, sir.'

Morgan raised an eyebrow.

'Could we sit down do you think?'

Evan Davies, feeling a bit like a referee at a dog fight, offered coffee to both men.

'No thanks, Evan. So what information can I supply you with now, Sergeant?'

'Well, it's like this. You know about the body we've found inside the Cob?'

'Well, I know what I read in the papers.' Morgan waited patiently for the man to come to the point.

'Well your name was one of the ones we were given as a source of history of the railway and we, er... we wondered if you could tell us a bit more about the Cob's history.'

Morgan felt his lips twitch, and caught the answering, slightly shamefaced, smile of Gareth. 'I know, sir. It's a bit awkward, but I'm not Inspector Jenkins and I've got a more open mind than him.'

'Hum! Yes, Sergeant!' Morgan smiled a bit more openly.

Taking this as a good sign Gareth took up his tale. 'We know it was '27 when the big winter storms swept the coast and breached the Cob. But no-one seems to be able to tell us where the breach was.'

Morgan nodded.

'And we're almost certain that the body was placed there during the breach so that ties it down to October '27 to March '28.'

'But you want to narrow the field a bit more, is that right, Sergeant? Well, there were several breaches as a matter of fact. Some of them just small holes, some that let the tide through to the other side. The winds took out the railings and track along the top too.'

Evan, who had begun to relax, said. 'It's funny, that, Willow was asking about the 'hurricane' as she called it, only last week.'

The two men turned astonished faces towards him.

Evan looked embarrassed. 'It was in those letters she's got, Morgan. Haven't you read that bit?'

'No.' He exchanged perplexed glances with Gareth.

'What letters are they, then, sir?'

Morgan shrugged. 'Apparently Miss Edwards' great-uncle was working in this area back then and sent letters back home to his mother and father. She's been trying to trace him.'

'There was a bit about the cup final too, when we won.' Evan exchanged grins with the others.

'I'd like to see that.' The sergeant nodded his head. He coughed. 'Anyway, sir. What else can you tell me?'

'Let's see. If the body was placed there too early then it would have been spotted; too late, say after the start of backfilling, and they'd never have got it in the hole. Now, they blocked the tide with wooden battens to hold it back to start with, and then built up the outside first, then started on the infilling.' Morgan pulled a scrap of paper over to demonstrate.

'How near to the outside was this body?'

'Right next to the outside line of boulders; that's how we spotted it. We had to send into town for some Vicks after we started excavating. It had been in a box, but last week's rain had eroded away some of the top soil and the box had broken so that we got a whiff. It's unmistakable that smell.' He wrinkled his nose as if still smelling the odour of decomposition.

'Is that why you use the Vicks, then?' asked Evan.

'Oh yeah! One of the best masks there is, Vicks Vapour Rub.'

Morgan had been pondering while this exchange went on. 'So if it was right next to the outer edge, there hadn't been much backfilling. That narrows it down to before Christmas if the records are right.'

'Well, that's helpful. A young male missing during the months of November and December of 1927. From the clothes we're pretty sure it was a labourer. He'd got leather shoes like they wear when they work on ships and docksides. The PM said he was between 25 and 30, according to his epiphyses.' The sergeant raised a comical face. 'Wherever they are.'

But Morgan didn't return the smile. He had a sinking feeling in his gut. 'What other clues have you got, Sergeant?'

'Well,' Gareth looked surprised at the serious tone. 'There was part of a tattoo on one of the arms. We can't make it out; it's just a stain in that fatty stuff. And we've got a watch so we don't think whoever killed him did it for motives of robbery.'

'Was it a murder then?'

'Oh yes, got the bullet rattling around in the chest cavity, and the matching gun, according to ballistics. We're still waiting on the Americans for information about that. They've identified it as one of their battlefield issues, but haven't found out who it was issued to yet. It's certainly First World War vintage anyway.'

He rubbed the back of his neck with a faint rasping sound. 'Not that that will prove anything, from all accounts those things got brought home and kept as souvenirs by all ranks of men, not necessarily the original owners, but it's worth a try.'

He sighed. 'Whoever did it will be as dead as his victim by this time. So we're unlikely to find out the whys and wherefores now, but I like to tie off my ends neatly.'

He offered a nice smile as he stood up. 'Thank you for all your help, Mr Williams. I appreciate it.' He smiled again, 'And tell that young lady I don't for a minute think she's murdered anyone. I hope she finds her great-uncle soon.'

Morgan stood up too, holding out a hand. 'Shake, Sergeant. I hope you'll keep me abreast of developments; I'm interested in your corpse. I'm hoping it doesn't turn out to be her great-uncle.'

The sergeant did a double take.

Evan, equally as quick on the uptake as Morgan, said, 'No it couldn't be!'

'Well, I haven't read all the letters yet, but he certainly fits the description. Age is about right. You saw the tattoo, Evan. What arm was it on?'

Evan paused. 'Hang on.' They watched as he mentally turned the photograph from the paper around in his mind, touching his arm and swinging his body. 'Left, I'm almost certain it was left.'

'So am I. Where was your corpse tattooed, Sarge?'

Gareth said slowly, 'Left.'

'Anything on the watch? Inscription, dedication? Something like that.'

'Dunno, it was a half hunter in rather terrible condition. The body fluids had got at it a bit. Hang on, I'll ring and ask.'

They all sat down while he pulled out a mobile and spoke to someone called Bert.

'Well, because I might have a lead, that's why.'

'I don't care if it is all manky. Go and find out.' He looked at the other two men. 'Kids, I have to work with squeamish kids.' He shrugged, waiting.

Morgan looked at the serious face, he estimated Gareth to be about thirty, but he was a sergeant in the police, so he supposed the man could be older. He was big as a barn door and certainly looked older at this moment.

Morgan thought back to the scene in the police station and then scowled. He was obviously an adrenalin junky to challenge this young man, suddenly he felt tired, he wanted to get back to Willow. He stirred restlessly as they waited.

After a longish interval while they all sat silent Gareth said, 'OK, let me write that down. 'To James Edwards in recognition of 50 years for the GWR.' What was that date again? 1921. Right thanks.'

He turned towards them. 'It's the right surname. But that would have belonged to a much older man.'

'Not if it had been passed to his eldest son.'

Morgan stood up again. 'I'm going to talk to Willow. Do you want to come with me, Sergeant?'

Evan looked rather enviously at the others. 'I'm baby sitting this afternoon. You will let me know what happens, won't you, Morgan?'

Morgan nodded. 'Of course I will.'

He and Gareth ap Rhys left the quiet street and headed towards the harbour.

'I wonder if you're right.' It was the only comment from the rather bemused policeman as they part. Each to drive separately, and rapidly, back to Minffordd and Willow's lodgings.

THE CHILD SWUNG ROUND on her grandfather's hand like a gyroscope. Dancing from foot to foot as Evan Davies stood in the doorway, talking in low and serious tones to Eirlys and Deniol. 'You'll take some flowers to the nurses, from me?'

'Yes, of course.' Eirlys spoke over her daughter's head as that young personage also spoke.

'*Taid*, you came, Mam said you were coming to look after me.'

'Yes, *Cariad*. Mam and Deniol have to go out.'

'OK.' Gwyneth stopped dancing and began to tug him indoors.

'No, sweetheart, you get your coat; you're coming with me to my house.'

'I've packed your bag, Gwyneth.' Eirlys smiled at her daughter.

Gwyneth stopped moving, she looked from her mother, to Deniol, to her grandfather. Then she burst into tears and flung herself at Deniol. 'No.' She clung tightly to the teenager's leg. Deniol tried to pick her up but she only gripped tighter, forcing him to stand still as her tears soaked into his jeans. His, *'Cariad'*, was overlaid by Evan's, 'Sweetheart.'

Evan bent over her. All three adults looked puzzled and distressed.

Eirlys shut the door. 'Gwyneth, darling, let go of Deniol, let's go and sit down and you can tell us what's wrong.'

Gwyneth continued to sob, deep wrenching sobs. Deniol finally managed to pick her up and carry her into the sitting room. He sat down with her on his knee and shushed her while the others waited for her to calm down a bit.

'I thought you liked staying with *Taid?*'

Through the tears, a small voice was understood to say she loved *Taid,* lots.'

Deniol hugged the small body to him. 'Why don't you want to stay with him then, darling?'

Gwyneth, trying desperately to get control of her voice just shook her head.

Eirlys glanced at the clock. Deniol saw the look. 'I don't care, Mam. Gwyneth needs to talk to us.'

'You'll miss the train, lad. I can stay here with the little one, if she doesn't want to come to my place.'

'No. I don't want you to go.'

'But darling, I'll be back tomorrow.'

'Then you'll go away again and again, until you don't come home, like Twm did. You'll die. They'll put you in a box, I heard Uncle Morgan saying.' And the sobs started up again.

Deniol looked mystified. 'Why would Uncle Morgan say I was going to die, darling? I'm perfectly alright.'

'You're going to the hospital, where the nurses live and people die.'

Deniol, trying to understand the workings of a five-year-old's mind, shook his head again in puzzlement.

'Wait a minute, Den.' Evan moved over to the settee where the two siblings sat. 'Gwyneth. What did you hear Uncle Morgan say? I want you to tell me, but before you do, listen to me. No-one is dying, and Mam and Den will be back again tomorrow, I promise. Do you believe me?'

'Yes, Taid.' Gwyneth sniffed and wiped her fingers over her eyes, then under her nose.

Evan pulled out a handkerchief and held it out. 'Blow.'

'Now what did Uncle Morgan say and when?'

'He said,' Gwyneth sniffed and gulped. 'He said to Sian, that she'd been a good friend and it wasn't her fault her young man would die. And that's Den. He's Sian's young man, like Uncle Morgan is Willow's young man; because I've seen him kiss her, like uncle Morgan kissed Willow.'

345

Eirlys and Evan cast a quick look at Deniol, who was turning a painful red. Then they looked back at Gwyneth.

'Uncle Morgan wasn't talking about me; he was talking about another young man, a friend of both Sian and me. He was very sick. He had an accident and that's why he died.' Deniol kept his eyes on Gwyneth and ignored all references to kissing, his little sister's distress was too important to worry about sly looks. 'But, not everyone who goes to hospital dies, *Cariad*.'

'Sian's mam did, and she died.'

'Our mam went to hospital and she came home with you as a tiny baby. She didn't die. Granddad Myrddin went to hospital last year, and he came home all better. Didn't he?'

Gwyneth gave a small nod.

'Now I'll tell you why we're going away for the night. But you have to promise to keep it a secret. Promise?'

'Yes, Den.'

'You remember Sian and I made a film for school?'

Gwyneth nodded. 'The one with the train. 'Stranger Danger.''

'Well our film is in the semi-finals. That means they have to choose between four schools as to who's going to win. And to do that they want to ask Sian and I some questions about why we made the film. The people, who have to choose live down in

London. Mam's going too, because it isn't right for Sian to come with me on her own.'

'But Taid said to give the nurses flowers, and they're at the hospital.'

'The nurses were very kind to us, and we just want to say thank you to them for all their care. One of them, who looked after Twm, has offered to let us stay in her flat for the night. OK?' Den looked at the serious face of his young sister.

'Twm was very ill, darling. Everyone did their best to make him better. Sometimes people get better and sometimes God looks after them instead. But Deniol isn't ill, I promise. Now will you stay with Taid?' Eirlys looked at her youngest child. She hadn't realised how much Gwyneth had understood, and misunderstood, about Twm's death, but they obviously needed to talk to her a bit more, and get rid of some of these fears. She looked at her father. He gave a nod.

'I'll talk to her, Eirlys. Make sure she understands. Off you go.'

There was a thump at the door and Sian came in, followed by her father. She looked in puzzlement at the scene.

'Are you ready, Den?'

Deniol glanced at her and began to blush again the heat crawling up his cheeks until he felt like one huge red blob. Sian looked at him curiously, then at Gwyneth. 'What's wrong, *Cariad*?'

'Nufin, Sian. I hope you have a nice time.' Gwyneth smiled at Evan, it was a bit wobbly but it was a smile. ''m all ready to go, *Taid*.' She held her tear stained face up for a kiss. Deniol gave her a big hug and kissed the little face. 'I'll see you tomorrow. Would you like a present from London?'

'No, Den. So long as you come back.'

'Just you try and stop me.'

He stood up, lowering her to the ground, and she went to her mother for a goodbye kiss.

Sian looked on a bit mystified. Deniol finally looked across the room, holding out a hand. 'Come on, Sian we've got a train to catch, and our strategy to plan.'

Mrs Dilys Jones was out shopping when they knocked on her door. This was probably just as well for the life expectancy of Morgan Williams and Gareth ap Rhys. Willow came down to answer the door and gazed at the two men with a dull kind of acceptance. She expected more trouble and just wished it would happen. Then she could sink back into apathy.

Morgan looked at her with concern as she let them in and turned and walked away into the kitchen without saying anything. He exchanged a glance with the sergeant, and then they both followed her.

Willow was sitting at the kitchen table. Her head propped on her cupped hands. She glanced at them as they entered but didn't say anything.

'Willow. *Cariad.*'

'Yes, Morgan.'

'Can we look at your letters?' Whatever Willow had been expecting it wasn't this. A faint spark of interest crept into her eyes.

'If you want to. They're in my room.' She didn't move. So after waiting a minute, Morgan left, coming back with a bewildered expression on his face and the folder in his hand. 'You've packed. Where are you going?'

He dropped the folder on the table and stood looking down at her.

She shrugged. 'Back to London.'

'Just like that?'

She gave another shrug. The Sergeant, ignoring for the moment the strange behaviour of the other two, stretched out a long hand and pulled the folder towards him and opened it. He pulled out the letters and other documents and after a quiet grunt settled down on a kitchen chair to read.

'You weren't going to tell me. You were just going to go, weren't you?' It was part statement, part question. But Willow shivered slightly.

'You don't own me, Morgan. I can do what I want, and go where I want.'

Morgan pulled her up out of the chair, holding both her wrists in his hands. 'No, you can't! You love me, I know you do.' He gave her a gentle shake, pulling her close, muttering in Welsh.

Willow stood unresponsive in his embrace. Sergeant ap Rhys, becoming aware of them, said, 'Hey, Hey,' and touched Morgan's arm. He spoke as Morgan had, in Welsh, 'Let her go, man.'

Morgan turned to him saying fiercely, 'She's mine. I won't let bloody Barry Scott have her. She's mine and I'm going to marry her.'

Gareth ap Rhys looked at the pair of them. 'Well, you'd better ask her in English, man. She hasn't a clue what you're saying.'

Willow looked from one to the other and stepped back, away from Morgan. 'You said that, what you just said, once before.' She turned to the policeman. 'Perhaps you'd be so obliging as to translate for me, Sergeant.'

'Oh no! He can do his own translating.' Gareth gazed at the pair; he'd as soon get in the way of a couple of she bears fighting over a tasty scrap, as between these two. 'I'm a bit in the way here. I've just got a couple of questions to ask, then I'll clear out and you can sort things out between you.'

Willow stood looking at him stonily. 'Yes, Sergeant.' She sighed. 'But I haven't killed anyone and I haven't helped them get into the country.'

Gareth blinked. 'Er, no.' He shook his head. 'What I want to know is, what was your paternal great-grandfather's first name?'

'Eh?' Willow was totally confused.

'That's what we came to ask you.' Morgan looked across at the pile of letters in the big hand. 'Do you think we might be on the right track, Sarge?'

'Well, I don't know.' Gareth spoke a bit testily, 'You haven't answered me yet, Miss.'

'James Gareth Edwards.'

The two men looked at each other, then at Willow. 'You said he worked for the railways. Which one?' Morgan took advantage of her confusion to get both arms back round her. He hadn't lost sight of the main issue in these interesting insights. If he had anything to say about it she wasn't going to be Edwards much longer anyway.

'Great Western.'

'Then I think we might have found your great-uncle.' he said slowly.

'Hang on, Mr Williams; we need to check a few more facts first.'

'OK, you check facts. I've got more important things to deal with.'

'Willow.' He addressed the young woman standing quiescent in his hold. 'I don't quite know what's going on but I'm not letting you go without a fight. Will you come with me? I promise to bring you back or take you wherever you want to go after, but come with me now. Please.'

'Well, can I take the letters?' asked Gareth.

Morgan rounded on the policeman. 'Do what you want. Just go away!'

Gareth looked as though he might have said something, and then thought better of it. His own love life was complicated enough without getting mixed up in anyone else's. He gathered up the letters putting them back into the folder, and turned to leave the oblivious pair to sort themselves out.

Willow finally yielded to the insistent tug of Morgan's hands.

'Cariad.' Morgan drew her out of the kitchen with Sergeant ap Rhys following in their wake; they all stopped in the hall.

'But, Morgan...'

He swung round with her jacket in his hand. 'Please, Willow.' Looking at his face she could see tension, desperation and pleading, and what she hoped was love overlaying them all.

He held the coat open for her to shrug into, then took her hand and drew her out of the front door and along the path. Willow thought she ought to protest, but couldn't somehow summon the words. She followed behind him; her emotions all tangled together, and allowed herself to be seated in the warm luxury of the car.

Gareth watched them go, and then swung the door shut. He hoped Dilys Jones had got her key, because he couldn't wait on her doorstep for her to come back. In fact he didn't want to be anywhere near said doorstep when she discovered he'd been to visit her lodger again.

'WHERE ARE WE GOING?' Morgan and Willow had been travelling for a couple of minutes before Willow thought to ask.

'Well, for the time being we're going to Portmerion to my accommodation, it's a nice quiet spot so that I can talk to you without interruptions.'

Morgan was driving through the now steadily pouring rain towards the seaside village. He pulled up outside what she belatedly realised was a Castle.

'This is Castell Deudraeth, they do wonderful seafood meals and it's very private.' He looked seriously across at her. 'I've got a set of private rooms here. Hopefully I can get you to listen to me without policeman and bodies dropping out of the sky and distracting us both. And I do want you to listen to me.' He turned in his seat keeping his hands on the steering wheel. What he really wanted to do was grab hold and never let go. 'I'm willing to listen too, Willow, because this is too important to us both for there to be any mistakes. The Sergeant was right.'

He did let go of the wheel then, taking both her hands in his. 'What I said back there,' he nodded his head in the direction they'd just come, 'was that I'm going to marry you. I don't know how you fight a corpse, but I won't let Barry Scott have you. I love you too much for that. If you don't love me, that's different, but I'll be damned if that scum gets you. Now will you come with me and explain why you were leaving?'

Willow sat looking at him. She hadn't a clue what he was talking about. And she was too tired of fighting her own emotions and his as well, to raise any fuss when he got out of the car and drew her out too.

He hoisted a light leather briefcase out of the boot, gathered up a newspaper from the back seat, and strode confidently towards the imposing entrance with Willow following reluctantly behind him, his handclasp ensuring her obedience.

They strode up an imposing staircase and he keyed in to a room with separate dining and sitting areas. Morgan dropped briefcase and paper on the table, and then lifted the phone, punching in a digit and speaking into the phone. 'Could you have them send up a pot of coffee?'

354

Willow was struggling to keep up with events and Morgan was counting on the opulence of the surroundings to keep her dazed long enough to where he could talk to her in private.

He gave her a minute to take in the warm and sweet smelling surroundings before he patted the double settee, and pulled her down next to him.

Morgan held her close for what seemed an eternity. 'You know I am so scared.' He spoke into her hair then drew back to look at her. Willow looked at him in astonishment; she could feel him trembling. This big confident man really was afraid!

'Scared. You?' She tried to lighten the mood.

'Oh, yeah! I've been scared for nearly a week now. I can't bear to lose you.' He pulled her close; enjoying the feel of her body after the fright of thinking he'd never hold her again. Then he grinned impishly, 'I like you on the engine, all serious and smelling of diesel, but I really like you like this, darling.'

There was a discreet tap at the door and Morgan looked down at her as he stood up. 'Don't go away.'

He opened the door to a young man who wheeled in a trolley of coffee and small cakes. Morgan offered a tip, and the young man said thank you so fervently that Willow wondered just how much the tip had been.

'Right.' Morgan wheeled across the trolley and seated himself again. 'I think I'd better talk first, or I may never get round to it.'

'First, do you love Barry Scott? Is that why you were going?' She felt him brace himself at her side, even though he kept his eyes fixed steadily on her face.

'What! No, of course I don't! I told you that before, Morgan.' She shook her head in bewilderment. She could see the tension in the strain lines round his eyes and realised for the first time that he wasn't a youth anymore.

'Well, why were you going, darling? You didn't believe that damn Inspector's insinuations did you? I swear I have nothing to do with sweat shops or the like.' She found she couldn't bear to have this strong man humbling himself before her.

'It wasn't you, Morgan, it was me. I seem to have got you into trouble from the moment we met. First you have to talk to that obnoxious Inspector about what you're doing, and then there's that American contract that I've mucked up for you, and now he thinks you're a criminal, and its all my fault because I took you to see Ivan.' Her voice gathered speed and pitch as she spoke, 'And you've got a beautiful mistress and you're a millionaire and I'm not a bit beautiful.' She all but wailed the last bit so that Morgan was totally nonplussed by the catalogue of worries and words.

'Oh! darling, come here,' He pulled her close as she started to cry in good earnest.

She made a valiant effort to pull herself together, and away from him, only to be frustrated by the iron hard hold that he took of her shoulders. 'I never heard such nonsense in all my life.'

''T'isn't' The word was muffled against his chest.

A faint chuckle greeted this. Morgan allowed her to snuffle her way to calm, then pulled out a handkerchief. For a second time that day a respectable man was asking a young woman to use a handkerchief. 'Blow!' He mopped her eyes, and then drew her closer so that she sat on his knee.

'Right. One: I already had my doubts about that contract and the firm involved before I discovered Scott's involvement. They weren't treating Jane right.' He felt her instinctive stiffening. 'We'll get to Jane in a minute. Sit still.' He pulled her more firmly into his embrace as she would have shifted.

'Two: the Inspector knows damn well I'm no criminal. He's just trying to save face because he knew he should have been on to the immigrant angle earlier. He isn't going to convict me of anything because I haven't done anything.

'Three: what was three? Oh, yeah! Mistress. I haven't got a mistress. I hope to God I'm soon going to have a beautiful wife though.' He looked at the blotched face so near his own, but she refused to meet his eyes. He sighed quietly and allowed her to pull away while he reached out for the jacket which was over the back of the settee. Pulling the jacket onto his lap he extracted his wallet. 'I have some pictures to show you.'

Willow, bewildered, took the small folder. Looking at his serious face; she looked down and found herself looking at the stunning brunette of the newspapers. She was posed holding a hand up to stop the wind blowing her long hair off her face, the hand against her face revealed clearly a diamond ring and a gold band on the wedding finger.

'She's gone auburn just at the moment and she's had her ears pierced recently, but that's my beautiful Jane.'

Willow felt the jealousy like a great cloud blocking her vision. She tried to thrust back the photo and stand up, but Morgan held her other hand fast. 'She's my twin sister, Willow, and she's a widow. When you first heard me talking to her, she seemed like a good camouflage. I wasn't too sure how I felt about you, and I still don't know how you feel about me. But I can't play those sort of games now, it's too important. I love you too much.' It was said so simply it took her breath away.

'I abandoned the poor girl and rushed back to Wales because I saw this photo in the colour supplement yesterday. I was planning on giving you a bit more time, darling, but events have rather forced my hand there.' He flipped through the colour supplement to the photo that Willow had seen previously.

'I couldn't risk you seeing this and disappearing on me. I thought I'd better come and show you myself.' Morgan looked at her.

When Willow still didn't say anything, he took both magazine and photo from her unresisting hands, and then held her hands tightly in his own. 'Well, say something, if only to put me out of my misery.'

'Mrs Jones already showed me the paper. She's beautiful, Morgan. She belongs in your world. I don't. I was trying to make things easy for both of us, but mainly for me.' Willow was no coward. She gently drew her hands away.

'Ah, yes!' Morgan ticked it off on his fingers. 'Four: so I'm a millionaire, according to the papers. I wish, but so what!'

'Barry said ...' She stopped at the dangerous look on his face.

'I don't give a damn what bloody Barry Scott said. Money might grease paths and buy nice things. It might allow you the freedom to travel first class and sleep in private suites, but it doesn't count with the important things, Willow.

'We might have more than enough money in the bank, but it didn't stop Jane losing her husband to cancer. My money couldn't keep little Twm alive, or Sian's Mum. It can't guarantee happiness. It doesn't mean you'll love me, or marry me.' He suddenly stood up, walking away to the far side of the room and looking out on the teeming rain coming down on the naked trees outside.

'I need you.' He spun round facing her. 'I need you in my life, and I'd need you to make me complete if I was working for a wage on the railway, just as much as I need you while I'm running my own business. Without love, life is a long slog through a grey day. Please Willow.' He walked back towards her.

Willow looked at the naked emotion on his face and held out her hands. Morgan took them, then drew her close. 'I need to talk to you. I don't ever want misunderstanding between us again, but first I need this.'

He pulled her gently into his arms and began to kiss her with the air of a man settling down to enjoy a banquet after a long fast. Willow, submitting to nibbling caresses across her jaw line, felt herself tip off balance again.

'Mmm! You smell nice.' Morgan appeared to be working his way purposefully towards her mouth, his hands holding her hair back while he darted tiny kisses on her lips. Then his lips closed on hers and Willow forgot everything in the moment.

GARETH AP RHYS WASN'T FORGETTING anything, even as he sat at his desk writing up reports he was thinking about the letters he'd taken away with him. He set the final report aside and picked up the folder of letters from Willow's great-uncle. He began to read the history of a man separated from his family by work. He thought he could get right behind the sentiments the letters expressed, even if it wasn't family, but the girl he loved, that Gareth was separated from.

> *'I've got the tickets, Mam, and I'll be home Christmas Eve. We're travelling via Blaenau and Chester. I hope that Seamus will come with me too. I've bought his ticket as a surprise Christmas present and I plan to pack his bag so that we can leave on the late afternoon train. I've borrowed the key to his room at the hostel, so that bit should be easy. He's a nice man, and I know you'll like him as much as I do. Maybe if he can see what a proper family is he won't want to be mixed up in all this IRA stuff and he'll stop being so bitter.'*

The scene at Dilys Jones Bed and Breakfast was fresh in Gareth's mind as he thought about his girl, Claire. She would be home for Christmas too, and he wanted to be with her. He'd decided that if she'd have him he was willing to live in Cumbria. He'd miss his family, but he missed Claire more. The phone rang just as he reached out a hand to it.

Gareth looked at the hand, and then the phone, and then picked up the receiver. An American voice assailed his ear.

'Have I got a police sergeant called Price in county Gwynedd, Wales?'

Gareth admitted that his name was ap Rhys. The voice sighed with relief. 'They said you all didn't speak English there, and my buddy has a computer ready to try and translate you.

Gareth grinned. 'That perfectly alright, sir, I'm fluent in both languages, though American might give me a bit of trouble. How can I help you?'

'I'm with the American military. My name is Captain Milo Haines. They sent some info' to me about one of our handguns, asking who owned it in the First World War. Apparently it's turned up over there.' The man sounded bewildered. 'I sorta wondered what you needed to know a hundred years later, that was so urgent. But I'll get to that.' Gareth could hear the clicking of a typewriter, down the line, as the Captain paused.

'Normally we would have taken months to get back to you all, but with this new graveyard going in over in France, and the work they've been doing on the bodies, DNA and such, and the bits found with them, we have quite a bit of research of artefacts going on too. You've heard about the new graves?'

Gareth agreed he had, it had been on the news, 250 skeletons discovered in a mass grave near the site of the battle of Fromelles, from the First World War, newly discovered, and now being reinterred in an official war cemetery in France. The Americans had been working with the British and Australians, asking people, who thought they might have relatives who had died in that sector, to submit DNA.

Haines continued, 'This hand gun you were enquiring about fits right into the time period. It belongs to a Seamus Donovan. It was issued to him via the 5th Army Division in May of 1917 when his troop was attached to us.'

Gareth, busy scribbling details, grinned all over again. 'Captain Haines I believe you've just solved a murder.'

'I have!'

Gareth could hear the incredulity bouncing off the satellite connections. 'I'll send you a report to let you know all about it, but I have to get to my superior with this information.' A few more pleasantries and Gareth cut the connection.

He rang Robin and then the super-in-charge of the investigation. He might not be able to solve modern murders, but he was sure he'd solved an ancient one. He picked up the phone and rang Morgan at the hotel.

Epilogue

I⊤ WAS THE NIGHT before Christmas. The moon was fitful, the air crisp, but inside all was cosiness and warmth.

'My dearest, darling Claire.

I shall think of you tomorrow as you celebrate Christmas, but, better than that, I shall see you on Boxing Day Eve. I have some mistletoe, it's covered in berries. We Welsh believe that every berry is worth a kiss! Will you let me collect? I feel starved of your company, Cariad, and your kisses. You do know I love you?'

Gareth smiled, as he finished writing the question. He'd been back to Cumbria earlier in the month and spoken to the Superintendent of Police, he'd also talked to Claire, and told her how he felt, and Claire, bless her, had admitted his feelings were more than reciprocated. He had only a few more weeks to serve in North Wales, and then he was going back to Cumbria as a Sergeant. Still in uniform, he'd rather wait for promotion than wait for his girl.

'I thought I'd let you know the final chapter in the saga of the 'body in the Cob'. I had a letter from Captain Milo Haines yesterday. They confirm it was Seamus Donovan who had the '45 in the Great War. The Americans are very through when it comes to tracking down members of their forces. They like to account for every piece of ammunition and every person that has served with them.

'Milo writes that Seamus landed in New York early 1928, he was very vocal among the Irish there, trying to persuade them to support the Irish in a peaceful way instead of sending money and guns. He joined the American Army Medical Corps in '42 and died on the beach on D day. Neither Milo, nor we over here, can prove that Seamus accidently killed his mate Tudor Edwards and buried him, but the circumstantial evidence is very strong.

'Miss Edwards allowed us to take a sample of DNA which proved it was her great-uncle. She and Morgan Williams have looked, but there don't seem to be any of her relatives still living. Morgan and she are, however, getting married soon so...'

MORGAN SPOKE AS HE met Jane coming down the wide staircase of his London home. 'Only two more days, Jane.'

'I know, every time I think about it I get frogs jumping in my tummy.'

Morgan swung an arm around her waist and walked her into the sitting room of his London house. Willow was sitting in front of the fire drinking coffee and talking quietly to a young man with hair cut so short it stood on end, and a pair of eyes that lit up as Jane walked into the room.

'Hello, *Cariad*.' Morgan smiled across the room and held out a hand. 'Jane says she's got frogs in her tummy.'

'Well, I've got butterflies.' Willow smiled softly at Jane, as she set down the cup and stood up, looking at Morgan. She had been a bit worried about meeting Morgan's sister but the two of them were now firm friends, so much so, that they agreed a double wedding would be wonderful.

Morgan looked at the young man across the room. 'How about you, Andrew?'

'You don't want to know. My stomach contents aren't in any reportable condition and won't be until after Boxing Day. I never thought I'd find myself wishing Christmas was over and done with.'

Morgan grinned, 'My sentiments exactly. The church is booked, the guests invited, all we have to do is turn up, and these young ladies will waltz down the aisle and issue us with the standard ball and chain.' He walked across and, pulling Willow gently into his arms, ignored both his sister and her fiancé. 'I can hardly wait.' He whispered as he kissed her, but Andrew heard.

Andrew grinned as Jane came and sat on his knee. 'Neither can I.' He glanced at the other couple and then, since kissing seemed like a very good idea just then, joined in.

About the author:

The author began writing after employment in numerous jobs. Among other occupations there has been teaching, interpreting, nursing, stoker on a steam engine and shop worker. This variety has coloured the writing and informed the writer as all lives do.

Married with children, the temptation to commit murder has been firmly repressed, especially when family life has intruded into the time set aside for the enjoyment of solving the puzzle that is murder. And why men and women commit the act.

The author has lived in a number of countries including England, Scotland, Wales, and New Zealand and travel as they say, 'broadens the mind and the vocabulary'. If the occasional expression is new, the motives and causes of death are not.

Also by the same author:

Relative Dating. (2008) {e}
ISBN 978 1 9997425 2 2

Tree Dimensional. (2009) {e}
ISBN 978 1 997425 5 3

Grave Doubts. (2009) {e}
ISBN 978 1 997425 7 7

Diverse Distress. (2009)
ISBN 978 184386 558 2

Smokescreen. (2010)
ISBN 978 184386 649 7

Collide and Conquer. (2011)
ISBN 978 190349 048 8

In the Loop. (2011)
ISBN 978 184386 702 9

Timeline. (2011) {e}
ISBN 978 1 9997425 9 1

Enter Two Gravediggers. (2011)
ISBN 978 190349 066 2

Disreputable Truth. (2012)
ISBN 978 184386 829 3

Discarded Images. (2014) {e}
ISBN 978 184386 558 2

Entrapment. (2017) {e}
ISBN 978 1 9997425 6 0

{e} indicates also available in e-book form

Printed in Great Britain
by Amazon

32730584R00222